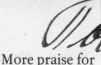

More praise for

Wherever You Go

"Who says the novel has lost its relevance? This one should be required reading." —Jonathan Wilson, author of *A Palestine Affair*

"Leegant's compelling debut novel weaves together the lives of three characters searching for personal and religious reconciliation in volatile settings. . . . But when an act of violence propels the intersecting of Leegant's characters' lives in a shocking climax, they are finally forced to confront the aftermath of their life choices."

—*Booklist*

"Leegant has taken this phenomenon of religious and political fanaticism as acted out by Americans in Israel, tempered it with more balanced perspectives, and turned it all into a finely wrought story that raises issues while it keeps the reader turning the pages."

—*Chicago Jewish Star*

"This is one of those novels that readers won't stop thinking about after it's finished, which is the measure of a great book."

—*San Francisco Book Review*

"The reader can't wait to turn the next page. This is a novel that will make you both think and feel." —*Cleveland Jewish News*

"It has taken seven years for Leegant to give us her first novel, and it was worth the wait. *Wherever You Go* . . . is a luminous journey through the lives of three young Jews struggling with issues of territory and home. . . . The novel is a small masterpiece, small only in that Leegant needs few pages to say a lot. Her book is eloquent, timely, and thought provoking." —Association of Jewish Libraries

"The lives of three New Yorkers looking for personal meaning in Israel collide tragically in short story writer Joan Leegant's debut novel, a quick and gripping read. . . . [T]he novel's real merit comes from Leegant's adept portrayal of her central characters' hearts and minds in a tale that rings true. The nebulous but timeless theme of searching for purpose in life is difficult to commit to the page in a sympathetic and engaging way, but Leegant does it."

—*Jewish Book Review*

[T]hose who seek politically charged stories brought to a human level, such as the work of Barbara Kingsolver, will not be disappointed."

—*Library Journal*

"Leegant is to be applauded for showing us Israeli society as seen from the outside. . . . With Leegant as our newscaster and narrator, we would all do well to tune in."   —*Lilith*

"Leegant is a talented writer with a sharp eye for detail, a good ear for dialogue (and interior monologue), and a knack for drawing characters that engage our interest and empathy. . . . She succeeds at building suspense with a variety of literary strategies and executes a clever twist in the plot's denouement to prolong the tension until almost the very end. . . . [She] provides insights generated with the benefits of both intimacy and distance that are becoming harder and more painful for Israelis and their American supporters to ignore."

—*Moment*

"*Wherever You Go* is a lively, full novel by an elegant, ironic writer who handles the topics of terror and messianic violence as agilely as she does love and redemption."   —*Miami Herald*

Wherever You Go

ALSO BY JOAN LEEGANT

An Hour in Paradise

Wherever You Go

JOAN LEEGANT

W. W. NORTON & COMPANY

NEW YORK · LONDON

For information about permission to reproduce selections from this book,
write to Permissions, W. W. Norton & Company, Inc.,
500 Fifth Avenue, New York, NY 10110

For information about special discounts for bulk purchases, please contact
W. W. Norton Special Sales at specialsales@wwnorton.com or 800-233-4830

Manufacturing by Courier Westford
Book design by Ellen Cipriano
Production manager: Anna Oler

Library of Congress Cataloging-in-Publication Data

Leegant, Joan.
Wherever you go / Joan Leegant.—1st ed.
p. cm.
ISBN 978-0-393-05476-7 (hardcover)
1. Americans—Israel—Fiction. 2. Jerusalem—Fiction. 3. Psychological fiction.
4. Jewish fiction. I. Title.
PS3612.E3495W47 2010
813'.6—dc22

2010006924

ISBN 978-0-393-33989-5 pbk.

W. W. Norton & Company, Inc.
500 Fifth Avenue, New York, N.Y. 10110
www.wwnorton.com

W. W. Norton & Company Ltd.
Castle House, 75/76 Wells Street, London W1T 3QT

1 2 3 4 5 6 7 8 9 0

For my sons,
Eliezer and Nathaniel

Do not ask me to leave you, or turn back from
following after you. For wherever you go, I will go.
Wherever you lodge, I will lodge. Your people will be my
people, and your God my God. Where you die, I will die,
and there I will be buried.

—BOOK OF RUTH

Alas, poor country!
Almost afraid to know itself.

—WILLIAM SHAKESPEARE, *MACBETH*

ACKNOWLEDGMENTS

My thanks to the MacDowell Colony and Yaddo for residencies during which portions of this book were written. The wonderful Judy Labensohn and the faculty of the Shaindy Rudoff Creative Writing Program at Bar-Ilan University in Tel Aviv—Allen Hoffman, Linda Zisquit, Michael Kramer, Ellen Spolsky, and Susan Handelman—welcomed me three times as visiting writer, even going so far as to provide me with the use of an incomparable Jerusalem hideout to work on final revisions. Special thanks to Peretz Rodman for everything from tracking down a copyright to chaperoning me to locations in Israel critical to this book, and to Nathan Ehrlich, who answered all my questions with wit and erudition at any hour of day or night. My agent Elaine Markson has been a ballast during the years when this project's ultimate shape as a novel was by no means guaranteed. Jill Bialosky at W. W. Norton brought to the manuscript invaluable insight and care. I am grateful to Eunice Reisman, Tehila Lieberman, Rachel Kadish, and Chris Noel for reading drafts at crucial stages and sending me in the right direction. For helping me discover that home is not a matter of four walls but of many great hearts, I thank Evan Fallenberg, Jackie Stein, Derek Stein, Shoshana London Sappir, Debbi Cooper, Lauren Stern Kedem, Miriam Laufer, my students in Israel, Andy Hurwitz, Marc Solomon, Lauren Solomon, Dan Shevitz, Amy Shevitz, Jerry Helman, Sandy Helman, Eliot

Abemayor, Susan Milsky, Peter Milsky, and a list too long to include of Boston friends and community (you know who you are) whose extraordinary kindness has sustained me, especially in the recent, unexpectedly nomadic years. Finally, I thank Allen Katzoff, whose love and support is behind every word.

PART 1

1

The metallic clanging. The loudspeakers blaring in five languages. The luggage carousel coughed up its half-digested suitcases.

Yona Stern dragged her valises onto a cart and wheeled it to the line for Passport Control, her brain on automatic after the twelve-hour flight and the surreal change in time—it was still yesterday at home—threading her way through a sea of Hasidim in inky black hats, as if a flock of crows had swooped down and settled on everyone's heads. The ones on the flight from Newark had prayed nearly continuously as the time zones slipped one into the next and the sun beckoned them eastward like a hungry lover, congregating every three hours by the bulkhead and the galley and the economy-class restrooms, prayer shawls draped down their backs like superhero capes. Yona was not a believer, had not attended a religious service in years, and found everything about them—their antiquated dress, their tribes of offspring—disturbing, yet their fervent shuckling in the cramped corners of the plane had provided a desperately welcome distraction. A spectacle she could follow with a kind of craven compulsion because it allowed her, if only briefly, to get her mind off herself.

The line snaked glacially; she pushed her cart a hopeful two feet. Far ahead of her, a jaunty cowboy hat teetered among the somber fedoras: a pie-faced young man chattering too enthusiastically with a redheaded officer in Passport Control. Yona had first noticed him, nineteen or twenty, when they landed, babbling his excitement in a deep Southern accent to anyone within earshot, starting with the old man next to him who appeared to know no English. Eager. Too eager. *Mah first time!* he'd said to Yona as they inched up the aisle of the plane. His leg was bobbing up and down and he seemed to be blushing, as if he were about to lose his virginity. She'd nodded, unable to think of anything to say—congratulations? good luck?— unable to even smile. She was a poor booster for him, an inadequate cheerleader. He should have been with a tour, one of those high-minded delegations with matching travel bags and name tags who sat in clusters on the flight and applauded and sang *Hevenu shalom aleichem!* when they touched down, then got on their knees outside and kissed the tarmac. He should not have been stuck waiting in the aisle with her, she who had a mission hanging around her neck like a set of deadweights.

The redhead was studying his passport; her finger moved like a little windshield wiper, telling him to stop talking, the way you dealt with an annoying child. He thought everyone would be as excited as he, and also as polite. He thought it would be like Texas. He would learn. And stunningly soon. Maybe within the next hour, when he stepped outside into the muggy soup of Tel Aviv.

"You. Miss. You." Yona snapped to attention. Black jeans, white shirt with the sleeves rolled up, a telephone wire by his ear. Handsome, inscrutable, oddly generic. It occurred to her there were probably two dozen of them in the room, all remarkably alike.

"Passport." The accent was thick. *Pessport.* He held out his hand.

She unzipped her pack, gave it over. Crisp navy blue with the haughty gold American eagle. He would not engage her in small talk, unlike the nosy Israeli she'd sat next to on the plane, would not ask if she liked traveling alone and why she wasn't married and whether she was planning on eating her dessert. He flipped pages. Her so-called love life, exposed. Paris. Mexico City. St. Maarten. All suspiciously short stays. It made her look like a drug runner.

"First time in Israel?"

"No."

"When before?"

"Ten years ago. I was a student here, had a different passport then."

"And since?"

No, she hadn't been back since.

An eyebrow went up. "You speak Hebrew?"

"Mah sh'ani zocheret." What she remembered.

He turned the passport around, studied her picture. Elias had liked it. He'd looked at it and called her *my little cherry.* The pouty lips, she thought. But she had not liked his expression then, his possessiveness, the leering. He was almost fifty. It was becoming salacious. Cliché. She went with him to the Caribbean and that was that, sent him back to his raven-haired wife.

"Where are you staying?"

"Jerusalem. At a friend's."

"Name?"

"Claudia Rozan. Tchernikovsky Street. She's away."

More flipping. The loudspeaker disgorged static. At a table directly across, two officers were questioning a family of Arabs, long loose dresses and white scarves for the women, neatly pressed pants on the men. One of the younger men couldn't find something; he kept zipping and unzipping the pockets of his pack. A document, she heard the officers say. Where is the document.

"You have family in the country?"

"Distant relatives in the north. A sister."

He looked up. A sister? And where did this sister live?

She studied him a moment. "Givat Baruch."

A pause. He took in her designer jeans, the sharp blazer, the close-fitting blouse. She didn't look like the sister of a settler. Certainly not those settlers anyway. "In the territories," he said. "Near Hebron."

"That's right."

"Your sister's name?"

"Dena. Dena Ben-Tzion." She might as well tell him the rest; he was going to ask. Because those in the territories weren't the patriots they'd once been. Or thought they'd been. Some of their names were on lists. And anyway they'd never been particularly law-abiding. "She's been there nine years. Her husband is Aryeh Ben-Tzion. They have five children."

He looked at her a long minute. "Five children but for you they have no room?"

I'm a soft American, no appetite for zealotry, she wanted to say but didn't. Because that wasn't the whole story. Or even close to it. "I prefer to stay in Jerusalem."

He waited, then looked again at the passport. "And you, I see, are Yona. Yona Stern."

"That's right."

"What is the purpose of your stay?"

You don't want to know. "To visit. Sightsee."

He handed her the passport. His face could have been chiseled. Square-jawed, like a model's. And just as unreadable. "Your sister out near Hebron. Dena. You know what this name means?"

Din. "Yes. Judgment."

A nod. Across from her, they were taking the Arab without the document away. The women were shaking their heads, worried, white scarves flapping like tiny sails. "And Yona. This name also you know?"

She nodded. The dove. As if she'd come with an olive branch in her mouth, a peace offering like an illustration from a children's Bible. "I know," she said. "But it can be, you understand, a burden."

. . .

Outside, a wall of heat. She smelled overripe fruit, roasting meat, cumin. The cowboy caught her eye, waved gleefully, ran off to the taxis. She pulled her suitcases behind her like recalcitrant horses— she had brought too much—found the Jerusalem-bound van and squeezed herself into the middle row between a woman with a sweaty baby on her lap and a man with a cigarette hanging from his lips. He was trying to open his window.

"Lo oved," the driver barked, slamming shut the back doors. It doesn't work. The window. Forget it. He came around front, started the ignition. They moved into the knotted traffic. The man beside her coughed, a phlegmy tobacco-tinged hacking. They were driving through a gritty haze of yellow dust. The remains of a *khamsin,* one of those broiling desert winds that come up from the south and blanket the country in heat and sand before changing its mind and retreating. As if it has come to remind itself that there's more to life than snakes and scorpions and the black-haired tents of the Bedouin. At the merge onto the highway a dented Volkswagen darted out and cut them off. The van driver hissed. *Kus emek! Your mother's cunt!* Yona closed her eyes. Elias had laughed when she told him where she was going. *What, looking for your roots?* She'd relented when he called a week before she was to leave, had let him take her out to dinner and of course come back to the apartment. Because she was weak. His family were rich rug merchants from Shiraz who fled when Khomeini came to power and then, after a brief sojourn in the Jewish State, which Elias described as lasting *no more than five minutes,* built a hugely successful business in New York out of nothing. Elias would no more want to go back to Israel than he would Iran. *Primitive. Run by a bunch of farmers.* He loved his demitasse, his Metropolitan Opera box, his bright shiny showroom on Madison Avenue, his nine-bedroom colonial in Westchester. *So, habibi, checking out the natives?* he'd said, and pinched her cheek. *Habibi.* Sweetheart. Like the catcalls from the construction workers when she was a student. From them it wasn't so bad but from Elias, paunchily naked on her

bed, a gold chain with a Jewish star resting like a nursing infant on a plump pink nipple on his hairy chest—*I've got nothing to hide*—the word made her nauseous. Elias made her nauseous. She should never have consented to dinner.

The van lurched, stopped. She opened her eyes. Sweat dripped into the small of her back. A snarl of cars under a hot orange sky. And cramped shops, narrow alleys, old women lugging plastic bags stuffed with produce, loaves of bread. A murmur rippled across the seats: what happened, why weren't they moving. Beside her the baby, curled like a kitten, breathed noisily. His head was a mass of damp ringlets, sticky and not quite real, like the hair on a stone cherub in Florence.

"Chefetz chashud," the driver said, killing the ignition. A Suspicious Object. An unclaimed package, a bag that didn't belong. Dozens of them each week. Did they think the only crazies were the ones who detonated themselves? The bomb robot would come now to explode it. The driver lit a cigarette, tossed out the match, then crumpled the pack and tossed that too. Yona leaned toward the window that wouldn't open. Where were they? she asked the man beside her in her rounded American Hebrew. It was embarrassing; she had never been any good with the accent.

Jerusalem, he said. He tapped on the grimy glass with a yellowed nail. "You see over there? The bus station. That's why the delay. They're always at the bus station, the bombs. That's where the Arabs put them."

"Lo nachon," the driver said into the rearview. Not true. If the bombs were always at the bus station, no one would ever get blown up because they'd never be taken by surprise. Instead they put them everywhere. In the Mahane Yehuda market. By the Jaffa Gate. In the downtown shops. Even where other Arabs go. They're killing their own. *Animals.*

The man beside her shrugged. The baby snored, shifted; his mother leaned against the side and slept. Yona stared out the dusty windshield. A cluster of girls, ten or eleven, in long skirts crossed the road in front of them, sucking drippy red popsicles, their mouths lip-sticky smears. A thunderous *boom!* then another. *Boom! Boom! Boom!* The girls looked in the direction of the explosions; one dropped her popsicle, laughed. The baby stirred, whimpered. His mother patted him, cooed in a strange language. *BOOM!* An earsplitting explosion ripped the air, and then a minute passed and the cars began to move. The girls disappeared down a side street. The driver mopped his face with a handkerchief, started the ignition. A twangy guitar whined from the radio, a seductive male voice. Oldies Israeli rock. *Olam u-m' lo'o nivneh b'ahava.* We can rebuild the world with love.

They crept out, crawled past the bus station. A triangle of police jeeps shuddered out front. Two men in bulky coveralls like what the astronauts wore yanked off thick tan gloves and boxy hoods, threw them into the jeeps. An acrid smell filled the van.

"*Baruch haba,*" said the driver into the rearview. Welcome to Israel. Behind her, someone snickered.

It looked, she thought, like a planned community in Florida. Pristine white sidewalks, a tidy square with a flower garden, a grocery, a bright playground with a plastic slide and a red-roofed playhouse, even a row of eye-catching date palms. Certainly no caravan outpost on a windblown hilltop with bands of outlaws standing their ground with rifles and bandannas, the womenfolk bringing provisions under cover of darkness and keeping the children out of harm's way. Not this place. The mood was forthright, outspoken. *Make no mistake,* the sunny streets of Givat Baruch said to the overheated passengers alighting bulletproof bus number 170 from Jerusalem in front of an amply stocked bakery café with trays of cookies and cakes in the window, a stop the bus made every hour and a half without fail after passing the concrete barricades and armed guards at the gate. *We're here to stay. No hiding, no ducking, and we want everyone to know it.* A brass plaque on a handsome stone obelisk in the middle of the garden commemorated its putative namesake, one Baruch Zinzer, a member of the Irgun who in 1947 was hanged by the British at age eighteen— *A fighter for our freedom, let his death not be in vain.* Though the community's true namesake, according to her friend Claudia, who paid attention to such things, was a different Baruch, an American from a neighboring settlement who opened fire on a phalanx of hundreds of prostrate Moslem worshippers in the nearby Cave of the Patriarchs fifteen years before, killing thirty before being beaten to death himself. A commemoration the Israeli government would not allow. So the founders unearthed a safely pedigreed Irgunist to be the cover and kept a smaller second marker beside the obelisk as a reminder, for those in the know, of their other spiritual father, the code words *For a holy man, who gave his life for the Jewish people and the nation of Israel* carved surprisingly crudely, Yona thought, into the stone.

"Rotza tremp?" Need a lift? Yona looked up. A soldier with propped-up sunglasses was standing twenty feet away by the driver's side of a dusty white Renault parked half on the sidewalk. He cocked his head toward the passenger door. He looked all of eighteen. "I'm going to District Gimmel, I'll drop you off."

She hesitated. She had supposed she would walk. But she hadn't counted on the heat. Or the steep incline. Another cock of the head and she went over, slid inside. The floor was littered with candy wrappers and crushed cigarette packets. He started the ignition. The Renault sputtered like a toy car with a dying battery. "Where to? I have to pass through Aleph and Bet to get to Gimmel." He made a stingy laugh. "Just like in the alphabet."

She looked at the slip for the hundredth time. Claudia had found the address for her. *You can always find somebody who knows somebody. Even in the territories. "Mishpachat Ben-Tzion,"* she said. The Ben-Tzion family. District Bet.

"You're an American." He could tell by the accent. Of course. He lit a cigarette, offered her the pack. She declined. It wasn't the time to restart a bad habit. She could always do that in New York, when all this was over. "Where'd you learn your Hebrew?"

"School. Twelve years of it." He glanced over, sizing her up. He was thinking she didn't look the type to have gone to one of those religious girls' seminaries. Though she'd put on a skirt and a blouse with sleeves for the occasion. She looked out her window at the orderly sidewalks and the ornamental streetlamps, their decorative ironwork painted a tasteful forest green, at the bicycles and double strollers left out in front of the buildings, children's riding toys sitting unworried on the dirt. No petty theft by the local Arabs here. Because they couldn't get in.

He took a long pull on the cigarette. "You speak pretty good."

"That was the best thing about the place." He didn't have to hear about the bitter used-up teachers and the oppressive modesty rules, the screaming matches she'd had with her father and the headmaster and the woman who frisked them every day for makeup and contraband earrings, the ones that exceeded the permissible quarter-inch circumference or dared to dangle a millimeter off the ear. The only reason she didn't get kicked out was that the principal owed her father. A towering rabbi even more towering than the headmaster, her father, once dean of the city's premier rabbinical college, had come to the man's rescue when a parent accused him of accepting money for grades. Yona never believed the headmaster wasn't guilty.

"Which Ben-Tzion?"

She turned. "What?"

"Which Ben-Tzion family? There are a lot of them."

So. A thousand Sons of Zion. They'd fled their stooped-over Diaspora names and taken on new, muscular Hebrew ones, cast their lot with the grand nationalist dream, the great utopian vision. Ben-Avraham. Ben-David. And the most grand of all, Ben-Ami. Son of the People.

"Dena and Aryeh," she said. "Five children."

A shrug. "Don't know them." The Renault chugged valiantly

uphill. He tossed the unfinished cigarette out into the tinderbox scrub. She expected it to go up in flames any second. He'd grown up there, he said, his parents among the founders. But he'd been away a lot, first for high school and now the army, and he couldn't keep track of all the new families.

"They aren't new. They've been here nine years."

He looked over at her. Dark-eyed and smug. Sure of himself. "That's new."

"Nine years? That seems a pretty long time to me."

"You're an American, yes?"

"So?"

"So these Ben-Tzions, they're also American?"

"Half. The wife. Actually, one-seventh if you count the kids."

Another parsimonious laugh. He seemed exceedingly pleased with himself. "Americans will always be new. No matter how long they're here." A stray dog wandered into the road, and he gunned the accelerator and watched the terrified animal flee. "They could be here thirty years, even fifty, and they'll still be new. Except maybe if they shed blood. Then maybe someone might say they belong."

The two girls squatting next to something at the end of an unpaved road were unmistakable, long-limbed with hair like burnt copper she'd know anywhere. The Renault sputtered away, and she walked down the hot street, boxy three-story apartments on both sides that seemed to have sprung up overnight out of the dirt, no flowers, no trees. A lone motorcycle sizzled on a narrow patch of asphalt.

A tiny lizard, thin and green, lay motionless in the dust.

"Is it injured?" Yona asked, bending over the girls.

"Maybe," the bigger of the two said. She looked about nine, the other, seven. Neither looked up; strangers with uncontrollable American accents were apparently not on their list of fears. "Usually they live on the walls," the older girl said, slipping into English and gesturing with her chin toward the white concrete barriers fronting the buildings. "It's not safe for them in the street. Too many cars."

"Let's move it," the younger one said, reaching.

"No." Her sister seized her wrist. "We mustn't. Ima said it might have a disease."

Ima. Mother. Yona's chest pounded. Dena was somewhere nearby. She resisted the urge to scan the windows. "If you get a twig," she said, trying to sound matter-of-fact, calm, normal, "I could push it onto a piece of paper and move it out of the road." The thing was maybe four inches long and light as a matchstick. It was also probably dead, but she didn't want to say so. She reached into her bag and pulled out a notepad. The younger one watched, openly staring. Freckles and a button nose. Norman Rockwell features that suggested an adorable cuteness, a wholesome naïveté, but cold hazel eyes that militated against it.

"Why do you keep a pad with you?"

"I don't know. To write things down, I guess. Names. Addresses. Directions."

"Are you a spy? Shin Bet?"

"A spy? No. I'm a visitor. A tourist. How do you know about spies?"

The older one took her sister's hand. "Don't talk so much, Anati." *Anat.* Yona had never been told the names. The bigger girl looked at her. Also blue eyes, but a softer version. "She doesn't know what Shin Bet is, she just hears the word." Her gaze lingered on Yona. Did she see something? Something familiar? "Anyway we'll get a stick and move him so he doesn't get run over."

They went to the side of the road. Yona forced herself not to look up at the windows. The street was eerily quiet. She'd imagined the place would be noisy, bombastic, the kind of cacophony that went with red-faced rebels chaining themselves to defiant trailers like what you saw on the front page of the *New York Times*. But it was hushed and still and reminded her of the place upstate where she'd spent summers when she was small, when their mother was still alive and you could sit outside for whole July afternoons and just listen to the buzzing in the grass.

They were back, holding out a frail twig. Gently, Yona pushed the lizard onto a piece of paper.

"Put him by the wall," the younger one, Anat, commanded. "Here," Anat told her, standing by a patch of scrawny weeds. "He'll wake up later and climb to where he likes to go."

Yona carried him carefully, keeping the paper low enough for the older girl to see. She was a grave child, looking somberly for signs of life. At the spot the younger one pointed to, Yona slid the body off. It lay limp in the dry grass.

"Do you think he'll live?" the older girl said.

"What do you mean, will he live?" demanded Anat. "He's a lizard, this is how it's supposed to be. They're born, they die, that's all. Don't waste your tears, Hila." *Hila.* "He's just an animal, not a person."

The door to the flat was open.

"Ima!" Hila called, and motioned Yona into a shadowy vestibule. Anat had gone ahead. "Someone here to see you!" Yona made out a front room stuffed with furniture and toys and mounds of laundry. The shutters on the back doors had been closed against the sun. Somewhere a fan cranked loudly. The smells of garlic and cooking oil hung in the air, and then Yona picked up another odor, more pungent, human. Diapers. Unwashed. Ripening in the triple-digit heat.

"Tell them just a moment, Hila," and again Yona's heart did its ricochet knocking: Dena's voice, from off to the right. She had imagined the encounter a hundred times and still hadn't been able to prepare herself. The girl glanced back at Yona, checking that she'd heard—*Hila,* named for Helen? Yona's dead mother?—then disappeared down the hall.

Footsteps on tile, baby sounds. *"Okay, I'm coming, here I am."* Weariness in the tone—five children, the end of a long hot afternoon, everyone hungry and now someone, unannounced, at the door. *"Sorry it took a bit longer than—"* She stopped. The baby in her arms turned to look. A glimmer of copper shone in the fine hairs of his perfect oval scalp. The same color as the damp strands peeking out of the cotton scarf on Dena's head. A hoarse whisper: "My God."

"Ima! I can't find my sh—" Anat, appearing behind her mother. "Oh. This is the lady I told you about, with the lizard." She looked at Yona. "What are you doing here?"

Yona found a voice somewhere in the back of her throat. "I'm here to visit your mother," she heard herself say.

Anat tugged on her mother's arm. "Ima, I can't find my shoes and I need them."

"Go ask Hila," Dena said, still staring. "Hila will help you, I can't do it now."

Anat exhaled loudly to register her annoyance, then walked off. The baby rested his head on Dena's shoulder, and Dena put her hand on it as if Yona might suddenly snatch him away. Her face was stone. "You have no right," she whispered.

"I know."

"You have no right to come here."

Yona nodded. Her eyes were welling up and her throat had closed. Everything she'd practiced, everything she'd rehearsed—vanished.

"No right to appear on my street and talk to my daughters and walk with them to my house."

Another nod.

Dena looked away. She wouldn't want Yona to see her face. Though all Yona wanted was to reach out and hug her. But she wouldn't. Because Dena would pull back and never let Yona near her again, and Yona would blow everything.

She forced herself to speak. "I know this is hard. I know you hate me. But this isn't good. Ten years. We have to try."

"I don't want you in my life." Dena still wasn't looking at her. "I don't need you."

"But I need you." The baby let out a tiny snore; Dena pressed him closer. "We have to try to move beyond the past. Move on to something else."

"There is nothing else."

"That's not true, Dena. There's always something else. Always something—"

Hooting and yelling just outside, a *whoosh* of small bodies crowding into the vestibule. Three little boys, breathless and soaking wet, dripping on the tile. "Ima!" one said, yanking Dena's skirt, "Binny got water guns from his grandparents in America! We're filling them up, then going back out!" The boy let go and rushed off with the others deeper into the house, leaving puddles on the slippery floor. Yona heard drawers opening, Anat screaming, *Don't touch me! You're all wet!*

"Your children are beautiful," Yona said.

Dena turned to her. There was a hardness about her mouth, and her face was thinner than Yona remembered. But she still had that unadorned beauty, that stoic proudness that defied decoration or anything artificial. The baby burrowed deeper into the curve of her neck. His head was a perfect egg, his fleshy thighs like soft butter. Yona had an impossible desire to hold him. "You have infinite ways to be cruel," Dena said.

"I'm sorry."

They stood there. A beat passed. The boys in the kitchen were calling; they wanted crackers, cheese, lemonade. Yona handed Dena a slip of paper. "My phone number. I'm staying in Jerusalem, my old roommate's, Claudia. I'll meet you wherever you want. Here. There. Just call. Please." Then she turned and left the apartment and went out into the unforgiving heat.

• • •

It's not that she expected dispensation. Ten years before, they had both come to the country, Yona to the university in Jerusalem, Dena, along with David Small, Dena's big love, together since college, to a two-room flat on the outskirts of the remote desert town of Arad, nothing out their windows but far-off clusters of tents and goats and donkeys and camels, the occasional pickup truck rigged with a satellite dish. Dena had by then a social work degree; David had finished law school. They would master the language, then come up to the cities or poor development towns on the periphery and find work. That was the plan. To marry there, start a family there, contribute. A life of purpose. Yona, twenty and bored in the Foreign Students Program, seized every chance she could to make the two-hour bus ride down to see them. Jerusalem was too crowded, too religious, too full of Americans just like her; she liked the quiet, the starkness of the landscape. There was something magical about the desert, she told Claudia.

"Magical?" Claudia said, trimming her nails and rolling her eyes. Her excellent English had an exotic Spanish lilt. She was from Chile. All the young Jews there spent a college year in Jerusalem, she said. It was a great way to improve your English. "Blistering hot days and freezing nights and absolutely nothing to do?"

"But look at this," Yona said, jumping off her bed and getting her sketch pad. Charcoal drawings of the Bedouin women who came to town in their elaborately embroidered dresses to sell sheepskins and woven blankets. Dozens of sketches, the tablet already half filled.

"You did these?" Claudia said, paging through. "Pretty damn good. Did you show your sister?"

"Next time," Yona said, taking back the pad. She'd told Claudia about Dena, how they'd never been close—the age difference took care of that—plus Dena had always been too busy for her, model student, model citizen, always running off to one project or another. But now they were in the country together, far from home. Maybe things would change. "By then I'll be better."

Her drawings did get better. But the Foreign Students Program nose-dived: a strike by senior faculty, leaving Yona with a single surviving class and yawning stretches of empty time. A third of the students went home; others abandoned the dorms. The extracurricular trips were cancelled. Yona took endless walks, rode the bus to Tel Aviv to wander around, prolonged her visits in Arad.

Dena, on the other hand, was thriving. By January her Hebrew was fluent and she had a job in a program for problem teenagers; within a month she was put in charge. David was another story. He was worried; it wouldn't be easy to be a lawyer in a foreign country. It wasn't like being a computer geek or a scientist, he said. You had to really know the culture. And the language; lawyers relied on the nuances of language. It was too difficult, he had too far to go.

"That's ridiculous," Dena said. He'd been sounding that way for weeks. "Thousands of immigrants have done it before us, including lots of lawyers." Yona listened from the couch where she was sketching a plate of strawberries. March, the end of berry season. Dena carried her cereal bowl to the sink, let it clatter against the porcelain. Yona had already witnessed one argument that morning. About the dishes. Dena was working, David was not, where was there even a debate? "You're smart, you're talented, you'll be fine. You've got to stop obsessing and focus on what's important. Get your priorities straight." Dena picked up her backpack and left the apartment.

David turned to the couch. "Sorry you had to hear that."

Yona shrugged. "It's okay. I know Dena."

David exhaled loudly, walked over and sank into the cushions next to her. "Tell me about it. She's so damn certain all the time. She can't deal with anyone's ambivalence."

Yona studied the strawberries. It was true. Dena didn't like weakness, doubt.

"She has no idea how hard this is for me," David said. "I'm not like her. I can't connect to the old Russians who play chess in the parks, or the Israelis who grew up here and work in the factories.

You've seen how she just goes over and talks to them." The truth was, he said, he felt alienated and awkward, an Ivy-privileged American from Connecticut who loved movies and cafés and bookstores and belonged in Tel Aviv or the leafier parts of Jerusalem. He would never relate to vast sectors of the population. That's why he wanted to be a lawyer: to have a prescribed role, a comfortable distance. But if he didn't get out there and be with the people, he would never learn the language, would never learn anything.

Yona listened, nodded, though it was cold feet talking and she knew it, Dena knew it, probably even David knew it. Her sister was right; he should stop worrying and concentrate on picking up the language more. But Dena's can-do determination bothered Yona too. It made her feel inferior. Lazy. It was how she'd always felt around Dena. Rudderless. Because Yona was also languishing. And not just because of the strike. Why didn't she use the free time to take a drawing class? Or volunteer? Or pull up stakes and go back to New York and get a job, sign up for the summer semester to salvage the school year? That's what Dena would have done.

David was going on about the quality of the government-run language course; his teacher wasn't pushing them, Dena's was much better, but hers was the most advanced class so they got the best instructor. Yona put down her charcoal, turned to him, murmured something sympathetic. She liked David; he was older, smart, good-looking. There was no one in Jerusalem who interested her, the handful of other foreign students who were still around foolishly lightweight or overly studious, the Israelis nowhere in sight, everything at the university at a dead standstill. And David was safe. He wouldn't—couldn't—want anything from her because he was taken.

He looked over at her. She lightly put a hand on his arm.

"I'm going out of my mind, you know?" he said, watching her.

"I can imagine."

He put his free hand on hers. "Thanks for letting me vent like this. I must sound like a prima donna, a real spoiled brat."

"Hey, it's hard." She gave his arm a gentle squeeze. He squeezed back.

"You're so different from Dena. So much more mellow."

Of course she was different. She was the empathic sister, the soulful sister. Not like Dena, Ms. Never-Stop-Moving, no time for anyone. She still hadn't shown Dena her drawings. She gave his arm another squeeze, longer this time.

He stopped talking. He pulled himself out of the cushions, leaned over, put his mouth on hers.

Afterward, he was a wreck. He had to tell Dena. He couldn't live with a lie. They had been completely faithful, it was the bedrock of their trust.

"Completely?" Yona asked, pulling on her shirt. "Not even once? In four years?"

"Not even once."

She made a low whistle. She didn't know anyone who lived like that. But that was Dena. Upright. Principled. Perfect. "Well, you can't tell her. That would be terrible. We both love her."

"I don't know." David was hunched over, his head in his hands.

"What do you mean, you don't know? Look, David, we have to forget about this." She reached for her jeans, slipped a leg through. "It was an impulse, that's all. This is what you get when people are unhappy and far from home. You should see the Foreign Students dorm." She stood and zipped up her pants, tried to lighten things up. "No one even knows which is their assigned room anymore; it's like musical chairs over there."

He didn't laugh. His clothes were still on the floor and he was just sitting there smothered in guilt. It was stupid, what she'd just done. Stupid stupid stupid. So maybe she felt like she and David were the discarded leftovers from Dena's industrious, purposeful existence. Maybe she was still mad at Dena for ignoring her her whole life even though you'd think Dena would've taken over some sort of mother role after their actual mother disappeared on them by dying when Yona was only twelve instead of throwing herself into more busy busy busy, sixteen and already Miss Competent, Miss Capable, Miss High-Minded Must Do Justice and Save the World—how many times had Yona been over this, with the high school counselor and the psychologist her father made her see and everyone else who pried their noses into her state of mind during the height of her adolescent defiance—but it was still stupid. All the hours listening to David, thinking she understood him better than Dena did, imagining herself as the sensitive sister, the sister with feelings, when really what she needed was to stop looking for sustenance outside herself and take charge of her own life.

She sat on the couch, fished for her sandals. And now she was ashamed, as much over her desperation for Dena's attention as for having committed this primitive trespass. It was as if the two of them, she and David both, had been reaching for the elusive Dena and instead found only each other. A consolation prize. Well, it didn't have to be the end of the world. She glanced at him. He was still bent over, cradling his head. They'd made a huge mistake but it didn't have to ruin everything; it could still be contained.

"Listen, David, it didn't mean anything, what we just did." She waited for him to look at her and when he didn't, she waved at the expanse of nothing out the window. "The desert does weird things to people, you can lose yourself." She paused. "Anyway, it would be better if I didn't come down here so much anymore. I have to try and make a go of things in Jerusalem."

He looked up. "Why? Why do you have to stop coming?"

"You know why."

He slumped toward his clothes. It was an effort. She reached down, handed him his shirt. He took it and looked at her with wet eyes. "This wasn't an impulse, Yona. I've been thinking about it for weeks. The fact is I'm in love with you."

"In love? That's crazy! You're just depressed! I'm a convenient diversion, a way to avoid dealing with the hard stuff."

"No, that's not true. Things with Dena haven't been good for, I don't know. Months. You've seen it yourself. And now all I do is think of you."

"That's lunacy! We're just friends. We let it get out of hand." She glanced at the window. Dena would be back at noon for lunch. If she hurried, she could catch the ten o'clock bus. "Look, I'm going to go. You need to pull yourself together. She's my sister. This can't happen."

"It's already happened."

Two days later, David showed up at her dorm. Yona made Claudia send him away, but not until he'd conveyed a message: he'd told Dena everything. It was over. He was relieved. He'd be staying at a friend's on the other side of the city to sort things out. He would call.

Panicked, Yona called Dena. Dena refused to talk. She took the bus to Arad; Dena wouldn't open the door. She wrote a note—she'd been reckless, David had been scared, it would never happen again. She waited outside the building, and when night fell and Dena still hadn't come out, she got on the last bus back to the city.

For weeks she tried everything. David told her he'd been in love with her all year. She said he was deluded, that he was running away from his fears—of marriage, of life—but he insisted he knew what he was doing and that if Yona didn't want him, he would wait until she changed her mind.

"Maybe he really does love you," Claudia told her. "Maybe your sister even knew it."

They were on a bench outside the dormitory in the hot spring night drinking warm beer. The strike had never ended and now the semester was over; Claudia was going home to Chile. Yona's father had called from New York that afternoon. He'd heard from Dena. Was it true what Yona had done? What kind of person was she?

"Actually, you've been pretty useful to your sister, if you think about it," Claudia said. The smell of orange blossoms was intoxicating. More than anything, this was what Yona wanted to remember. "Being David's sounding board," Claudia said, "his personal worry beads. She's not exactly a font of warm and fuzzy. Took a load off her, if you ask me."

Yona looked at her. Was Claudia serious? Did she think Dena actually wanted this outcome?

Claudia took a long sip of beer. "Well, she did leave the two of you alone an awful lot. You have to ask yourself what that was about."

When her one exam was over and she had nowhere else to go, New York not an option, facing her father not an option, Yona moved in with David in a second-floor flat on Hapalmach Street and took a summer job handling the English correspondence for an elderly professor. David studied for the New York bar. She told him she'd sleep with him but that she wasn't in love. He said he didn't care.

Dena moved to a settlement over the Green Line. She found work immediately and two weeks later met Aryeh Ben-Tzion. According to one of Dena and David's former friends, Ben-Tzion was looking for recruits for a new and more radical settlement deeper in the territories near the city of Hebron. It was important to establish a presence in the region, fingers of Jewish population, Ben-Tzion said, to keep the Arabs from believing the area could ever be their own state. The chemistry was immediate. Aryeh's commitment to the country, to his principles, was absolute. A third-generation Israeli with roots in anti-Semitic Poland, he knew exactly where he stood. It was for him an immutable truth that all Jews belonged in the land of Israel. And that Israel meant Greater Israel, the Whole Land, not just the castrated allotment carved out by the armistice lines in 1948 but the territories liberated in the Six-Day War. Lands that had been given to the Jewish people by divine edict four thousand years before, when the patriarch Abraham bought a burial place for his exalted wife Sarah. It was their task and privilege now to populate these lands with generations upon generations of Jews so that they would never again be taken out of their people's hands.

One month after meeting, on a steamy August afternoon ten days after the annual mourning of the destruction of the ancient temple in Jerusalem by the Romans, in a parched clearing that would one day be the bustling hub of the nascent settlement of Givat Baruch, Dena Stern and Aryeh Ben-Tzion were married. It was a small ceremony. In attendance were Aryeh's brothers and their wives, all of whom lived in a string of illegal settlements across the Judean ridge, as well as his parents and grandparents from Holon and a few of his friends from school and the army. No members of Dena's family were present. A week before the wedding, exhausted from life's burdens, weary from years of husbanding his grief over the premature death of his wife and shouldering sole responsibility for his two headstrong daughters, Yona's father suffered a heart attack in the backseat of the taxi on the way to the airport—and no one else had been invited.

She caught the bulletproof 170 back to Jerusalem, then a taxi to Claudia's. Her hastily opened suitcases lay like gaping mouths on the living room floor, garments strewn over the couch like a child's discarded dress-up clothes. She peeled off the sticky blouse, stepped out of the skirt, showered, changed, surveyed the apartment. Bedroom. Bath. Balcony. And in the living room an overstuffed velvet couch. A pole lamp with a red shade and gold fringe. A curtain of beads in a doorway. And on the floor, a tangle of water pipes, a low brass tray on spindly legs that served as a coffee table, a jungle of plants. Classic Claudia. Garish. Dramatic.

And generous. The refrigerator, on which Claudia had hung a smiley note saying how to reach her in Chile and commanding Yona to try to have a good time, was stocked; stuffed, really. Claudia's way of reciprocating. Three months before, in June, she had stayed in Yona's apartment in Manhattan for two weeks while Yona went with Elias to Martha's Vineyard. Though *went with* was something of a stretch; Elias had installed her in a luxury condo a block from the beach, to which he would escape between outings with the black-haired wife and their two newly married daughters and dutiful sons-in-law—both of whom worked in the business with Elias—whose names and physical descriptions Yona didn't want to know. It was better that way. Though a couple of times she was certain she saw them, two young, stylish, dark-haired pairs at a bar in Edgartown or renting bikes in Vineyard Haven. But she never asked Elias about them. She wasn't naïve; this wasn't the first such arrangement she'd ever had. Elias, the others, they didn't want to think about family when they were with her. Neither did she. That was the whole point.

She poured herself a glass of orange juice and carried it to the low table where it settled with a tinny echo, then opened the sliding doors to the balcony. A peppery sharpness rose up from the geraniums in the window boxes below. The sky had softened into pink, a water-color wash of approaching dusk, and she heard birds in the distance. Soon there'd be hundreds of them, maybe thousands, little punctuation marks in the sky, signaling the start of evening with their raucous *chit chit chit chit chit!*—some things you never forget—warning the inhabitants like anxious beacons. In the building across the way, someone was turning on the lights, little squares of gold, like foil-wrapped chocolates. She had thought she would never come back. *Why are you still doing this?* Claudia asked her when she returned from the Vineyard tanned and lean and disturbed. The handsome, happy couples in town, the look from the condo manager as he watched her getting out of the pool each day as if she were for sale: she didn't like it, it seemed different this time, cheap, tawdry, worse. *You need to stop punishing yourself. Ten years. It's enough.* That was the beginning. The seed. Claudia's question. Because Claudia knew better than anyone. A month later she went with Elias to St. Maarten and told him it was over, and when Claudia wrote three weeks after that to say she was going to South America to see her family, Yona stunned herself by asking to use the flat.

Jerusalem? You're coming here? Claudia wrote, incredulous. *Finally!*

Yes finally, Yona typed back, the steamy New York summer enveloping her like a shroud. *Because I have to. Because it's time.*

2

He was a fake. An impostor. It was all falling apart and he couldn't stop it. He ought to pull off the yarmulke, the tzitzit fringes, throw them into the trash. Everything was unraveling and he didn't know why, only that it was slipping away from him like so much water from his fingertips. One day it's the organizing principle of your life, and the next it's nothing. Gone, evaporated. Thirty-six years old, and suddenly you can't remember what it once meant to you, or why.

The train lurched and the doors slid open, the slouching silent filing out. Fifty-ninth Street. Greenglass had missed his stop. He got out, the urine stench of the cinderblock station-cave coming back to him—it was amazing what you could get used to—and hauled himself and his suitcase up the littered stairs. He'd walk the six blocks. The steamy drizzle was strangely refreshing, though he never missed New York weather. Not a drop permitted in Jerusalem until November, he liked to tell his brother in London, Scott, who was barely able to lift his eyelids by now, so sodden by the mist of the English fall.

He turned onto Sixty-fifth Street, the rain fogging his glasses. He could do it in his sleep. It made no difference how long he'd been away. Nine minutes from the park, six minutes from the corner. His suitcase was too heavy, he'd brought too much. The books especially. Why so many? Protection? Armor? Wasn't the beard enough? The tzitzit? The mocking black yarmulke that was now plastered, stiff, onto his hair? His raincoat was sticking to his back.

"Hello, Carlos."

"Ah, Mr. Greenglass." The doorman held open the door and smiled his obsequious smile, the one that made Greenglass cringe, even if Carlos had to do it. "I heard you were coming."

"Yes indeedy." Greenglass put down his bag and brushed the damp off his coat and smoothed back his hair. He took off the yarmulke, slipped it into his pocket. He had, of course, another one, but it could wait until the elevator. He straightened his coat sleeves. "Look okay?" he asked, though he already knew the answer.

A toothy grin. Carlos needed dental work, a man who grew up poor and was now working for the rich and pretending he didn't mind. "Looking fine, Mr. Greenglass," Carlos said, smiling, always smiling. "She's upstairs. Waiting for you."

His mother had been a beautiful woman. But now, fifty-nine, the decline was starting. The dimpling at the chin, the yellowing under the eyes, the eyes themselves dimming and shading into gray. Not that she was going to go down without a fight. The corrective work was beginning, if it hadn't already begun—God only knew how many times the wrinkles had been stretched back or puffed out or whatever it was they did, what sort of architectural renovation she'd undertaken on her body since he'd left. Felicia Greenglass was, always would be, had to be, a glamorous woman. Why else would anyone have noticed her, she'd once told him, an ordinary girl from Brooklyn whose own mother, a seamstress with aspirations to become the next Coco Chanel, viewed her daughters as fungible commodities, mere dress models whose purpose in life was to advertise their mother's unrecognized gifts to a waiting world? Thelma Rothstein's girls weren't allowed out of their Canarsie four-room without passing a merciless daily inspection. One had to maintain appearances. Thelma's fashion dreams came to nothing, but by the time Felicia had graduated high school, a lifelong compulsion for self-enhancement was under way. Whatever she wasn't born with she would invent, beginning with her name, the perfectly workable Phyllis not good enough for a nineteen-year-old coquette at City College who was aiming higher. The prize for becoming Felicia was to be wooed by the fabulously successful Lenny Greenglass, ten years older and already rolling in it by the time he was twenty-nine, though his would be one of those fortunes that would be won and lost repeatedly in the decades following. But in the early years, before anyone knew that, Felicia had been certain they were destined for only grand things, and she'd wanted to change Lenny's name too. Maybe to the French Léon, with the accent, or to Laurent or Leonid, or even the never-used Leonard, but Lenny drew the line, leaving his wife to channel her designing energies into their various domiciles and their two pliable sons.

"You take cream in your coffee, Mark?" she called now from the kitchen, the clicking of her heels on the marble already unnerving him, in the apartment for ten minutes. It was all cascading back, his mother's need to be the peacock admired by the resident dull hens. Waiting for him on a rainy Wednesday afternoon in a twelve-hundred-dollar blue silk pantsuit and high heels may have been unnecessary but it certainly wasn't an afterthought. What else could he say after their hug but *You look great, Mom*. And she did.

"Please," he called back, twisting his fingers, hunched over on the couch. It was a mistake and not a mistake to stay there. But he couldn't very well be teaching six blocks from their apartment and stay in a hotel. Anyway, there was no money for that in the stipend.

The *clack-clack-clack*ing warned him like Morse code, and then there she was, like a piece of the sky, the robin's egg silk glowing, brightening the dim room, the eternal Manhattan gray seeping in through the streaked windows despite the soft lamps, the carefully placed pendant lights, the white couches, the white carpet. *Like a wedding cake. Or a marshmallow,* Scott had written after he'd seen the new redecorating. Still, it was his mother. He couldn't judge her. He had no reason to. Because he loved her.

"Here we are," she said, singsong, like when he was a kid and she brought him tea and toast in bed when he was sick. She rested a perfect black lacquered Japanese tray on the table, then handed him a mug, put out a little plate of fancy cookies. They had long ago stopped wrestling over the kosher business. He didn't ask and they didn't tell. He ate what they put in front of him. If they were ignoring the labels, not checking the ingredients, lard in the pie crusts, animal rennet in the cheese, he needed to let it go.

He poured in the cream and stirred. She drank hers black. You didn't stay a size six by using cream.

"You got a call from the institute, a Mr. Wasserman?" She handed him a slip of paper. A message for Moshe, not Mark, another subject he and his parents chose to ignore, the Hebrew name never rolling off their tongues, his mother's out of awkwardness, his father's on principle. "Your father will be home by seven. We thought maybe dinner out? There's an adorable little place nearby we're just dying to try. That is, if you're up to it, after all that exhausting travel of course."

"Sure." He sipped.

"I wish your brother could have been here." She glanced out at the rain as if Scott might materialize at the window, like Peter Pan, or Tinkerbell. "I pleaded with him, but he had to fly back. So close. A week earlier, and we could have all been together."

He took a cookie. "What can you do."

She sighed and watched the window. "Right. What can you do."

He walked Felicia to her dentist two blocks away, a loose crown acting up the night before; she was apologetic, hated to spoil the reunion. The rain had stopped, and the buzz of jet lag propelled him. He found himself on the corner of Fiftieth Street and Tenth Avenue and turned into the dingy building, a hard pit forming in his stomach. He knew he would get there eventually but had imagined it would happen later, after he'd marinated longer in the city's grimness.

"Hello? Anyone here?"

The door opened like a whisper. She never kept it locked, she'd once told him. Because what difference did it make? It would just get kicked in or busted anyway.

"Regina?" he called out, and forced his way through the rooms. Though the windows were open, nothing moved. He tried to ignore what he passed on the floor, the spilled ashtrays and greasy food wrappers and empty cans, not even B-movie material. A tired, stale story. Who in this city cared about this one life? A thousand stories just like it in New York. Ten thousand.

She was in the back, sitting on a bed tangled with sheets, smoking. He hadn't seen her in a year. Her eyes were glassy and she was rail-thin, her bare coltish legs curled beneath her. She had on a man's too-large checked flannel shirt, and her hair was pulled back into a stringy ponytail. There was a book by her side. So she probably still read, still could read. She had once been so brilliant she read a book a day and skimmed half a dozen more. She was going to be a writer or a poet or a professor or who knew what but it didn't matter because she had so much dazzle and shine she could have been anything.

Instead she'd become this. "Hey, Regina. It's me, Mark."

She watched him from her perch on the mattress, wary, like a cat. Her hand shook as she brought the cigarette to her mouth. She should have been dead twenty times over.

He knew not to go closer. "How're you doing?"

"What do you want?" There was almost no voice left, just a rasp. Her skin seemed transparent; he could see the bluish veins. She looked fifty, not thirty-five.

"I don't want anything, I just like to see you when I'm in New York. I don't live here anymore, remember?"

She took a drag of the cigarette and blew out smoke. He didn't know how she survived. She had a mother somewhere on Long Island who used to come in once a week to get her to eat something before they started to throw things at each other, and a sister who lived for a time in Virginia. He didn't know where either of them were now.

"I moved to Jerusalem. Three years ago. But you know that, I told you last time."

She closed her eyes and inhaled. She probably never saw anyone except her dealers and the lackeys she had to screw because he was realistic, how else could she be kept stocked in junk? The thought made him sick. What kind of people got their rocks off screwing a zoned-out junkie who was slow-dancing with death and could hardly speak?

"I'm here just for a week. Teaching." He glanced down at the fringes. They were supposed to direct the mind to heaven. Though he didn't think they were going to direct anyone's mind to heaven now, least of all his own. "Still into religion. Though religion's not helping me much these days. A temporary salve, it appears. Had a good long run, but something's happened, I don't know what. I go through the motions, but I don't feel it. Not anymore."

She finished the cigarette and crushed it into the metal ashtray on the bed. He soldiered on. "How's your sister? Lisa, right? Still living in Virginia?"

She went for another cigarette. She was gone, checked out. Forget Lisa, forget Virginia. Still, he kept going. "You remember that apartment on St. Mark's Place? Years ago? How we used to joke, Saint Mark? How we'd say I was no saint? Well, then I tried to be a saint." He waved at his clothes—the pressed white shirt and the dark pants and impossible fringes, and then finally at the beard. The this-is-what-God-looks-like beard. "I tried to be good and repent for all the bad stuff we did and what happened to you, and I did it for a long time, but now it doesn't work anymore. But it all started with that place we had in the Village. St. Mark's Place and the big joke we made. Saint Mark Greenglass."

"Yeah." The voice was a thread. A fragile gossamer thread. "I remember. We were kids, weren't we. Just kids."

His eyes filled. She was still in there somewhere. Beautiful, brilliant Regina. *Regina*. An old-fashioned name. From the Latin, for queen. He had loved her so much. His first love, the purest there was. "We were," he said. She was closing her eyes. He had to go. "Just a couple of lost kids."

They had fallen into it together, in college, practically still children, but it was Regina who got him out. That was the crazy part. They were in that apartment in the Village trying to stay in school, trying to keep their heads above water, years of being stoned every day and then tripping and speeding and snorting, finally dealing, parents who might as well have been on Jupiter as far as communication was concerned, his personal demons within inches of engulfing him for good, when she began to give him the books. Books about the war and the history of the Reich and the doomed Jews of Europe and the methodical plans for extermination that had taken place country by country by country, and he'd been stunned. Shaken. An old cultural memory awakened in him with a cry. All those deaths, just because they were Jews. Suddenly he wanted to be a Jew. A real Jew. Not a Jew like his mother, who thought Jewish meant a few foods from Brooklyn, or his father, who'd just as soon forget he was one. Or like his college friends from Long Island and Westchester who'd had bar mitzvahs in little suits and that was that. He wanted to be a true Jew, a serious Jew. A bell rang somewhere in a far corner of his ragged mind, a message penetrating the dope-addled torpor telling him that there was something still worthy in him. That he could still make a life of value. One day she took him to an Orthodox synagogue, to her family's rabbi, in Rockaway, where she'd grown up. Rabbi Kleinfeld. Oskar Kleinfeld. A shriveled survivor who ministered to a community of wounded souls. Including Regina's family. That was the beginning.

It became a truth that never ceased to awe him. That he had been rescued by those who had died. And by Regina, who was still dying.

Pinchas Wasserman was as his name implied: sunk deeply into middle age, doughy, with the thick New York accent of a man who'd never been out of the yeshiva, who without apology ate a pound of brisket every Friday night except when there was chicken, who couldn't understand why a Jew would live anywhere but New York or Jerusalem, who thought bicycles were strictly for children and considered Montana a foreign country. He also had a Ph.D. in Talmud, another one in physics, plus rabbinic ordination and a master's in philosophy just for the hell of it.

"Good. So, staying by your parents is working out?" he said, taking off his glasses and massaging the bridge of his nose. He'd been looking over Greenglass's lecture notes and, like God, had pronounced them worthy. Ordinarily Greenglass would have been offended—who asked a visiting scholar to screen his notes before he spoke?—but in this case he didn't mind because Wasserman knew everything. Besides, Greenglass would rather hear in advance if he'd made any errors since the attendees at such lectures, despite their adherence to precepts of piety ostensibly precluding nasty ad hominems, were notoriously merciless with their criticism. If he made mistakes he'd be ripped to shreds, and they wouldn't hesitate to do it immediately, to his face. Politeness was not a virtue in that world. The opposite: it was a sign of weakness, lack of spine, intellectual laziness. Verbal sparring for this crowd was essential recreation, a physical sport.

"Working out well enough," Greenglass said.

Wasserman nodded, replaced the glasses, and paged through Greenglass's notes once more, perfunctory, a way to prolong the conversation because looking up and holding a heart-to-heart was out of the question. He moistened a stubby index finger as he turned each page and said, "Just so you'll know. You're welcome to come by us any night for dinner."

A casual invitation, hence the lack of eye contact, because of what Wasserman was saying and not saying: that Greenglass, staying at his heathen parents', could either transgress or be stuck eating cold fruit and yogurt straight from the container with a plastic spoon for ten days, and that Wasserman knew it.

"Thank you," Greenglass said, and since the last place he wanted to be was in this man's apartment with his surely rigorously devout wife and equally devout children where his raging spiritual confusion would be on full naked display, added, "Tell you the truth, I'm looking forward to trying some of the new places around here. Change of pace from falafel, you know?"

A barely perceptible nod as Wasserman continued to lick and turn, lick and turn. Case closed. No one wanted to discuss it, least of all Wasserman. How Greenglass chose to bow to the divine will was his own business. Wasserman had done his part by extending the invitation because you had to be sure not to in any way cause someone else to sin. Beyond that, no insistence was required. Wasserman stopped paging and piled up the stack and pushed it across the desk to Greenglass.

"You've got a good enrollment. Already we're at maximum capacity." Walk-ins of course would not be turned away. You didn't deny anyone who wanted to learn, and you also didn't pay attention to the Gentiles' rules, like the city building inspector's occupancy limits, the concern of non-Jewish bureaucrats who understood nothing about the inviolable primacy of studying holy texts. A mere inconvenience, these numbers. A trifle no one bothered even paying lip service to.

Wasserman reached into a drawer and pulled out a packet and inspected the contents. Instructions, lists, administrative details. His institute ran classes fifty-two weeks a year, Greenglass one of twenty guest lecturers. In exchange for round-trip airfare from Israel and a stipend that equalled what he could earn in Jerusalem in three months if he was lucky, for a week Greenglass would lecture twice a day and in between oversee four hours of small group study. Satisfied, Wasserman slid the packet across the desk. His nails were cut square across and were surprisingly yellow for a man Greenglass put at no more than forty-five. Where, when, who, it was all in there, Wasserman said, gesturing at the envelope, though Greenglass would not find any tax forms. Too much of a bother, and why give the government any more money than necessary. It was all an honorarium, as far as Wasserman was concerned, up to Greenglass if he wanted to report it. But he had better not slip and fall because there was no workers' compensation either. Then Wasserman smiled at his joke and extended a fleshy hand and welcomed Greenglass to the Diaspora.

It had been during the preparations for Wasserman's course that the trouble began. Greenglass had wanted the job. He'd heard of Wasserman and had contacted him, gotten people to put in a good word. His life, like that of every teacher like him, was a constant hustle, an ongoing pitch game to be a scholar-in-residence, a guest lecturer, an honorary this or that to help cover because you couldn't make a living in Jerusalem.

And Wasserman's gig was a thousand times better than most, a serious outfit run by serious people for serious students. Unlike the usual offerings, soul-crushing marathons put on in Miami or Beverly Hills or Shaker Heights where you prostituted yourself for a week or a string of weekends at an event bankrolled by a rich congregant or federation donor who made his money in furs or plumbing supplies and was underwriting everything to impress his friends with his wealth and piety. Greenglass had done his share and had sworn to himself: no more. The obligatory stay in a mammoth trophy house, the lavish catered meals served by a fleet of uniformed black maids, the Filipino houseboy hovering in the corner waiting to hang up the coats. The food may have been kosher but the ethics reeked, company presidents who wouldn't ride on the sabbath or put milk in their coffee after their pot roast, their sons huddling beaverlike over their Gemaras in the next room, snarling about how the unions were strangling them or the government's OSHA rules were destroying their profit margins. He'd go through a weekend in Highland Park or Teaneck among the tax lawyers and real estate moguls and feel like he'd allowed himself to be bought—worse, raped—packing his suitcase and tucking his check into his wallet, his gut filled with deli and pastry and bile, and tell himself: never again.

But then Wasserman came calling. Or, more precisely, came answering. Because Greenglass had needed the money and had pushed. It was a job he thought he could handle. No *Architectural Digest* homes. No exploited dark-skinned help. No rich doctors or rich doctors' wives. Real teaching. Interested students. Good but not exorbitant pay. Greenglass was costing Wasserman more because of the overseas airfare, Wasserman told him, but it was worth it for the role modeling. The men should see that a life in Borough Park or Riverdale wasn't the only option. And Greenglass had a good reputation. A smart boy, even for a Johnny-come-lately, Wasserman said, a guy who'd been studying texts less than a dozen years; most of these guys had been at it since the age of five. Clearly Greenglass had a gift. Greenglass accepted the offer, relieved. He'd catch up on his bills, get himself ahead of the eight ball instead of behind, and visit his parents. The seminaries in Jerusalem who employed him told him to take whatever time he needed. Two weeks. Three. A month. The jobs would be there when he got back.

But then. The preparation began—and died. He'd pulled out his notes, Tractate Brachot, Maimonides' Mishneh Torah, the Tosefta, material he'd taught dozens of times and loved, intricate enough to occupy a man for three lifetimes, all now suddenly flat, mechanical. Soon the ritual was mechanical too. He'd lay tefillin in the morning with the intentionality of a robot, fail to get himself to a minyan in the afternoon, then spend his nights reading old issues of *Time* or walking the hot streets of his neighborhood. The peace he used to feel at dusk when he readied himself for prayer in a stone shtiebl off an ancient alley, a dozen men swaying as the light outside the windows deepened to crimson, then lavender, then a velvety sapphire—*Blessed are you, Master of the World, who opens the gates of heaven and arranges the stars in their watches in the sky*— gone. All gone. He'd stand with the other murmuring petitioners and be mute, the language of devotion lost to him, as if someone were slowly erasing it from his mind, wiping the slate clean. A silence moved into him. Something inside was dying, a fire that had blazed in him for twelve years going out. He felt like he had a hole in his heart.

Days. Weeks. He suited up every morning like a person putting on a costume and went out into the world and pretended. He forced himself to work. A free Talmud course for the disaffected looking for a way in. A weekly lesson for secular Israelis. A youth group from Long Island he had to take on an inspirational walk to the Wall, the experience suddenly terrifying to him, idolatry, worshipping stones. He listened to himself talk as if there were two of him: the Greenglass who was lecturing and the Greenglass who was on the periphery, whispering *Who are you? What are you doing?*

Until finally it was September and he could pack his things and get on a plane to America. Hide in Wasserman's institute and his parents' apartment and the anonymous indifference of the numbing city and hope that something would change.

. . .

His mother had left a note. *Out on errands. Guest room all ready. I'll wake you for dinner.* He methodically unpacked, slowed by fatigue and the inertia of the room, an enveloping cocoon of mauve and ivory, like a giant raspberry cream truffle. As she had in every other square inch of the apartment, Felicia had endlessly redecorated this room too. Last time he'd visited it was green—celery, she said—the time before that a shade of yellow that was also a fruit or vegetable. Melon, or summer squash.

He slid his suitcase into the closet, a few of his old shirts rustling on the hangers like ghosts, relics of another life—a gray and white pinstripe, a hippie sixties-style pink madras plaid that was unbearably loud and once his favorite, Felicia's not so subtle attempt to get him to wear something other than the standard religious person's uniform of white shirt and black pants—then took off his shoes, his glasses, and lay down on the bed. Soft, puffy, a mountain of frilly pillows and bolsters and useless little bedrolls in a quilted floral design. A flowery scent rose up, as if from the linens themselves, detergent or air freshener, his mother addicted to products that banished anything that smelled of unhappiness or decay or, heaven forbid, the natural life of the body. He used to wonder how she'd ever managed to give birth until he realized she'd more or less not been there. *Totally doped up,* she told him brightly. *They put me out and the next thing I knew I had a sweet little baby in my arms and a brand-new pink satin bed jacket on, a dozen matching roses from your father on the nightstand.*

The ceiling was all swirls, icing for the living room cake. From beyond the sealed windows the traffic droned. He knew he should get up and pray. That it was time. Past time. He had skipped the afternoon and evening prayers the day before too, though he hadn't had to, could have done it silently, by heart, on the plane or at the airport; he'd certainly done it in transit countless times before. And the morning ones: he'd skipped those too.

And now he was going to skip them all again. In the place where the whole business began. New York. Where he'd descended with Regina and climbed back out alone. The irony was not lost on him. He was giving it up in the place where all that hot desire for the holy had first taken root.

3

*A*gain the bus was hurtling downhill. Again the terrified old man sitting next to Aaron Blinder fell against Aaron's shoulder, mumbled something, and righted himself, tightening his grip on his plastic bags of cucumbers and tomatoes. The news was on, and the old man had to listen. The country was addicted, broadcasts an astounding thirty-six times a day, always introduced with those insistent beeps. *Beep beep beep beep, kol Yisrael m'Yerushalayim! The voice of Israel from Jerusalem!* As if everything were always an emergency. The finance minister indicted. A shooting outside a synagogue in Paris. A fact-finding visit from former American president Jimmy Carter. Aaron stared out at the monochrome bleached-out yellow—yellow buildings, yellow fields, yellow sky—plumes of coppery dust rising up from the rutted road. *A peanut farmer. A lock-jawed Georgia peanut farmer.* He couldn't believe the guy was still alive. He hated Jimmy Carter and his phony Golden Rules, his smug Christian charity. They were so naïve at home in America; they had no idea who they were dealing with. You didn't *make concessions* here. You didn't give back to *play nice.* The Americans, the Europeans, they thought it was like some giant sandbox argument. *Now, children, you must learn to share.*

The bus veered sharply and the old man clutched his bags

tighter. They'd been charging up and down hills for twenty minutes, the driver maniacal. Aaron edged up closer to the window, pushed a greasy knot of too-long hair off his face. He should shave the whole thing off, like the Israelis did, half the country walking cue balls. He looked too American, too soft with his Day-Glo yellow T-shirt and hiking boots from L.L. Bean. The Israelis could tell a mile off; they talked to him in English before he even opened his mouth. The bus swerved again and the old man trembled. Aaron felt sorry for him, scared of a bus ride. If he ever got that old and scared of life he hoped someone would off him. Kaput, over, finished. *Carpe diem*, a professor of his once said, a smarmy married forty-year-old who thought his ponytail entitled him to sleep with any girl in the class but who was right about one thing: *Seize the day*. Because that's all you're certain to get. Like at the end of a Bugs Bunny cartoon. *That's all, folks*. So here he was, seizing.

An Arab boy lazily grazed his goats along the narrow sloping shoulder, inches from the bus. He seemed oblivious to the traffic, almost as oblivious as his animals, who didn't look up though the road dipped steeply and the engine roared in their ears. Pickup trucks with Palestinian plates, army jeeps, white vans of yeshiva boys: what did they care which vehicles polluted their air, whose road it was, who was in charge? It was all the same to the goats. Aaron pulled a slip of paper from his back pocket, glanced at it, then resumed his vigil at the window. No need to look for official signs. The place he was going wouldn't have an official sign, they told him. *Adamah*. He loved that name. *The Ground*. They had a handmade wooden post, the guy on the phone told him. Then a little snort at the other end because of course they wouldn't get a proper sign from the government. They wouldn't get anything from the government. Because they weren't supposed to be there. But no one bothered them either. That's how the country was built, the guy said. People just staked out a place together, started living there, and that was that. Even right outside the Jerusalem city limits. The post would be painted blue and white. Aaron should watch for it. If he went past the decaying Crusader ruin stuck in a field between two ancient olive trees, he'd gone too far.

He got off before the trees, the only one to disembark. The bus rumbled away in a cloud of exhaust. He crossed the road, a humming electric stillness, ten in the morning, already ninety degrees. There were two moshavs down this road; he could tell they were nearby from the stench of manure. The dirt path he was looking for would be just beyond the iron gate of the first one. He walked toward the smell, an eerie moaning beginning to thread its way through the silence. He knew what it was. He'd seen these places before, hundreds of cows penned in, unable to move, lying in their own excrement. *Man, who has dominion over all the beasts.* The moaning got louder, a long, low keening from a thousand constricted throats. A wave of something vaguely sickening began to churn in his gut.

He stopped and took off his shirt, wiped his face with it, then tied it around his waist. The heat was like a cloak, airless and suffocating. *This is how it is here,* the Israelis told him. *If you don't like it, you can go back to Brooklyn.* As if they knew. Because the last place he wanted to go back to was Brooklyn. Ever. His pack was heavy and his boots were too hot. He should have worn sandals. He should have brought less. He should have worn a hat. The cows keened and the air stank. The wave curdled and rose into the back of his throat. He pulled his canteen from the pack and drank. He should have brought more water.

The place had once been a cooperative just like the others down the road, given over to South African and Australian immigrants in the 1970s, but the new occupants, city people homesick for nightlife, for cafés and music and dancing, didn't like farmwork so they trickled away, and by 1980 it was deserted, the livestock and machinery sold off to the neighboring collectives, the buildings left to bake and rot in the blistering sun. A succession of indecisive governments had been unable to settle on what to do with it, using it at various times as a school for delinquent boys, a training center for Jerusalem's police recruits, even a home for unwed pregnant teenagers for a few shameful years until it came out in the papers that the girls had been sent there against their will and were surrounded by a barbed-wire fence and watched over by a guard tower, conditions that struck a chilling chord in a populace permanently hemorrhaging from the concentration camps. The facility was immediately shut down, the few remaining residents hurried off to prosperous country-club kibbutzim to finish out their gestation in style. After that, no one seemed to have any more ideas, and the place was left to disintegrate, ignored, neglected, forgotten.

"Which is fine with us," the shorter of the two guys showing Aaron around said. They were passing a crumbling cinderblock building splattered with graffiti, once the dining and community hall, not just for meals but for administration, the post, a tiny store, the occasional cultural event brought in to alleviate the isolation. That's how all these collectives were built, the guy said. Tents, a watchtower, and a community hall. The original commune. Just like the hippies but with a purpose. Best way of life. The two taking him around were both Americans, the short one with a nasal pronunciation Aaron instantly recognized as New York, the other sounding flatter, more Midwestern. They'd asked how his Hebrew was—*pretty good, good enough*—then glanced around as if checking and proceeded to give him the rundown in English anyway. "So we do our own thing and no one interferes," the squeaky New Yorker said. "The government doesn't even notice we're here. And who needs them? We've got generators for electricity and we haul in our own water."

The Midwesterner made an exasperated sigh.

"What, we don't haul in our water?" the New Yorker said, flashing him a look.

The tall guy rolled his eyes and looked away. Aaron took in the broad patches of dry scrub, the ruined flower beds. Haul in water from where? There was no place to haul it in from except their neighbors. Which meant they were doing some kind of guerrilla diversion, or poaching, or out-and-out theft.

"Looks to me like you do fine," Aaron said, because he liked the idea of getting by on your wits, of not going by the rules. They had a higher calling. Why should they be bothered with having to become official just to hook up to the water and power, having to deal with the byzantine bureaucracy, having to pay? They should let the farmers next door supply them with water.

"Oh, you haven't seen the half of it," the New Yorker said. "Out there? Past that tin shed? Date palms. A whole fucking row of them. And we've got olive trees too. Just beyond that."

The Midwesterner was looking off in another direction, shaking his head.

"What's the matter, Davidson," said the New Yorker. "You have a problem with my explanation? Don't like my spiel?"

Davidson kept shaking his head, looking the other way. "I just wish you'd tell the truth, Barney," he said. "Just tell the kid the goddamn truth."

"It is the truth, Davidson. And it's not Barney anymore. It's Ben-Ami."

The truth was that the palms and olives were technically on their land but had been neglected for so long that the neighboring collective had taken over their care and cultivation because they couldn't bear to see perfectly healthy trees left to waste and die. But if the members of Adamah went out there to pick the resulting bounty whenever they felt like it, what was the harm? It's not like the people over there didn't have plenty of trees of their own; they had groves and groves of them, Ben-Ami said, and a lot more abundant and closer to their processing plant than these. These stragglers near the boundary meant nothing to them. Besides, you were supposed to leave the corners of your fields for the poor. That was in the Torah. So let them call Adamah the poor. They were doing that collective over there a favor, giving them a chance to do a good deed.

"Just ignore Davidson. He's got this thing about honesty, wouldn't take a damn paper clip if it wasn't his," Ben-Ami said. Davidson had left to lie down. He'd been up all night doing guard duty in the tower. A staple of every collective as far back as a hundred years because you could never relax, Ben-Ami said, never let down your defenses. Especially there, practically butting up against the Green Line. Not that Ben-Ami believed in those bullshit distinctions. As far as he was concerned there was no line, green, blue, purple, or any other color, because the land was all theirs.

They were sitting in a sliver of shade against the side of the old infirmary drinking warm orangeade, courtesy of a crate of army rations stored inside. Aaron didn't ask how they got the rations and Ben-Ami didn't offer to explain. "Yep," Ben-Ami said, answering some unuttered question, "Davidson and me, we met in the old country. Hebrew school buddies, Skokie, Illinois. Met him when we were ten, throwing spitballs at the teacher, Mrs. Berg. My family moved back to New York but Davidson and I kept in touch. Naturally when he said he was coming to Jerusalem I told him he should stay with me. I had a place there." He took a long swallow, wiped his mouth with the back of his hand. "I've been in the country four years. I told you that, right? I was in the army. Demolitions." He finished his drink, set down the bottle, and leaned back. "Had to twist Davidson's arm to come out here, though. He could care less about the situation. But he'll come around. Got to open his eyes, you know what I mean? Get him to see what's really going down in this country. We're talking about the forces of light against the forces of darkness." He leaned toward Aaron. Aaron thought he could smell marijuana on him. "Era of Redemption, you hear what I'm saying? Jewish people got to stand up for what's rightly ours."

"Absolutely." Aaron watched Ben-Ami open up another bottle of the syrupy drink before taking a long swallow of his own. You wouldn't exactly say it quenched your thirst. The sun bore down on the ruined buildings. Somewhere a cat shrieked, sounding like a crying human baby. Aaron took another thick swallow. For the thousandth time that day, he wished he'd brought more water.

Naftali Shroeder, early fifties, steely blue eyes and a bushy gray beard, was a big man who in another life might have been a linebacker or a forklift operator or the cold-blooded CEO of a corporation that did whatever it wanted and didn't let anyone stand in its way. He looked Aaron up and down outside the shed that doubled as his office as if he were surveying his next meal and finding it wanting.

"Hebrew only, you understand?" Shroeder barked, letting Aaron know the terms of the encounter. It wasn't simply about which language they'd converse in. Aaron was being assessed, evaluated. The line he'd been given over the phone—*actively recruiting new members, come down and see how you like it*—wasn't the whole story. It wasn't going to be up to Aaron. Not like when you checked out an apartment to see if you could stand living with the existing roommates, or like a fraternity, which admitted you if you could survive their stupid attempts to make you throw up or hurl yourself butt naked off the frat house roof. This was something else. Something new and different and unnerving.

"He has great Hebrew," Ben-Ami said before Shroeder threw him a look. *Shut up.* "Hey, he'll tell you himself."

"It's decent enough," Aaron said, which was true. An intensive course in the winter during his aborted semester abroad before he got kicked out on account of their so-called *academic standards*, followed by three wasted months at a kibbutz cleaning out the chicken coops. But before that, there'd been a million years of Jewish day school shoved down his throat by his father.

"Good," Shroeder said, eyeing him, because only Hebrew was acceptable, did he understand? This was a Jewish country. The Diaspora languages of the Jews were for shit—Yiddish, Ladino, Judeo-French. Dzhidi. He bet they didn't know that last one. Judeo-Persian. Did they know there were sixteen hybrid Jewish languages in the world even today? He knew because he was once a student of such things. Back when such things mattered to him. He had once cared about the Jews who were far-flung, their customs and histories and dialects. He'd thought they were his brothers and sisters, worthy of his sympathy because it had been their misfortune to be born far from the Jewish homeland. All they needed was some understanding and they would all come there, where they belonged. He would study them, learn their ways, know everything about them.

But the more he studied, the more disgusted he became. *Parasites,* he said, using a word that sounded to Aaron like the word for insects. And sycophants. *Sycophantim.* They sucked off the Diaspora's wealth and prosperity to feed their gargantuan personal appetites, and then they sucked off Israel to feed their shallow Jewish pride. They puffed up with glory when Israel won a war or a UN seat or even a fucking soccer game. But then they stayed in their big American houses and their uppity British universities and their frou-frou French apartments and refused to budge. They sent over their parasite money and sometimes they even brought over their parasite selves, not just the tourists—the tourists he didn't mind so much— but the ideologues too. Did Aaron want to know a secret? Shroeder said, leaning closer. He reeked of tobacco and sweat. The ideologues were the worst. That's right. Arab-baiters who thought they were just like Shroeder, on the same side, clasping hands in solidarity, egg- ing Shroeder on to do more and more to punish the enemy where he lived, to take over his villages and fields, and occupy his warren-like apartments in the holy city of Hebron, firing Shroeder up with easy money and promises of sending over droves of eager supporters—and then they left, flying out ten days later on Continental to go live in the soft cunt of America, leaving people like Shroeder to do the dirty work. He hated them; hated their money and their drooling, vicarious lust. He tried to keep them away but they found him anyway, armchair phonies practically shitting with glee in their expensive American Levi's when they arrived so they could play out their tough-guy macho fantasies, their cowboys-and-Indians games, for an exciting week or two before returning to their bourgeois castles to write newspaper articles and letters to the editor, as if those mattered one stinking iota. As if what they said in America, in their American newspapers preaching to their smug American friends, mattered one bit. They made Shroeder sick. Did Aaron understand?

Aaron nodded. He understood, understood completely, he said. Shroeder pulled a pack of cigarettes from his jeans pocket, lit one, and blew out smoke. He didn't offer either of them the pack. Ben-Ami stared at the path, at a rangy black cat with a gash like a bloody red ribbon in its side. They listened to the moaning cows and smelled the manure and the smoke and the garbage rotting in the ferocious heat. No one spoke. Finally Shroeder tossed down the cigarette and ground it out with his sandal.

"Inside," he said to Aaron, tipping his head toward the door of the shack. To Ben-Ami he said nothing.

The lunch consisted of the standard chopped tomato salad, oily fried potatoes, and a gristly stewed meat that was hard to swallow even after it had been exhaustively chewed. Aaron gave up after forcing down two sinewy cubes, afraid he would choke, hiding the rest under his napkin because you didn't waste food in a place where resources were scarce, even meat that was probably the unsellable parts of the cows next door. Everyone ate methodically, quickly, with little conversation, the way he imagined an army unit might, or prisoners. There were thirty of them spread out at tables outside under a long lean-to, a mix of accents—Russian, Spanish, French, English. And of course Israeli. The youngest looked twenty, the oldest sixty. Some of them had families, Shroeder had told him, wives and children, and went home on weekends. The mission of Adamah was to recruit and motivate people to settle in the territories, and to defend and fortify those who were already there. This was a divine moment, Shroeder told him in the shack. The Jewish people were destined to have the Whole Land, from the Jordan River to the sea—Samaria, Judea, all of it. It had been delivered into their hands in 1967, and to turn their backs on it, to allow themselves to be distracted by pressure or hardship, was a rebuke to the Almighty and His plan. Sometimes the government was on the right side, but mostly not. Gaza—if anyone wasn't yet convinced—was proof: Jews expelling Jews. After that, what government could you trust? So Shroeder and a lot of others were going ahead and making things happen on their own. Because their leaders had lost their way. And one must never follow an authority whose moral compass was broken. If a few more Germans had thought that way, there'd be a couple more million Jews in the world today.

But Aaron needed to understand that Shroeder and the others did not hate the Arab. To the contrary. Sometimes he could even respect the Arab. The sons of Ishmael were a formidable enemy. But they were in the way. Just like the Canaanites and the Hittites and the Jebusites before them. Which was why they had to be disposed of. Not literally of course, Shroeder said, crushing his cigarette into a sand-filled plastic dish; Lior, Shroeder's big-shouldered lieutenant, had by then come into the shack and was standing to the side, arms crossed, watching. The sons of Ishmael simply needed to be given the incentive to move to a more hospitable locale. Motivation to speed up their departure. A little push. Just as the Jews in Syria and Iraq and Egypt understood in '48 that they were no longer welcome, so too the Arabs here. This is how it goes in the Middle East. Everyone changes places. Meantime, their task at Adamah was to present the truth dispassionately. To explain the divine promise and expose the facts about their foe. Because the enemy was brutal; they thrived on the taste of blood and had no regard for human life. Yet they were clever at public relations. They cast themselves to the world as the tender David equipped with only a slingshot against the mighty Goliath. So the world had to be shown the truth. At Adamah, they needed members to educate and be examples.

And they needed labor. They needed to fix up the buildings and refurbish the kitchen and dining hall. They had money, donations from abroad, even if the donors were the very same parasites that made Shroeder sick. But it was only temporary, he told Aaron. Sometimes you had to just hold your nose and take it. Writing fat checks made the parasites happy, and meanwhile it would get them the construction materials they needed. A trade-off Shroeder was willing to make for the sake of the greater good. For now.

"What about the actions?" Aaron had asked. "You know. The planned incidents."

Shroeder looked at him a long time. "Who told you about that?" A thick pause, Shroeder lighting another cigarette, then tossing the pack to Lior, the stifling shack like purgatory. For a few minutes Aaron thought he might pass out. The trapped heat, the curling smoke, the man's X-ray gaze, like sitting before God. "Are you the one whose father is the big writer? The guy with the novels about the camps and the refugees and the stinking vermin Nazis?"

"Yes."

A torturously slow inhale. The unwavering gaze. The quick sizzle of Lior's lit match. "You're not ready for that. Maybe later. When I say so."

Now, in the makeshift dining tent, Aaron sipped his sticky orangeade, tuning out the prattle of Ben-Ami beside him who was talking to a couple of olive-skinned Israelis about the cost of Adidas in New York. A fraction of what they cost here. Ben-Ami had been assigned to babysit him but the guy annoyed him; he was too talkative and gave Aaron a headache. After Aaron got up to get himself a glass of smoky tea, he didn't return to his seat. Instead he walked past a clutch of whispering Australian girls visiting from some Jerusalem seminary and found Davidson, who was eating alone at the end of an empty table.

"Mind if I sit here?"

Davidson shrugged, dug into his salad.

"Though I guess we better talk in Hebrew," Aaron said.

"What're they going to do? Whip us? Throw us into the brig?" Davidson picked up a glass of murky water. "It's not a prison camp, for godsake."

"Why are you here? I get the feeling you don't like it."

Davidson put down his glass. He had dark circles under his eyes, as if he hadn't slept in days. "I don't. Place gets on my nerves. But I don't have anywhere else to go. I'll split when I come up with something."

"Ben-Ami said you were staying with him before, in Jerusalem."

"Barney? I was staying with Barney, yeah. But then he left to come here so I had to come too." Davidson hunched over his plate, shoveled up the food. It didn't explain things. There were lots of Americans in the city, lots of places a guy like Davidson could have crashed.

"I've been living in Jerusalem too," Aaron said, watching him. "Ever since I quit the lame semester abroad. Bunch of spoiled rich kids, waste of time. In between I went to a kibbutz. You know. Volunteer. Be their slave." He waited for Davidson to say something but Davidson kept shoveling in his lunch. "You go to college?"

"Two years. Messed up, failed a couple courses." Davidson sopped up the gravy with a square of bread. It turned a slushy brown. "But I'm going to try again. Community college in Chicago, near my family. I want to go home, start fresh. Get my degree."

Aaron watched him cram the soggy square into his mouth. "Not me. I was out of that dumb overseas program in a month. Pissed off my parents but good. Not exactly parents; my father and step-mother. It's all they ever talk about. Israel Israel Israel, Jews Jews Jews. That and school. My father's mortified that the only college I got into is way the hell out in nowhere, practically the Canadian border. Gottsburgh. State university, you can major in, like, for-estry and animal husbandry." He was talking too much; sometimes he did that. He'd go off on tangents, people always told him. But the guy just kept eating. And he'd hardly said a word to anyone all day. "Weird thing is I was actually thinking of doing it. The animal stuff. Took a couple courses, really liked it. But my father went bal-listic. 'What are you going to be?' he said. 'Some kind of farmer? Jews aren't farmers.' He was too embarrassed to tell his friends I was even going to that school, let alone that I might do something with my hands. I once heard him tell someone I was at college upstate and let the person think it was Colgate or Hamilton or, if you can believe it, Cornell." He had to stop. Talking about his parents both-ered him. He was sick of thinking about them. After he dropped out of the semester abroad, his father threatened to yank him home if he didn't find something official to do, so he went to the kibbutz. He also promised to call once a week—collect, he didn't have a cell phone—and when he did, all his father ever did was harangue him about when he was going to come back and finish his degree or transfer somewhere respectable, start doing something with his life, twenty-one, kids he'd grown up with were applying to law school and medical school while Aaron hadn't been able to last a month in a program everyone knew was an academic joke. That's what his father had called it. An academic joke.

Davidson picked up the water glass again. Pretty soon Ben-Ami would come looking for Aaron; he wanted to show him his collection of spent shells, claimed he had a fragment of a Katyusha in his room. Aaron didn't want to see them.

"In Jerusalem I'm crashing on Gad Street," Aaron said, watching Davidson. He wished he'd been assigned to him instead of Ben-Ami. There was something off about the other kid. This guy seemed at least normal, even if he didn't talk. "You know where that is? Near Bethlehem Road. This dude's family owns a sweet apartment there, he lets in anyone who needs a place. Parents live in England. They're loaded. They've got these pearl-handled hunting knives, supposedly belonged to one of the kings? I'm not kidding. They keep them in a special drawer." Davidson took a long swallow. Aaron didn't think he could drink that water, it looked polluted, like things were living in it, swimming around and doing everything else living things do. As it was, his stomach was always giving him grief. He'd brought enough antacids from America to last a regular person years. "Eli Cooper's the kid's name. Maybe you know him; everyone knows him. He's the one who told me about Adamah. Where were you staying in Jerusalem? You and Ben-Ami?"

Davidson put down the glass. There was an oily film where the water had been. "Some guy's apartment, I don't remember the street." He pulled his dessert plate toward him. A rectangle of yellow cake with a wet canned peach on top.

"You couldn't stay there? Without Ben-Ami?"

Davidson stabbed a piece of the cake and stuffed it into his mouth. He was a big bear of a guy, six four, six five, two hundred and fifty pounds, probably hungry all the time. Probably never got full. "The guy wanted him out. So I had to go too." Davidson worked on the slippery peach, which kept sliding away from his fork.

"Maybe you could stay at Eli Cooper's. I could ask him. If I come here, maybe you could take my place. Probably wouldn't even charge you. He doesn't need the money."

Davidson shrugged, kept going after the peach. It was clear he didn't feel like talking. After another minute, Aaron took his glass and went back to his table. He hadn't even asked him his first name.

• • •

When the meal was over he told Ben-Ami he wanted to walk around a little before catching the bus back to the city. Ben-Ami said that was cool, probably so he could smoke more weed before he had to go to work. He'd been assigned gate duty, the most boring job on the planet, he told Aaron. He had to fortify himself.

Aaron hoisted his pack, left the dining tent. The heat had intensified—it had to be a hundred degrees—and the letter was burning a hole in his pocket. That letter. He'd managed not to think about it all day until this very moment, a record, but now here it was, poking its big fat head into his thoughts, the envelope with his name and address in that flowery script he could hardly decipher. He didn't know why he kept carrying it around. It had arrived at Eli Cooper's three days before, and he'd read it and stuffed it into his pocket and left it there. She was back at school, upstate, and just wanted him to know that she was thinking of him now that the fall semester was starting, and that she was sorry he'd had to leave the overseas program and that they hadn't stayed in touch, and that she hoped that whatever he was doing was meaningful to him. She'd gotten his address from someone in the program who'd heard where he was staying. The writing was in that oversized loopy script she had, and she'd signed it *All the best, Julie*. Julie. All the best.

He sat down in the bus shelter, dropped his pack by his feet. Someone had spray-painted *Am Yisrael Chai! The Nation of Israel Lives!* in red on the concrete. The thing about Julie wasn't that she was so good-looking. She wasn't. But she was appealing in that friendly, girl-next-door sort of way. The kind you saw in TV movies, fresh-faced and wholesome. Happy. When he met her at Gottsburgh the beginning of junior year, he was living in a giant quad of dingy cement dorms, four no longer white towers built in the sixties meant to be clean and spare but which looked like a pod out of a futuristic novel or a showcase village in Communist China where they brought foreign dignitaries to impress them with how modern and progressive they were. She came over to his table on a Friday afternoon in the quad's hangar-like cafeteria, hugging a clipboard to her chest like a camp counselor.

"It's a petition to fund a faculty advisor for the campus Jewish group," she said in an obviously scripted speech after introducing herself. He imagined a whistle hanging off a plastic lanyard under her pink sweater. "We're a small organization but dedicated, and we're asking all students to sign, whether they're Jewish or not. We hope you'll support our right to practice our religion and honor our heritage in a way that allows for full and meaningful participation in the college community." She smiled quickly and held out the clipboard and a pen.

He studied her a few seconds. She was upbeat. Perky in that eternally optimistic way of someone who never got depressed, never doubted herself, never wondered what was the point of living. "Where are you from?" he asked.

"Massena," she said. "Thirty miles from here. Almost on the Canadian border."

"And you're actually Jewish? From Massena?"

"Oh yes," she said, serious. "And let me tell you, we don't take it for granted up here. Not like the kids from New York City, or even Rochester and Buffalo." She held out the clipboard again. "I'm very proud of my heritage." She nudged the petition an inch closer to him. "Will you sign?"

He shrugged, picked up the pen. The last thing he cared about was some faculty advisor. The fact was, for two years he'd scrupulously avoided the tiny Jewish Student Alliance, the hokey flyers they put up announcing a Purim party or a bagel brunch, measly offerings that the school, a Jewish wasteland compared with the other New York public colleges, had managed to cough up. It didn't interest him. More than didn't interest; it positively turned him off. After twelve years in Jewish day school and his father's relentless obsession with World War II and Europe and the Nazis—*Never forget! Never forget!* the mantra his father put in all his books and essays and speeches and every single thing he wrote—he'd had enough Jewish in Brooklyn to last fifteen college careers. Twenty.

But something about her plaintive appeal, her sincere pitch, moved him. Or maybe it was because he'd been eating by himself in the miserable echoey dining room for three weeks and had hardly talked to a soul, the handful of people he'd met in his first two years who hadn't changed schools or quit now housed in the more human-friendly dormitories on the other side of the campus.

"Aaron Blinder," she read when he handed back the clipboard. "Well, Aaron, thank you very much. The Jewish students of SUNY Gottsburgh greatly appreciate your support."

He nodded. "And a good shabbos to you too, Julie."

After that, she could hardly leave him alone. He refused to go around collecting signatures, but she got him to attend an Israel Day picnic and a concert by a group called the Klezmamas who agreed to play for free since they were on their way to Montreal anyway. The same fifteen or twenty pimply students showed up for each event, city kids who'd tried and failed to get into the harder schools and couldn't wait to transfer or graduate, counting off the days until they could get back to civilization as they'd known it.

Aaron, though, had come to like his rural surroundings. There was something soothing about the upcountry location. He liked the rolling scenery, the well-tended farms surrounding the campus, the sight of cows grazing peacefully in the broad green pastures, the horses that stood in the middle of the fields in the crisp fall sunshine flicking their tails. He liked the sleepiness of the town's main street where he went to buy toothpaste or batteries or to just wander around. It may have been a crummy school by his parents'

standards, who never missed a chance to remind him that they'd
have sprung for private college tuition if he'd have made the grades
or done better than his stunningly tepid SAT scores, but Aaron was
happy there. The classes weren't too hard, for the first time in his life
he felt he could actually breathe the air and hear himself think, and
no one bothered him. No one was on his case every five seconds telling him to pay attention, to stop letting his mind wander. He passed
his courses and started taking an interest in the barns. He got used to
the quiet and solitude.

But then Julie had come along. And suddenly his contentment
was gone. He could've told her to take a hike, to leave him be, but
the truth was he liked her company. He'd never been any good with
girls; they'd avoided him at the day school where everyone had been
together since first grade. He knew they thought he was stupid. Julie,
though, was nice to him. The space-age quad had become noisy and
chaotic, people coming and going at all hours, the new party address
on campus after some hare-brained resident advisor got the idea that
what the place needed was a revolving-door policy of all-night beer
and blasting music, but Julie was too friendly, too eager, too insistent
to let him sit alone in his room with the door closed. She dragged
him to artsy films and English contra dancing and even to a couple of
Jewish events because, she said, he knew more about all that and had
better Hebrew than anyone she knew, and that he had to share his
wisdom and experience with those who had less to offer.

Then one early November lunch hour in the drafty dining room,
the wintry cold moving in for the long haul, she announced her
intention to go to Jerusalem. February. Second semester. Junior year
abroad. Gottsburgh was just too small, too limiting, too un-Jewish.
She'd talked to her parents and they were willing to pay for it. Why
didn't Aaron come too? There was still space in the program, it
would be good for him. There might even be some scholarship
money around if he got on it fast.

Jerusalem? Abroad? Why in the world would he want to go

there? Even his father hardly went anymore, saying he didn't need to fly six thousand miles so he could be surrounded by a few hundred million anti-Semites in kaffiyehs who'd like nothing more than to permanently wipe the Jews off the map. The enemies of the Jews were everywhere, his father said. He didn't need to go traveling to find them.

But Aaron hated his dorm, he had hardly any friends, and soon the whole of St. Lawrence County and all his beloved scenery would be locked into the frozen winter, not a cow or horse in sight. And then there was Julie. For two months nothing had happened between them, only best-friend bear hugs and playful kisses on the cheek and all-night bull sessions that were just talk talk talk. But he had hope. She seemed to really like him. He'd never seen her with any other guys. And he had to admit he liked her too.

"Maybe I'll do it. It's a possibility," he told her in the awful cafeteria, polishing off his greasy sub and wiping his mouth with a napkin. "I'll check with my parents." Though of course they'd agree. Anything showing a glimmer of intellectual or—even better—Jewish curiosity on Aaron's part was instantly reinforced in the Blinder household. *Finally*, they'd say. *Maybe you got something out of that primitive upstate backwater after all.*

She broke into a wide grin and, abandoning the second half of her overprocessed grilled cheese, jumped up from her seat, ran over and threw her arms around him, and gave him a kiss full on the lips, long and sweet, and he knew, at that moment, that he was home-free.

But he wasn't home-free. Julie's interest in him evaporated almost immediately after their arrival. She was still smitten, but with the country, not Aaron. She wanted to sightsee, to ride the buses and walk the streets and try all the exotic foods and soak up the language, to be out every spare minute poking through the Arab shuk and signing up for hikes in the desert and staying up for hours gabbing with the other overseas students. She was like a kid in a candy store. They had to branch out, she told Aaron, make new friends. That was the whole reason you went on junior year abroad. To *broaden* yourself. You didn't waste time with someone you already knew, someone whose stock of what he could offer had already been exhausted. In Gottsburgh, all he had to do was breathe something Jewish—*hamantaschen, challah, Tel Aviv*—and she'd smile and make him feel like a million dollars. But here, everyone was breathing Jewish; everyone was saying *falafel* and *b'va'kasha* and *Ben-Gurion*. In the Siberia of extreme upstate, Aaron was a lifeline, an intoxicant; in Jerusalem, he was just a drag.

For three weeks, through an interminable orientation featuring rainy bus trips crisscrossing the countryside, a frigid predawn climb up Masada on no sleep, a float in the Dead Sea where the salt irritated his skin; through boring visits to the Knesset and Herzl's grave and the Museum of Illegal Immigration and a miserable half-day spent in a claustrophobic cave at an archaeological dig, and at practically every other tourist attraction in the country, he watched Julie having a great time. Everyone liked her. Loved her, even. She was so friendly, they said. So refreshing. They were sick of cookie-cutter Jews like themselves from Boston and Sydney and Johannesburg. She was different. She was fun. Everything was new to her. Which made it new for them.

Then one night they were walking back to the dormitories, the whole group, after getting pizza downtown. They'd taken placement tests that day for the mandatory Hebrew-language classes. Aaron, one of a handful who'd attended full-time Jewish school, placed into the most advanced group. A couple of people complimented him. He must have a good ear, they said. He must have a knack. Julie was walking ahead of him with a gaggle of girls. She hadn't heard any of it.

"Yeah," he said, watching her. "I do okay with the language. Maybe that's because my father is a writer. Maybe some of you have heard of him. Emanuel Blinder."

"Emanuel Blinder? That Emanuel Blinder? Wow. I've read almost all his books, they're on my school's required reading list. Holocaust stuff. Wow."

More people crowded around. Was it true? That was his father? Julie kept walking, oblivious. She'd hardly looked at him all evening. That's how it was now. Like he didn't exist. Like they'd never been friends at all. A guy with curly red hair like from a cartoon was walking next to her. His name was Philip and he was from London, and when he talked, which was always too loud, he sounded snotty and rich. He turned around and told everyone he'd placed in High Beginner and wasn't that pathetic considering he'd had ten years of afternoon religious school, which was serious in England, really serious, he said, laughing, and Aaron wanted to punch his stupid freckled face that looked like Alfred E. Neuman. He was such a phony in his woolen peacoat with the collar turned up and a scarf knotted around his neck like some fake British movie star.

They were at the dorms, everyone standing around, cold, rubbing their hands, waiting to go inside. Philip turned somber and admiring and looked over at Julie and said that she had placed in High Intermediate and was too modest to say so herself so he was going to do the honors. Julie looked at the ground and moved in closer to her girlfriends but Philip kept on talking. Julie was just amazing, he said, looking at her. Bloody amazing. She must be a natural genius to have learned so much entirely on her own with no formal lessons whatever, and especially because she'd been stuck at some awful New York public college way the hell out in nowhere with nobody to talk to and where everyone else Jewish was a virtual loser, isn't that what she'd said, Julie? A bunch of losers, how lame was that? So no wonder she'd had to learn on her own. Philip laughed and Julie looked away and someone said it was late and they ought to go inside. Julie moved off with her friends but not before Philip gave her a wave and what looked to Aaron like a nauseating wink.

The next day Aaron tried to talk to her, but she told him she was late and had to rush to class, and when he tried again she told him she was busy and had to go. A couple of weeks later he started skipping classes, oversleeping, ditching the homework. His roommate, a kid from Michigan whose idea of studying was to get shit-faced over his books, helped him on a paper and then spread a rumor that Aaron must have gotten a 300 on his verbal SATs because he couldn't write a decent sentence to save his life. The one kid Aaron got along with, Dave Something from Massachusetts, went to the States for a family wedding and didn't come back.

When the program social worker met with him and asked if everything was okay, he said he was fine. When she pressed and asked if he needed academic support, he said he'd think about it. A week later he didn't turn up for a test. The social worker pleaded with him to come in for help, but he shrugged her off. When he didn't show up for the makeup exam, he told her he didn't care and that they should kick him out if they wanted to.

"What about your father?" she said. "Don't you want to make him proud? He's so happy you're here."

He looked at the floor. The woman said she didn't want him to leave. But it wasn't fair to the other students, the ones who did all the work. They'd wonder why they bothered. What would he propose they do?

"Just kick me out," he said. Because the truth was, other than the Hebrew class, even before he began blowing things off, he didn't get what was going on a lot of the time, couldn't grasp the reading, couldn't even finish the reading. It was too complicated and dense and boring, he kept falling asleep over the pages. And then there were the handouts. Sheets stuffed with facts and dates and names of prime ministers and presidents and secretaries of state they were supposed to memorize. But he was no good at digesting and regurgitating that kind of information. Even if he attended every class, he'd never have passed the tests. It was stupid of him to ever think he could.

"My father's going to have to deal," he told the social worker.

She looked at him with sympathetic eyes. Was he sure? Why didn't he think it over? Call home. Or talk to a friend. The program was ready to assist. He just had to make an effort.

"No. Just let me go," he told her.

And so she did.

4

he older girl, Hila, was waiting in front of the bakery; Yona could see her from the window of the 170 from Jerusalem, copper-haired and somber as she watched the bus come to a stop. Yona had forced the invitation.

I keep leaving messages but you don't call back. I'm here only a short time. Please.

A thick silence. She thought Dena might have hung up. Then: *You can come on Friday, Hila will meet the three o'clock bus.* No chitchat. No questions. Just: *You can come, Hila will meet.*

"The van is this way," the girl said, pointing to a battered white Toyota across the street. "It takes people up the hill, you don't have to pay."

They waited while the driver got a coffee and for more riders to collect on the sidewalk. Yona pulled down the sleeves of her blouse, trying to keep them at her elbows, be respectful, meet Dena halfway; it wasn't the time to raise the feminist flag, dredge up the old argument about who owns women's bodies and why Middle Eastern female dress codes always seemed to operate on the assumption that men have no self-control.

"Anat says Ha-Shem must be punishing you if you aren't married and have no children."

Yona turned to the girl. "Excuse me?"

"My sister. Anat. She says you're being punished because you don't live in the land. That you live like the goyim in America. That's what her teachers would say."

Yona had to look away. Her father would turn in his grave. That's not how it was supposed to be. The laws, the ritual, everything they were required to do, was supposed to help them be a righteous people. God's partners in creation, to make a better world. Not some holier-than-thou standard-bearers.

The driver was crossing the street with a takeout cup. Afternoon shadows fell across the square in narrow hopeful swaths, cooling the sidewalk, the sun-scorched garden. Two teenagers in long denim skirts and running shoes, giant backpacks hanging off their shoulders, came up to the van, talking in American English about another girl who wasn't answering her phone. They smiled at Yona, slid off the packs. *No More Disengagement!* screamed the canvas in thick black marker. *Refuse the Population Transfer!* Orange cloth ribbons hung off the straps. Gaza. The outrage seethed still, nursed and kept alive by those salivating for a repeat in the West Bank—let the government dare even mention withdrawal—so they could fulfill their promises of Jewish civil war.

"Anyway, I don't agree with my sister," Hila said, watching the teenagers.

"No?" Yona said. One of the girls moved the top flap on her pack. *We Must Not Forgive, We Must Not Forget!*

"No. I don't think it's right to judge. Only Ha-Shem can judge."

"And who taught you that?"

"No one. I thought of it myself."

The van began its labored ascent. White boulders pocked the dry hills in the distance while black dots moved across the inhospitable terrain: goats and sheep belonging to the Bedouin who lived in the valleys below. Yona had been startled on the bus ride from Jerusalem to see donkeys roaming unattended on the road and, once, a tiny gazelle leaping through the brush.

The driver shifted with effort. The van lurched, progressed unconvincingly; Yona imagined them all piling out, the American girls and she and Hila pushing the thing uphill while the driver steered, sweat staining their blouses, their skirts dragging in the dust. The teenagers opened their pocket-sized prayer books. Of course. The Traveler's Prayer. Required recitation before every school trip of Yona's youth, technically to be done while standing, but in a pinch, seated would do. Meant for long journeys, or dangerous ones. Though what constituted danger, she supposed as the vehicle strained and hiccuped up the hill, contemplating the prospect of spending two days in a home where she wasn't wanted, was open to interpretation.

The girls flipped pages, silently moving their lips. *May it be your will, Eternal One, to lead us toward peace and allow us to reach our destination alive. And may you rescue us from the hand of every foe, ambush, bandit, and wild animal along the way.*

Dena's hello was brief, barely courteous. She showed Yona where she'd sleep, tripled up, like another child, with Hila and Anat on one of their bunk beds, then declined her offer to help with the cooking, the laundry, straightening the house. *No thank you. Not needed. We're fine.*

The other children were warily curious, like forest animals sniffing out an intruder. They accepted Yona's gifts with muted acknowledgments: toy cars for the boys, embroidered change purses for the girls, a soft small teddy bear for the baby, candy and wine for the dinner. Everyone had their chores. Yona's was to stay out of the way.

By five-thirty, Aryeh, Dena's husband, had not appeared. The children took turns in the bath. Yona had been there nearly three hours and Dena hadn't said more than two sentences to her. Now

Yona sat on the sofa reading a book to Hila in English about a frog and a toad at the girl's request. Anat was setting the table, which had been opened to accommodate twenty—there would be company, another two families, ten more children—taking plates from a stack and listening. The apartment's furnishings were adequate but emphatically functional: brown Formica bookshelves, a serviceable brown couch, nondescript tables, chairs, lamps. If there was anything whose purpose was to beautify, anything decorative, however small—a colorful ceramic pitcher, a piece of pretty fabric covering a pillow—Yona hadn't found it.

"Don't set for Abba," Dena said, passing Anat on her way from the kitchen to the bath where she would retrieve the last two in the tub. "He won't be home."

Yona looked up from the book. So this was why Dena could invite her.

"Is your father in the reserves?" she asked when Dena was gone. Every man up to age forty-five served for a month, sometimes longer.

"No," Hila said. "He's with a new group somewhere. Kiryat Tzvi or Hebron Bet or Adamah."

"Adamah, Hila," Anat said, annoyed. "Didn't you pay attention? He's with Naftali. Abba's very important," she said to Yona. "He explains why we mustn't listen to the Americans who don't care if the Arabs drive us into the sea."

"Who's Naftali? Is he one of your uncles?"

"Of course not," Anat said.

"Naftali is Naftali Shroeder," Hila said. "He's our father's teacher."

"Not teacher, Hila," Anat said, a hand on her hip. "His *rav*. There's a difference."

Rav. Yona got it. A mentor, guide. The person you turn to, follow, sometimes for life.

"The Arabs all want to kill us, you know," Anat said. "They

shot at my friend's car and made her sister blind. Did you know they leave their girl children to die in the desert if they already have too many? It's true."

"Stop dawdling, Anat, and get the soup bowls," Dena snapped, appearing with the baby, who was wrapped in a towel. He was a beautiful child, wide-eyed and smiling, pudgy in all the right places. When he wasn't napping, Dena had him in a playpen in the kitchen. Yona would have gladly held him or taken him outside for a walk but of course Dena wouldn't have allowed it. "Hila, come take Daniel and dress him," Dena said. "And tell the boys to clean up the games on their floor so the littler ones can play in there later without choking."

The room emptied out. Yona sat alone on the couch, sunken and useless. Claudia had emailed that morning. *You're doing the right thing. Take heart. When you get back to Jerusalem Saturday night, go out for a drink.*

Anat was bossing around one of the little boys in the kitchen, demanding that he count forks. Dena had gone to the balcony to collect the wash. The sky was coloring itself a dusky lavender. Yona marshalled her courage and stood. A pale minaret pointed heavenward from the village on the nearby hilltop. Three hundred thousand Jews among two and a half million Palestinians in these territories. Hardly what Dena had in mind ten years before when she and David Small had come to the country to make a difference. But that was a long time ago and much had changed.

"If you'd like to go to services," Yona ventured, and Dena turned around, a small T-shirt draped over her arm, another in her hand, "I'd be glad to watch the children. And finish up whatever's needed here."

Strands of wet hair had escaped Dena's scarf and were stuck on her cheek, making a spidery, copper-colored spray on her face. She was wearing a loose cotton skirt, its decorative stitching almost gone, a decade older than anything Yona owned, and a pink blouse a size too small. And then Yona saw it. What she'd noticed and not noticed. Dena was pregnant. Just. But pregnant nonetheless.

"Hila will watch them." The reply was cold, brusque. "She knows what to do."

Yona nodded. *I'm not the source of all your suffering,* she wanted to say. *I didn't cause our father's heart attack. I didn't kill our mother. I did a lot of bad things but those weren't among them.*

Instead she said, "That's fine. Maybe I'll join you."

"Suit yourself." Dena turned back to the clothesline. Yona retreated into the shadowy dark of the living room. From the corners of the apartment came the noises of industry: Anat in the kitchen, Hila cooing with the baby, the boys picking up their room. Yona took another glance at the balcony. Dena was bent over the laundry bin, the folds of her old skirt swaying slightly, the ties of her scarf trailing down her back, and she looked for a brief moment like a painting Yona once saw in a museum, the biblical Ruth gleaning barley in the fields of Boaz for her mother-in-law Naomi. Ruth, the loyal daughter of Moab who'd given up her own family, her own country, to join the strange and alien one she was part of now. *Wherever you go, I shall go; your people shall be my people, and your God shall be my God.*

Abruptly Dena straightened up, caught Yona staring. For an instant Yona thought she saw a softening, a fleeting expression of interest, kindness, even forgiveness. *Talk to me.* But then it was gone, and the stoniness was again there. Dena picked up the plastic basket and left the balcony, Yona stepping back to give her room to pass.

All weekend Dena avoided her. It wasn't difficult. Twenty people at dinner, a chaos of babies and children, of feeding and serving and cleaning up, following which Dena, up since dawn, went to bed. In the morning, Dena and half her neighborhood went to the synagogue down their street, Yona tagging behind like the unpopular teenager with acne no one wants to talk to, though the watchful Hila silently kept to her side. Lunch was at another apartment, where thirty more people crammed around folding tables, and a few charitable souls politely inquired if Yona was having a nice visit. Then Dena went home for a nap. By the time she woke, nursed the baby, sat with her study group for an hour, prepared and served the religiously mandated third meal with yet another two families—by then Yona had figured out that the constant stream of people had been designed to eliminate the already remote possibility that she and Dena would ever be alone—it was dark and time for Yona to go. She said goodbye, to which Dena and the other adults responded with nods, and Hila walked her to the van's pickup point at the end of the street.

"I'm going to visit America one day," the girl said. She was looking out at the blue-black sky. There were jackals in the distance, she'd told Yona. Others found their howling scary, but she liked it. If they were lucky, they'd get to hear it. "My teachers say it's like Sodom there, but I don't think that can be. Because my mother came from there. Like you."

They waited in the silence. "Our father was a rabbi, you know," Yona finally said. "Your grandfather. He was a very respected scholar."

"Oh. I didn't know that." A pause. The girl tipped her head, listening for something. Then she righted herself and said, "Ima doesn't talk about America because it's the galut. Like Babylon. For when we were in exile. But we're not in exile anymore."

A soft high-pitched cry rolled toward them, as if unfurling from the neighboring hills. The girl put a finger to her lips. Then it came. A ribbon of sound, a plaintive yearning. Yona closed her eyes, letting the sadness in the howls wash over her. She was so tired. She had tried so hard to be good. To smile at Dena, to befriend the children, be polite to the neighbors. To be pleasant and interested and harmless. And it had come to nothing. Dena would hold on to her anger like a lifeline. She would never let it go. It had cemented itself around her heart and become stone, part, finally, of the heart itself.

"They have a lot of different calls, the jackals," Hila said, and Yona looked over at her. The howling had melted away but the child was still staring into the distance. A tender soul in a harsh landscape. "Yips and growls and hisses. We think it's all meant to frighten, to scare away predators. But some of it is to welcome their friends." Headlights appeared. Two bright giant disks. The van, coming to take her down the hill. "That's the thing about animal cries," the girl said. "About any creature we don't understand. Some sounds are hostile and others are friendly, but we can't tell the difference."

5

At the first dinner, at the adorable little place where the bill came to half of Greenglass's monthly rent, his father had been on good behavior, coached by Felicia to keep his mouth shut, but now, the fourth night in the city, the restraint had worn off and Lenny Greenglass couldn't keep himself from being who he was. Greenglass sat across from his father at the dining room table and watched him eat. It was nine-thirty at night. Despite having a fortune that would have allowed him to retire and live in style to the year 2500, Lenny put in the working hours of three people combined.

"So what's the job this time," Lenny said, efficiently cutting his steak, not lifting the sentence into an interrogative because he didn't expect much of an answer. None of Greenglass's jobs ever satisfied his father because none of Greenglass's jobs made any money, and money was all that counted for Lenny. Unlike his and Felicia's acquaintances, Lenny, the son of a dry cleaner who'd grown up in a four-room apartment above the store, didn't pretend that academic status was just

as worthy, or that artistry or bookishness or any of the other effete
or intellectual things others occasionally gave lip service to merited
applauding—the friend's nephew who overnight became a success
because finally he sold a play, the cousin's son who at thirty-two got
tenure at Yale. *So what?* Lenny would shrug, consistent to the core,
a trait his son found oddly admirable; at least he wasn't a hypocrite.
What do they get up there in New Haven? Forty thou? Fifty? Dreck.

Greenglass played with a bottle cap from his father's soda. "Just
another teaching gig, Dad," he said. The cap had sharp little ridges
that he pressed into the pads of his palms. The early mother-son supper added to the infantilizing, though in this instance it was Felicia's
attempt at sensitivity; she and Greenglass had had a specially prepared salmon mousse she'd picked up at Lombardo's after scanning
the ingredients, but Lenny had to have his steak, and she'd wanted to
keep the milk and meat at least nominally separate. She was trying
hard and Greenglass appreciated it, though nothing was really working for any of them; they were all miserable if they had to be in the
same room with each other for more than five minutes. Greenglass
pushed the bottle cap into his hand, then moved it away and looked
at the fluted circle imprinted on his skin, like a little flower. "Nothing
different from the usual."

Lenny stabbed a piece of lettuce and nodded at his plate. He ate
vigorously but virtuously: steak, salad, diet cream soda, black coffee. He'd been a fat child, with two fat parents who'd died young,
and like a reformed smoker, had a missionary zeal against anything
that suggested a lack of willpower or control. Sentimentality. The
welfare system. Religion. Most especially his own. A crutch for the
weak-minded who needed someone else to be in charge. He worked
on the iceberg. Neither he nor Greenglass had looked at each other
because what was the point? Greenglass would see only the disappointment in his father's eyes, like the dollar signs in the eye sockets
in the cartoons, and Lenny would see an expensive waste of talent

and brains. Greenglass knew the litany, his father didn't even have to say it. Thirty-six years old, a degree from Columbia, followed by seven years holed up in a Queens yeshiva living the life Lenny's grandparents couldn't wait to escape, now dining on a wimpy soufflé with his mother and teaching a bunch of semiliterates who hadn't gone to college about arcane second-century laws that had no use whatsoever. What the hell was the matter with him?

"Pay any good?" Lenny said, trying to make conversation—his only subject—pushing aside the small potato knish Felicia had purchased for him after she'd bought the mousse. It had looked so delicious, she told Greenglass, who felt sorry for her because it was she who'd really want to eat it, not his father. But of course she wouldn't allow herself. From a back bedroom, the tinny sound of canned applause erupted. Felicia had excused herself to watch TV but everyone knew it was so Greenglass and Lenny would talk. She was desperate for them to talk, had been desperate for thirty years.

"Good as any other."

Lenny finished off the steak, wiped his mouth with his napkin. He was a fastidious eater. He pushed away the plate. The knish, now soggy with steak drippings, was untouched and Greenglass knew his mother would have to fight an army of demons to keep herself from consuming the thing in a single bite when she came in to finish the dishes, though eating it would ruin her night, possibly her entire week. Yet the waste of it—three dollars, fresh and handmade from the famous Brooklyn factory that shipped them all over the country—killed her, as it killed Greenglass. She may have had money to burn now, but it hadn't always been that way. "You and your brother," Lenny said, picking up his coffee, black as tar. "Two peas in a pod."

"Two peas in a pod, Dad," Greenglass said, reaching across and taking up the wet knish and popping it, whole, into his mouth, not looking up at his horrified father.

• • •

If Mark Greenglass was a disappointment to his father, Scott Greenglass was a curse. First a ballet dancer, then a gourmet chef, a set designer, and a decorator, Scott not only failed to make good money but he also never ate steak and his idea of fun was to pull out his sewing machine and whip up something pretty. He barely made it out of college alive, the object of nearly homicidal ridicule in a Neanderthal dormitory at a small school upstate until Felicia took pity and let him come home and finish up at NYU. Everyone was relieved, then, when four years before, he went to England with his lover, an Italian waiter named Mario, to run an antiques shop. He came to the States regularly on business, and though he and Felicia always had a good time poking around the galleries, Lenny could barely contain his horror. *He looks at me like I've just crawled out of the sewer,* Scott wrote Greenglass after his latest visit. *At least he sees you as aboveground.*

Though the truth was, Greenglass's piety wasn't any better than his brother's limp-wrist homosexuality. They were both anathemas to Lenny, who had missed the live-and-let-live Age of Aquarius sixties, too busy making money, or worrying about it, his sons' life choices signs of not just weakness but abnormality. Jew and queer were words he uttered, when he thought his sons couldn't hear, with equal loathing, shuddering at the costumery of both, the yarmulkes and ritual fringes on one, the turned-up collars on the other.

Not that his boys hadn't tried. A year before, they'd all converged on England for a family reunion. The idea was that if Lenny could see his sons as full-fledged grown-ups, with real jobs and respectable friends, he might show another face. Greenglass got himself invited as a visiting scholar at a posh synagogue in London; Scott and Mario prepared for weeks, cooking and cleaning and meticulously refurbishing a guest room for Lenny and Felicia as if it were Buckingham Palace. They found high-demand tickets for the shows and took everyone on a tour of the Lakes District, and invited straight couples and their well-behaved children to visit, polite people who listened to Lenny's jokes and complimented Felicia on her smashing outfits while Greenglass watched from the sidelines waiting for the other shoe to drop.

For seven long days everyone killed themselves to impress Lenny and drive home the message that his adult sons were managing pretty well in life. Mario was considerate but self-respecting, having come a long way from his waiter days, demonstrating a flair for business and planning to double the floor space of the shop, looking at a second location in a promising district that was gentrifying. The guests admired the plans. Felicia beamed over the house, the food, the store's spectacular inventory. Even the weather seemed pleased.

It didn't matter. By the end of the week Lenny was still himself. The shop would amount to nothing. Greenglass's ritual habits—the hand-washing before bread, the Theodor Herzl beard—were primitive. Scott and Mario's expat friends were in England because they couldn't cut it back home. God only knew where his sons came from, Lenny said on his and Felicia's last day, shaking his head at the breakfast table while Mario, embarrassed for them, got up and began to clear—the perfectly prepared French toast, the homemade marmalade, the fresh local cream. It certainly wasn't his doing, he said, wiping his mouth with an ivory linen napkin. Probably was his wife's.

Three days into his course Wasserman wanted to see him.

"Scheinberg cancelled," Wasserman said. The office window was open but there was no breeze. Indian summer. A special name. As if New York wasn't always steamy and exhausted in early September. "Last minute. Family emergency." Would Greenglass stay a second week and fill in?

Joel Scheinberg. A big scholar. Mysticism. Pompous and full of himself but a genius. Greenglass would get flayed at the lectures if he tried to fill Scheinberg's shoes.

Wasserman read his mind. "You don't have to teach Kabbalah. No one can do it right anyway. Not even, with all due respect, Scheinberg." He shrugged. He had sweat marks under his arms the size of grapefruits. "I bring him in just for the hell of it. Like to jolt the boys a little, shake them out of their Talmudic lethargy."

"What would I teach?"

"Whatever you want. Maybe something to rile them up a bit, make the mind tick a little faster, if you know what I mean." Another shrug. "Your choice, Greenglass. You're a bright boy, you'll think of something."

Greenglass looked out the grimy window, the size of a pizza box. Wasserman's office was like a cell. The sky was a washed-out gray, the gorilla heat and slanty sun mingling and trying desperately to break through the gloom and failing. Everything about the city depressed him. Except the money. Which also depressed him because that's why he was there.

"Things working out okay with your folks? Good to stay a little longer?"

He turned back to Wasserman. He tried to imagine the man's life. Tried to see his accomplishments, his obvious brilliance, but all he could think of was too many kids and a cramped Brooklyn apartment and Dickensian headmasters ordering sadistic tzitzit checks at the schools, making the boys pull up their shirts to display the fringes and whacking them if they'd forgotten, and ignorant teachers saying that airplanes crashed because Jews on the plane had eaten shrimp and that mothers died of cancer because they were being punished. He had heard of this stuff for years, the seamy side of the religion, the fire-and-brimstone side, and he'd written it off, the beautiful made ugly by small and petty minds. So why was it coming to him now? He had loved the tradition madly, the way you'd love a woman, and it had saved him, stopped the terrible free fall of his life, but now it was over, like at the end of a relationship and you couldn't see the good anymore, only the flaws. How she eats too fast or laughs at the wrong times, how she repeats herself and has foolish opinions on things that suddenly matter. The great disappointment, the love of your life proving herself to be imperfect. Worse than imperfect. Impossible.

"It's fine," he told Wasserman. "My mother will be happy."

"I'll throw in a couple hundred extra. Wouldn't want you to be a burden on the family."

Wasserman's eyes were red-rimmed and had a permanently sickly look to them. Greenglass wondered if the man never slept. "You don't have to do that," he said.

Wasserman shrugged. "We were going to pay Scheinberg more anyway. I still come out ahead."

"I've come into some extra cash. I'll buy you food with it, dishes," Greenglass told Regina. She was in the kitchen when he arrived. Though kitchen was stretching things. No stove or table but there was still a sink, a prewar-model refrigerator. He didn't want to open it and look inside.

"I don't need food." She sat on a folding chair and smoked and looked out the window, taking tiny sips from a bottle of Coke. He didn't see any glasses. Last year he was sure there'd been a stove. Who would steal a half-functioning, trashed-up stove?

"Later I'll bring you some stuff. You like turkey? Cheese? Ham?"

She looked at him. A glimmer of recognition. "Ham?" she said.

"Yeah, ham. You like ham?"

She shook her head, blew out smoke.

"You know why you don't like ham, Regina?"

She looked at him, made a long, slow nod. "I know."

He nodded, satisfied.

· · ·

Why did he insist on bringing her food? Why did he keep going to
see her? They had stopped living together—and he had stopped taking care of her—ten years before. But he had never stopped caring
about her. He couldn't. And not just because his was the name on the
emergency card in her wallet until he left the country, his the number
they called each time she ended up in a hospital or police station or
strung out at four in the morning downtown or up in the Bronx with
no way of getting herself home. Even if they'd never called him, he'd
not have been able to stop caring. She was his other half, the self-
immolating half that could have, should have, taken him over and,
but for the grace of—what? God?—would have.

And so from the day he moved out of their apartment in the Village until that very morning waking up in Felicia's melon-infused
guest room, he had not been able to let her go. Not because he still
loved her—and God knew she no longer loved him—and not because
she needed him, because she didn't, but because he was responsible.
It was as simple as that. He had walked with her down that same
treacherous path, shared with her their ferocious headlong dive to
self-destruction, without understanding that she might never be able
to get back out. That the luck of the draw—for it was luck and only
luck—had made it so that his parents were born in New York City to
the children of unremarkable immigrants who'd left their dead-end
ghetto on the western border of Russia at the turn of the twentieth
century because they had nothing to lose, while Regina's forbearers
had been prosperous Hungarian businessmen who stayed behind to
contribute to the flowering of European culture, doomed to pay for
the privilege of such contribution by perishing, nearly all of them, in
Hitler's ovens. A betrayal that ran through the generations of Regina's family like an open wound. A wound Regina was driven to salve
with whatever tonic, however false and fleeting, was at hand.

So if Greenglass was to be accused of paternalism, of manifesting that deeply disturbing diagnosis, survivor guilt, he stood, Your Honors, culpable as charged. For his was no psychological projection, no *syndrome,* no merely imagined sin; he *was* in fact guilty. He had been Regina's co-conspirator, her joint and willing partner, and for this he owed her whatever care and concern he could, however minimally and feebly, however foolishly, still muster, mindful of the fact that, since he'd decamped to another continent, his caring at such a distance was indeed minimal and feeble. And that it was offered as much to satisfy his own shameful needs—for he wasn't blind, wasn't unaware of his desperate hunger to appease the guilty survivor within—as hers.

He brought her a secondhand card table, a set of glasses, plates, two bags of food. Bread, turkey, mustard, a six-pack of Coke, bananas. He considered apples but wasn't sure about her teeth. He found strawberries, a pint of imported figs. He wasn't going to pretend he was her savior. But that didn't mean he couldn't bring her groceries.

He made her a turkey sandwich and put it on a new plate, poured a Coke into a new glass.

"Why are you doing this?" she said, eyeing the food. She had let him set up the table, looking at it as if it were an exotic creature she'd never seen before, four legs, a dark flat back.

"Old times," he said.

She tested the sandwich with her index finger, as if it might move. Maybe it looked alive to her. Maybe everything did. It once occurred to him that she'd been using for so long—cocaine, heroin, acid, speedballs—that she was probably mentally ill by now. He knew how it went: the drugs could make you lose it. You could disappear.

He inched the plate closer to her. She looked at it, suspicious. A scuffling came through the walls. Mice.

"When we lived on St. Mark's Place and I brought up food, you always liked salami. I'd go to the last Jewish delis on the Lower East Side. Where your grandmother lived. Remember?"

She looked at him. Her eyes were watery but it wasn't tears. She was sick, very sick. She picked up a sliver of the sandwich, which he'd cut into eighths. She'd eat a quarter maybe. A whole, even a half, impossible.

"She was a nice lady, your grandmother." The fact that the old woman almost never left her apartment, paralyzed by fear, had escaped him back then, just as it had escaped him that Regina's mother was also not in such good shape. No one in that family was. She nibbled on the sandwich, sipped the Coke. He looked at the cracked linoleum and the sallow yellow paint. He had paid a kid from the secondhand shop extra to help carry over the table and the groceries, then told him to wait on the sidewalk. As if the kid couldn't guess what was inside. Because it was no secret, the building a warren of roach-infested apartments for nickel-bag dealers and street-scum pimps and anyone else whose life couldn't sink any lower. The first time he went there, after he'd moved away, he stayed for fifteen minutes, then rushed into a restaurant men's room down the block to vomit. He had known that she was spiraling down, but she'd held it together for so long, keeping up appearances, that he'd been shocked when he saw the place. And her. Glazed eyes, dangerously skinny. His once meticulous Regina, who'd showered twice a day and insisted they change the sheets every week and fussed over the ingredients of everything they cooked because she didn't believe in preservatives, now living with rodents and subsisting on greasy leftovers from the twenty-four-hour Spanish grocery across the street.

"Turkey good?"

She nodded.

"Good. Eat some more." He looked at his watch. He had to go teach. "I'll come back tomorrow."

They had loved each other, and then they'd nearly destroyed each other, and then finally he had to leave. But leaving her hadn't come easy, just as nothing between them had. He was then twenty-six years old, through with the drugs, pulling himself back from the brink, finishing at Columbia three years behind schedule. He had been meeting with Rabbi Oskar Kleinfeld in Rockaway for a year, and it had given him a shred of hope. He learned: *The world is based on three things: Torah, worship, and acts of loving-kindness.* He learned: *One hour spent in good deeds is worth more than an eternity in the World to Come.* He learned: *Whoever saves one life, it's as if he's saved an entire world.*

Regina had long since quit the university, had started mainlining, moving on to more dangerous stuff. Greenglass began to worry, to make calls. Hospitals, clinics, doctors, all quoting unthinkable fees. In October he called his brother to ask what to do, then swallowed his pride and called his mother and told her he might need money to help a friend. Felicia assumed a botched abortion or a baby and offered without questions. In November, Regina agreed to go to rehab; she couldn't live this way anymore, she wanted to change. Greenglass found a place in Massachusetts and made the arrangements. He would drive her up the Monday after Thanksgiving and pay for the first three weeks with his mother's cash.

On Thanksgiving Day, he went to his parents' apartment at two, as requested; Regina would be going to her mother's in Rockaway to tell her the plans. He arrived exhausted, up late for days doing schoolwork, managing his part-time job as a stock boy at Pathmark, staying close to Regina to keep her from her cokehead friends, making sure she didn't slide. He made small talk through the Bloody Marys and hors d'oeuvres. He was trying to be better with his family, less of a hothead with his father. The two of them had been at it since Greenglass hit puberty, but the drugs had taken the lid off. Given him guts. He'd let his father know what he thought of him and his money, his bourgeois businesses, including a brief and miserable stint as an owner of an uptown apartment building, Lenny as Harlem landlord, what could be worse. Greenglass had been snide and ugly, using flashy buzzwords and catchphrases from his political science classes, classes taught by burned-out anarchist Marxists with nowhere to go but burned-out political science departments, secretly banking on the hope that Lenny, without a college education, might not actually get it; that the stinging insults were flying past him and that he didn't really understand. But Lenny did understand. And later Greenglass knew it.

Thelma, Felicia's mother, was there from Brooklyn with her latest boyfriend, a sixty-five-year-old former tennis pro who gnawed on a cigar and bragged about his game. Scott, twenty-one and sprung for the weekend from his penal servitude at the college upstate, wordlessly picked at the fancy cheese. At three, they moved to the table. Turkey, stuffing, mashed potatoes, string beans, coleslaw. A black woman Greenglass had never seen before served them, silent, poker-faced. Lenny was in top form. He rolled his eyes at Thelma's attempts to pass herself off as sixty instead of her actual seventy and suggested that the tennis player demand a birth certificate before their next date. He announced that the pie would be off limits to Felicia because he was sick of listening to her obsess each morning on the bathroom scale. He told Scott to pull himself together and stop sulking like a girl.

Then it was Greenglass's turn. As the maid began to clear the dishes for dessert, Greenglass got up to help her. Lenny told him to sit down, and when the woman was in the kitchen, said that the girl, though she was as old as Felicia, was being paid to do the job and that Greenglass should stop being such a castrated, guilt-ridden, liberal bleeding heart.

Greenglass froze. "What did you say?"

"You heard me. You've got to stop being such a doormat, Mark, letting the whole world walk over you. Especially the females."

Greenglass looked around the table. Thelma shook her head. The oaf with the cigar rubbed his chin and watched. Scott stared out the window. Felicia was begging him with her eyes. *Please. Don't*

start. He didn't want to start. He'd been studying with Kleinfeld, trying so hard to change. *He who curbs his tongue shows sense.*

Lenny was sweeping up crumbs with his napkin. Again Greenglass caught his mother's eye. *Please. Not today. Not now.* He looked
away. He could make it worse. Cross the line.

Or he could do something different for a change. Not act. Find
another way.

He kept quiet. The maid brought out coffee. Felicia nibbled at a
sliver of pie. The oaf blew cigar smoke and asked Scott if the girls at
his college were the easy lays everyone said they were. At the first
opportunity, Greenglass excused himself, pleading an overdue paper.
A fluke snowfall had begun, thick heavy flakes that would turn into
a blizzard and cause traffic tie-ups and subway delays, paralyzing the
city for days. When he got to his apartment Regina was there, high
and wrecked with three of her friends. She'd never left, never tried
to go to Rockaway. When Greenglass yelled and called her a liar,
she laughed, and when he persisted, she shouted that he didn't own
her and that she was going to do whatever she damn pleased, which
included not going to any fancy-ass clinic on Monday and he could
go screw himself if he didn't like it. He sat in the darkened bedroom,
and when the others had left and she'd fallen asleep on the couch, he
packed his things and went outside.

He sat on his suitcase in the falling snow and began to cry.
Where was he going to go? To friends? They'd all drifted away long
ago. Back to his parents'? He couldn't live there, had never been able
to live there. He closed his eyes. He had made such a mess of his life.
Who was he kidding, thinking he'd changed? *Misfortunes without
number envelop me, and my wrongdoing has caught up with me. Though
my mother and father forsake me, God will take me in. O Merciful One,
do not hide Your face from me.*

He opened his eyes, watched the swirling snow, then got up,
dragged the suitcase along the wet sidewalk to a pay phone, and
dialed the number. Oskar Kleinfeld, who told him to take the next

train. Which he did, getting the last one before they were halted by
the storm.

They didn't notice his lack of piety at the lectures. It was Mishnah,
Gemara, law. No great religious inspiration required.

A wide-eyed student waited for him after his afternoon talk.
They would reconvene in the study hall in twenty minutes. Everyone
needed time to smoke, to get coffee, clear their heads before sitting
for two hours to work through the material again on their own.

"Yes?" Greenglass said, collecting his notes on the podium, taking off his glasses. "Can I help you with something?"

The boy—he couldn't have been more than seventeen, a preco-
cious type already done with high school—was searching Greenglass's face. He seemed to be stuttering internally, afraid to get out
what needed to get out. He had acne and thick lips and was not destined to be one of those who made the girls swoon from across the
divider at Saturday morning services.

"Please, you can speak," Greenglass said, not unkindly. "What
is it?"

"You're . . . you're a good teacher," the boy stammered, blushing. "The way you took apart that pasuk. I want . . . I want to be like
you."

Greenglass regarded him. He'd seen that look before. Love.
They fell in love with their teachers because they didn't know any
better. They thought their teachers could save them; that if they
learned everything, they'd have happiness and contentment, all the
answers in the universe, and then the world would cease being a place
of crushing confusion and loneliness and sorrow.

"You don't want to be like me," Greenglass said softly. "Believe
me, whoever you are, you don't want to be like me."

• • •

He emailed the seminaries in Jerusalem who hired him to say he wouldn't be back for another two weeks and to give away his teaching slots, recommending names of people who needed the work. He wished, not for the first time, that he had someone he could talk to. A woman. He wanted to talk to a woman. About Regina and his parents and the ground that was slipping out from under him every time he saw the prayer book on the dresser. Every time he looked in the mirror.

But there was no one. The women he met in Jerusalem, newly devout women his acquaintances insisted on fixing him up with, nice women, women with fine intentions, he couldn't talk to. If he hinted about his confusion, they'd back away. They didn't want to hear. It wasn't how things were supposed to be. They were good women, kind women, but they were like him; the religion had saved them. So of course they didn't want to hear. Whatever he had to offer, it frightened them.

Not that he could blame them. Every day, he frightened himself.

6

They put Aaron on the painting crew with a couple of square-jawed Israelis who talked only to each other in machine-gun Hebrew that was hard to understand, but when he asked to be moved—to construction or the kitchen or anything—Lior, Shroeder's lieutenant and the work assignment czar, dismissed him with an annoyed flick of the wrist, like so many gnats buzzing in the dust, and told him to go back to work because did he have any experience in construction, in cooking? Did he know how to pour concrete or install plumbing or make soup for fifty? Did he know any of that?

Aaron shook his head and quickly left the airless shed before there were any more questions because he didn't know anything about painting either.

At night, after the oily suppers and his attempts to wash off the turpentine and sweat, Shroeder lectured. The man might have been brusque and imperious but he was also a genius. He knew every inch of the country, what it was called in the Bible and which king or doomed king's son had ever walked there, which caliph or British general held sway until the Jews took it back, and in what battle or siege, the details of which he also knew. His knowledge was encyclopedic; there was nothing about the land's geography or history or topography he didn't know.

Including its destiny. He had no doubt, Shroeder told them, sipping muddy black coffee in the makeshift dining tent in the half-dark, a dim propane torch in front of him, Aaron and the others listening from hard wooden benches, smoke from their cigarettes curling up around them like fifty little pillars of cloud, that the land, all of it, from the Litani in the north to Sharm in the south, would eventually be in the hands of the Jewish people. Because it had been covenanted to them by God. It was as simple as that, Shroeder said, his face ghostly in the flickering light, his beard ragged as a prophet's, the jagged pink mountains looming behind him like Mars, and if anyone claimed otherwise, they were afraid of the truth. But it would not be easy. In every generation a new Amalek rose up to try to annihilate them—the Philistines, the Greeks, the Romans, the Christians, the Turks, the Brits, the Germans, the Arabs. Yet the Jews always survived. Why? Shroeder asked, leaning past the torch, his ice blue eyes glittering in the cold glare. Because they were physically strong? Because they were numerous? A shrill laugh. No, because it was their inheritance. Their right. It was a privilege to fight, Shroeder told them in the fluttering half-dark. For millennia Jews didn't have that privilege, barred like Moses from entering the land. How lucky they were. *How good are your tents, O Jacob, your dwelling places, O Israel.*

After the lectures, Aaron, exhausted, hungry, went back to the room he'd been assigned in a crumbling barracks that had holes in the walls and cockroaches the size of turtles, and knew that everything Shroeder had said was true. And that being there was his destiny too. His whole life had been leading up to this. The suffocating Jewishness he'd grown up on—the nightly discussions with his father and stepmother, Professor Anne, analyzing every article in the *New York Times* to see if what was written was *good or bad for the Jews,* the drumbeat of his father's Nazi obsession—*Never again!*— the miserable years at the day school feeling like a loser while everyone else was piling on the AP courses and climbing over each other to try to get into Harvard—it had all brought him to this. Even the two years at his lonely college upstate had brought him to this. He had been in that Judenfrei outpost in the middle of nowhere, minding his own business, happy among the horses and cows, but then came Julie pushing him to the overseas program. The failure of which was also his destiny. Because it had brought him to the kibbutz where he met volunteers like himself who told him about the apartment on Gad Street and Eli Cooper, who took him to settler rallies and free lectures where they talked to him about the importance of real Jews like him, loyal Jews who'd come to Eretz Yisrael and were not afraid to do whatever was necessary to redeem their rightly granted land, and where nobody cared about his SAT scores or what college he got into, and where they told him about Adamah.

He lay on the hard cot watching the cracks in the ceiling. It was all lining up just right. He could feel, even, the hand of something greater at work. He was never a big believer, never one to buy into the whole God thing during the endless morning services at school with their robotic stand-up sit-down take-three-steps-back choreography, and now he knew why. Because that was the wrong God. An eviscerated God, neutered and sanitized for their tender American ears. A God of peasant stories and do-good mitzvahs. Visit the sick. Donate your birthday money. Honor your mother and father. Or a

God of follow-the-rules. Do this, do that. Don't eat this, don't say that. A God who rewarded good little boys and girls if they did as they were told, like a jolly Jewish Santa.

But that wasn't the real God. The true God, the Israelite God in whose midst he now lived. The fiery God of the Hebrews who thundered to them to reclaim their ancestral lands and smite their ancestral enemy. The God who in his ferocious power had drowned the Egyptians and killed all their firstborn and incinerated the priests of Baal and ordered the slaughter of thousands whenever they got in the Israelites' way. They were afraid of this God in America. He embarrassed the Jews there who wanted, like Jimmy Carter, for everyone to just get along. So they taught their children about the Golden Rule, to do unto others, and they hid the true Jewish God, whitewashed him, so that he was bland and palatable enough not to frighten the neighbors.

But the real God was here, in this place, and Aaron knew it. He felt the hand of the Almighty Avenger guiding him, touching him on his very shoulder, looking down at him from this cracked ceiling in this miserable outpost on the edge of the scorpion desert where a hundred battles had been fought and where so much blood had soaked into the earth that even the mountains had turned red.

7

hen she wasn't leaving futile messages for Dena, Yona walked the city. On a soft early morning when the cool of the night still lingered like a protective canopy, she stumbled upon a small sculpture gallery nestled behind lemon trees in the old artists' quarter by the windmill, clay figures resembling archaeological finds

in a lucite display out front. She stopped to inspect. Females, graceful and elongated, like Modigliani's swan-necked women. They were
ten or twelve inches tall, painted in muted shades of sand and coral,
high rounded bosoms and narrow hips, and serene, contented faces.

Of course: fertility goddesses, updated. She'd seen the originals
in museums. Faceless characters who were all pointy breasts and out-
sized reproductive organs, short and squat and beleaguered. But these
in the case were lithe and stylish, goddesses who wore their potency
with ease. With, even, attitude. Classy, and a bargain at sixty dollars
each. They'd make good gifts. But for whom? Elias? She was finished with Elias. Anyway, he only liked shiny new things. American
shiny. Glass and chrome and as futuristic as NASA spacecraft. He
was sick of the Middle East, he'd told her. All dust and religion. For
Dena, then? Dena would smash them on the ground like the biblical
Abraham had, abominations reeking of idolatry. Anyway it's not like
Dena needed them; she was doing fine on her own.

"Yafe, ken?" Nice, aren't they?

A woman had materialized from behind the lemons. Forties, a
single dark braid, jeans, and a T-shirt. She held a half-filled glass of
black coffee, sharp with cardamom, a sediment of grounds on the
bottom. She placed it on a stone ledge, unlocked the case and took
out a figurine and handed it to Yona. A creamy pinkish coral, smooth
and cool to the touch, like porcelain. Bits of gold leaf were flecked
onto the paint.

"They're modeled after the Canaanite goddess Asherah," the
woman said, looking with Yona at the statue. "We've given her a
modern spin. Israelite women worshipped her long after it was outlawed, the prophets are full of diatribes against it. That's how we
know the practice continued."

"The Book of Kings," Yona said, turning the figure. "I remember that. Altars to Asherah are all over that text."

"So I don't have to convince you," the woman said. "Jeremiah
called her the Queen of Heaven, which was not meant to be flattering;

it was probably code for temple prostitute. She was highly threaten-ing to the ancient monarchy. And beyond. There's evidence that she was revered as late as Talmudic times." She cupped Yona's hands, lift-ing them. "Isn't that gold leaf wonderful in the light? We use a special bonding technique. The ancients kept them in their houses and made little personal shrines. We associate them with fertility, but women prayed to them for all sorts of things. Just like every other female object of worship—Mary for the Christians, the Shekhina for the Jews. They were all God's girlfriend, if you ask me. The Gospels sanitized her into a mother and the Talmud turned her into a vapor, but originally she was probably this. An equal partner, with powers of her own."

Yona carefully turned the figure over again. The specks of gold caught the sun, sending forth dazzling bits of glitter. "Do you make them yourself?"

"Together with my sisters. We're all potters and sculptors. There are four of us. It's a family business, you could say."

Yona looked over at the woman. "That sounds nice. You're lucky."

The woman smiled. "It has its ups and downs. Are you a sculp-tor as well?"

Yona reddened. "Oh no. Just an admirer."

"Not an artist? I'm surprised. That's who typically finds us. Especially at seven in the morning." She picked up her coffee glass. The sediment slid along the sides. *Botz.* Mud. The Israeli version of Turkish. Boiled four times and strong as a triple espresso. Yona hadn't had it in years. "Would you like a coffee?"

"Thank you, maybe I will. But first, tell me, what besides fertil-ity did women petition them for?"

"What do women wish for anywhere? Hope for the future. The fullness of life—love, joy, all kinds of procreation, not just babies. Peace in the house." She made a little laugh. "Harmony among sisters."

In that case, Yona said, she'd take it. Because she needed all the help she could get.

8

*G*reenglass came to an unspoken agreement with his parents: early dinners with Felicia, followed later by half an hour of strained conversation with his father in the den while Lenny kept the stock pages open and the television news running and gave his son the benefit of his opinions. Knee-jerk fools, Lenny said, eyes on the screen, during a report about a new watchdog agency charged with curbing executive salaries. Not everyone was a Bernie Madoff or an Enron CEO, for godsakes. Without those salaries the American people could kiss half its industries and even more of their jobs goodbye; it was the profit motive that made this country great. If they took that away, Lenny said, waving at the television, they might as well call themselves Cuba. Or Finland or Sweden. So maybe everyone had health care in those frozen countries with their sky-high suicide rates—which was no wonder with their six-month-long nights; who wouldn't pitch themselves off a roof?—but the quality of it probably made it more attractive to drop dead in the street. Lenny had been to some of those semisocialist countries and, believe you me, he told Greenglass, eyes still on the screen, life there was no picnic. Those people would give their right arms for a little more good old free-market American capitalism. Greenglass sat beside his father in a matching leather lounger and wondered if he wanted Lenny to look over and make eye contact, or if maybe it was better this way. At least there'd been no fights, no words they'd regret. Lenny had been no diplomat when, after miraculously managing to collect his degree from Columbia years behind schedule, Greenglass went to the yeshiva and the yarmulke and tzitzit appeared, but

Greenglass had given his father plenty of nasty pieces of his own mind before that.

Jerusalem flashed onto the screen. A speech by the prime minister. Then a cut to a house smothered in smoke. A rocket lobbed into Israel from Gaza. The Israeli city of Ashkelon had spent the night in shelters.

"What the hell do the Arabs want?" Lenny said, hand flying at the television. "The Israelis pulled out of there four years ago. Such a colossal waste. The Palestinians could've made it their own country. Instead the place is in flames."

Greenglass watched the images—a smoldering empty field, the shattered windows of a hothouse full of flowers. He and his parents never talked about Israel, Lenny's comments just a way to fill up the room, keep the silence from collapsing on itself; he'd been doing it for twenty minutes, talking to air. No one wanted to talk about Israel because no one wanted to talk about how Greenglass lived his life. Lenny and Felicia had no idea why Greenglass had gone there, what he found in the place, and Greenglass hadn't tried to explain. In three years, he'd never suggested they visit. Nor had his parents brought it up.

"Country's practically a war zone," Lenny said, eyes fixed on the TV. "Future scares the hell out of me."

"Well, that's the thing," Greenglass said, watching his father, who was still watching the screen. "To live there, you wouldn't know it. Life goes on. It's a beautiful country really." A crew-cutted general who looked like George C. Scott in *Patton* was talking at a podium now, a giant American flag and the seal of the United States above him. Reports of a different bad-news war. "Maybe you and Mom can come visit sometime," Greenglass said, surprising himself. Yet there were hotels, restaurants. Museums, archaeology, architecture, all the things one went to exotic places to see. Maybe everyone was ready.

Or maybe not. "I'll have to think about that," Lenny said, shifting his gaze to the stock pages, though Greenglass knew he wasn't really seeing anything there; that his father couldn't look at him because, while Lenny was no saint, Greenglass had hurt him too, and that they had a long way to go before they could be father and son in a room together talking reasonably face to face. "Have to see if I can get away. We already have plans for a week down in the Keys after you leave. I'll have to check when I can take off again. And of course when your mother's free, what's good for her."

The George C. Scott look-alike had been replaced by an honor guard shooting rifles into the air next to a coffin draped in an American flag. Greenglass pulled himself out of the chair. "Sure. I understand. But give it some thought, okay?"

Lenny nodded at the paper. "Right. I'll think about it."

Felicia was at the kitchen table reading a magazine. She looked up at Greenglass and smiled hopefully. If only her husband and sons got along. If only her sons lived on the same continent as them, or as each other. If only things had been different. If only.

She closed the magazine. "Having a good stay?" she asked as he pulled up a chair. If she knew he saw Regina, she didn't let on. Even ten years ago she pretended not to know. "Enjoying the job?"

He wanted to tell her the truth. Say that he was going to give it up—the teaching, the ritual, the discipline, everything. That the passion had deserted him and he didn't know why, only that it had something to do with Regina and that now he only felt empty. But he looked at her bright eyes and anxious smile and knew he wouldn't. She loved him, but she would find what he had to say disturbing. He was confusing to her, this son who had needed to be so different from them. Why couldn't he be a regular person with a regular profession, a wife or girlfriend, aspirations for a nice condo or house in Westchester or on the Island, normal vacations, normal things? What was so wrong with that?

"It's fine," he said. "Good students. Stimulating colleagues."

"I bet you're a wonderful teacher," she said, inching a plate of cookies toward him. Lenny's pre-bed snack, all laid out and ready, an hour in advance. "You always had such a talent for explaining things. You were so good with Scottie when you were both small." She smiled. The good times. "And what a feather in your cap that they invited you to stay longer. You have someone watching your apartment for you?"

He took a cookie. "A neighbor. She lives downstairs."

"That's nice. What's her name?"

"Rachel. She's just a friend, Mom." Actually, he hardly knew her. A few chats in the hallway, a wave now and then. She was in the hip arty crowd that hung out at the Cinematheque and trendy bars in the old Russian compound, and that wanted nothing to do with bearded religious types like him. But she'd offered. So he'd accepted.

His mother was suddenly examining the contents of her teacup. He'd hurt her feelings. Shut her out. Again. But he never talked about his personal life; no one in the family did. "Sorry if I snapped, Mom. I didn't mean to."

"No, no, it's nothing." She took a sip, busying herself with the important business of drinking tea.

"I guess I'm a little tense," he said. "I don't have the enthusiasm for the work that I used to."

A nod. She was afraid to say anything lest he snap at her again. He had been such a tyrant to her once. To both of them. Because it hadn't only been directed at Lenny. God only knew what he'd said to them during those terrible years.

"Maybe I'll look into something else," he ventured.

"As long as you're doing what you enjoy."

"I don't know what it would be. What else I could do."

"I'm sure you'll find something."

He made a quick smile. It was as far as he could go. As far as they both could go. From the other end of the apartment came the sounds of a door opening, footsteps in the hall. Lenny, coming to the kitchen for his dessert.

"Things going all right?" Wasserman said the next morning from behind his messy desk. A half-finished Styrofoam cup of coffee perched precariously close to his elbow alongside the remains of a powdered donut. Greenglass restrained the impulse to move it. He occasionally saw Wasserman in the halls, the man perspiring heavily and shuffling along like someone twice his age, though Greenglass had heard a rumor that he had a new young—second—wife who'd been his student at a women's seminary where he'd moonlighted after a day job at the city's preeminent rabbinical factory. The affair scandalized religious New York and got the still-married Wasserman fired. One former colleague had called him a Lothario who'd taken advantage of the natural sex appeal afforded him by virtue of his position and learning. Looking at the pasty sweating man fanning himself with a folded-up copy of the *Forward*, Greenglass found it hard to picture.

"Fine," Greenglass said. "It's a good group. Lively. Prepared."

Wasserman nodded, put down the paper, seemed to be considering his words. Greenglass wondered for a moment if one of the students had complained. The wide-eyed kid? "Found a jazzy topic for this crowd?"

"Oh yes. The *sotah*." A rush of heat bloomed across Greenglass's cheeks. The laws of adultery. He hadn't made the connection; they'd been studying the text for days before he'd gotten wind of any Wasserman gossip. Gossip, he now realized, evoked by his choice of subject matter.

Wasserman was unperturbed. "You got some work lined up for your return? I heard you gave away your regular jobs. News travels fast. Even from Jerusalem."

Very fast. Greenglass had gotten a panicky email from one of the headmasters he worked for within fifteen minutes of writing the man's assistant. *You need more money? Name it, it's yours.* Greenglass, without uttering a word about his history, had become one of the premier lecturers in programs across the city for seekers with pasts like his looking for salvation and a second chance. There was something about him, the rebbes and principals who hired him said, that made these young people relate. *Whatever it is, Greenglass, you're doing a wonderful thing for these kids. For all of us.*

But now he was not going to be doing a wonderful thing. Or that wonderful thing. And so, no, he didn't have any prospects, he told Wasserman. He'd have to find work when he got there.

Wasserman pulled a paper from one of the piles. "Maybe this'll interest you. Last-minute opening."

Greenglass skimmed the page. Something called Olive Branch International, an address in West Jerusalem. The note was from a Seamus Hurley, Dean of Faculty. It was addressed *Dear Pinky.*

"Just a part-time thing," Wasserman said. "But it might tide you over."

"What is this place? I've never heard of it."

"Don't imagine you would have." Because, Wasserman said, it had nothing to do with religion. A Scandinavian women's college that concentrated strictly on the arts—music, painting, literature, dance—determined to distance itself from everything that roiled the city, including its toxic sectarianism. They had a few other small campuses in Europe; a wealthy Dane had endowed the Jerusalem program in the 1920s. A haven of high culture, they spoke only the King's English, like a miniature Cambridge. Hurley, the dean, had been Wasserman's upstairs neighbor a decade before when Wasserman was on sabbatical in the holy city. A Shakespeare scholar from London, Hurley kept himself encased in a cloud of professorial pipe smoke and dragged Wasserman out for a beer whenever the opportunity arose, an experience Wasserman recalled with consummate pleasure, bar-hopping not a part of his social repertoire in New York. Religion, Wasserman said, was all but banned at Olive Branch; they had no symposia on the subject, didn't offer it as a field of study, and had once barred all official discussion of same.

"But as you see," Wasserman said, pointing to the paper, "they've had to respond to changing times. Students have been asking for the basics if they're going to spend nine months swaddled in the cradle of monotheism. They get top-notch people teaching all the biggies—visiting Islam scholars, Christians of all stripes. They had a guy lined up from Vanderbilt to do Judaism but he bailed at the last minute. Seems the fellow's wife, a tender flower from Louisville, got cold feet. Too many bombs on the nightly news." Wasserman sighed vigorously and looked at the dingy window as if searching for something. An elusive thought, perhaps, floating on the smoggy air above the skyline. "Strange little place, if you ask me. Trying to pretend they can divorce themselves from everything around them. Art in a vacuum. Which leads to a certain prettification, if you know what I mean. Blind slavishness to the pursuit of the lovely." He turned back. "All a bit too Keatsian for my taste—beauty is truth, truth beauty. I like better what Picasso said: 'Art washes away from the soul the dust of everyday life.'" A shrug. "At least I think it was Picasso. Anyway, that's neither here nor there. If I put in a good word, I think you'd get the job. "

Greenglass read the letter again. Two hours a day, a modest stipend, those who taught there described it as highly rewarding. They could offer a talented student body from all over Europe, a congenial faculty, a pleasant facility consisting of a large mansion—with an excellent full lunch, gratis to the staff—and the intimacy of a conservatory, fewer than fifty students. Fall classes started in two weeks. If Pinky knew of any qualified candidates, the dean would be most obliged.

Greenglass looked up. "I don't get it. There are a thousand Jewish scholars in Jerusalem. Why is he writing you, and why are you telling me about it? He could have his pick."

A tip of the head. "The dean has, shall we say, some rather specific requirements. Foremost of which is that he prefers his Jewish scholars not to be too Jewish." Wasserman drummed the desk with his fingernails. The donut trembled. "A strictly academic approach. Cool and cerebral. His Islam scholars come from Princeton and Yale, his Christians from Oxford doing research for their fifteenth or twentieth book. He doesn't need some local hothead to teach Mishnah or how to read a midrash. He needs a detached expert. Someone who knows the stuff cold but isn't caught up in the conflagration. Someone with distance. Not, let's say, a devout practitioner. You're Jewish, Greenglass, but other than that I'd venture to say you qualify. Now, anyway."

So Wasserman had sniffed him out. There was no need to ask how. Greenglass probably oozed ambivalence, despite the persistent costume. Perhaps it was his unambiguous no-thank-you's to the invitations for the sabbath meals—he'd spent the weekends with his parents, nominally observing since technically he wasn't the one to turn on the lights or use the remote for the TV, even if he sat in the room. His most Jewish experience had been watching *Seinfeld*. Or perhaps Wasserman the adulterer had an eye for trespass. A sixth sense that could tell when someone was starting to stray. Anyhow, it didn't matter; Greenglass needed a job, and he was grateful to the man for the help and told him so.

Wasserman waved off the gratitude. "You're a bright fellow, Greenglass, I have no doubt you'll do fine."

"Well, I certainly wasn't expecting anything like this to fall into my lap. Tell you the truth, I hadn't really thought through my decision to give up the other gigs. It was kind of impulsive, took me by surprise."

"Life is full of surprises," Wasserman said, sounding like a man who could prove it. He sat back. "Let me ask you something. You married?"

Greenglass flushed. Totally inappropriate, but the rules here were different. "No."

"I recommend it. Keeps a man balanced. Even at its worst, it keeps a man balanced. The messy grit of life." He gestured at the desk, aimed at the donut. "I'm not a man for asceticism, as you've no doubt noticed. Don't think it's healthy. Just the flip side of excess, really. A sort of spiritual anorexia when applied to religion—to lift a word from the current lingo." He glanced toward the doorway, then back. "Too much rigidity: this worries me. When I see our boys out there scrutinizing the ingredients on a can of vanilla Coke like it's the Gemara, I worry." He leaned forward again. His shirt was perilously tight, the buttons one sneeze away from bursting. "Don't be so hard on yourself, Greenglass. It's not all black and white, goodness or sin, Torah or bars. I learned that from my friend Seamus Hurley. You can toss back a few beers and still be a good Jew. And I'm not just talking about alcohol. There are a lot of ways to be a holy person."

Regina was flying when he got to the apartment. Greenglass hadn't seen her so high in years. The bed was a tornado of twisted sheets and clothing. Shirts, underpants, an ominous-looking leather belt. Men's shoes were piled haphazardly in a corner.

She was also furious.

"Why do you come here, Mr. I'm-So-Righteous, I'm-So-Perfect? You're going to liberate me? Release me? Rescue my sickened soul?"

"No. I just care about you."

"Well, go fuck yourself and care somewhere else because I don't need you. You and your Jewish savior complex."

She turned her back to him and began to strip off her clothes, to taunt him or mock him or maybe just to take a shower, and he walked out and sat in the folding chair in the kitchen. He stared at the yellow walls. Why was he there? Out of pity? She refused pity. But he certainly wasn't there out of piety. Who was he, this new Jew, this Johnny-come-lately, to tell this old Jew how to live? An old Jew whose family were experts at suffering? What could he tell her? To read Psalms? *Have mercy on me, O God. I seek refuge in the shadow of your wings.*

She came into the kitchen, her hair damp, her clothes smelling of tobacco and ash, and sat on his lap and draped herself over his shoulder, her chest racing, her foot bobbing. She was a windup toy whose battery was running down but couldn't stop.

"Talk to me," she said into his neck, her breath a powder puff of hot sour air. "Anything. Just talk." He could feel her heart beating like a child's. Fast. Too fast.

A shadow was stretching across the wall just above a dark square where the stove had been, deep yellow, like a cornflower. He knew that he was going to lose her and that it would be soon. That after all this time, she was finally going to exit his life, exit this life altogether, and that there was nothing he could do about it.

"Please. Talk."

"Remember Roger?" he said, and held her close to him. "The guy who lived upstairs from us? How he said he was going to be an anarchist and a dentist?" He felt himself starting to laugh though he knew he was going to cry. "Remember how funny that sounded? And then we found out he was actually doing it. How, when he finished dental school, he got some donations and started a free walk-in clinic. You went down to the piers to get those bums to come in— remember? You were so good at it, they all loved you, you got a whole slew of them to go."

She was tapping his back, taking short bursts of breath. Her knee was going, up down up down up down, and she was light as a bird. She was fluttering, a creature almost not of this world, already on her way out. He took in the stale cigarette smell, her skin moist from the shower, or maybe sweat. She had been so magnificent. A mind like a laser, cutting through all the junk and garbage. The first person he'd ever met who told the truth. The real truth, not reality glossed over, eyes averted, or, like Wasserman said, prettified to be made palatable. *We have a choice between truth and ease,* she once told him. *But we can never have both. Emerson.* They had made love and were in bed, smoking a joint. Her hair was fanned over the pillowcase, dark and luxuriant, like mahogany. It smelled of apples. He wanted to bury his face in it.

So which do you choose? he said, running a hand along her shoulder and under the soft curve of her neck.

She'd looked over at him and smiled. As if he didn't know.

"More," she whispered now. "Say more."

He stroked her damp hair. He wondered if her mother was still alive. Her skull was round like an egg, smooth and tapered. Her hair was very, very thin; maybe it was falling out. "Remember Amy and Ken who lived with us one summer? How it was so hot and they were always fighting and then making up with the loudest lovemaking, and how we'd leave the apartment then and get ice cream and how you said Amy had to be faking because no woman ever sounded like that except in bad movies?" He stroked the fine hair, the egg skull, felt her heart pounding against him. He had loved her so much. Eighteen years old. They met the second week of school and that was that, inseparable for eight years until he had to get away. "Amy turned up in Israel a couple of years ago. I ran into her on the street. It had been a rough ride, she was trying to get back on her feet."

The knee slowed. The breathing became more regular, less frightening. Maybe she was falling asleep; maybe whatever she'd shot up or swallowed or snorted would only put her down for the night. "We had a nice talk, me and Amy. Actually, not really. I was a pompous ass. I said something about finding the right path. Trying to get her interested in the religion. I was an idiot. She went off to a kibbutz and I didn't hear from her again."

He stroked her bony back. She was asleep. He had tried so hard to save her but maybe he hadn't tried hard enough, too busy saving himself. He looked down at her frail form, watched it move up and down with each feather breath, the life still in her, and silently, as he'd done so many times before, asked for her forgiveness.

A steady rain had begun to fall. He wasn't ready to go to his parents' apartment. He went into a coffee shop, took a table by a big window. Water sheeted against the glass. A grim dusk descending. The headlights of the traffic threw long white beams down the wet asphalt, crisscrossing the road like searchlights. At the table across from him, a young couple, seventeen, eighteen, snuggled together, giggling, sharing a piece of cheesecake, a pyramid of strawberries and whipped cream on top. The girl wore bright lipstick and one of those mod caps from the seventies, a little pink beanie with a rim, her dark brown hair sweeping her shoulders. They were taking turns feeding each other, first the boy, his baseball cap flipped backwards, then the girl, wisps of airy cream trailing on her red lips. Between bites they kissed or laughed, oblivious to everyone else in the coffee shop, as if they were all that mattered in the universe, and a wave of loneliness washed over Greenglass, and something stopped inside him. There it was, right in front of him. The truth: love. He had avoided love his whole adult life. He'd told himself it was because of the religion, that he'd be with a woman only in the proper way, with chaste dates and a correct betrothal, or else that his life was too uncertain, too unstable, that it wasn't the right time or the right place.

But it had all been an excuse, an evasion. Because the only person he'd allowed himself to love had been Regina. And if Regina could not be saved, if she could not have happiness, then he couldn't either. It was as simple as that. That's what he'd told himself for ten years. He was thirty-six years old, and he had denied himself the most important thing in the world.

The girl glanced up, caught Greenglass's eye. Flushed, he looked away. *The Merciful One desires the heart.* He wished, suddenly, that he could pray. Not the rote phrases of the thrice-daily services, the Eighteen Benedictions or the mandated Psalms, but just words, ordinary words. Why couldn't he call upon He Who Has No Name? The One to whom he'd turned all these years, his sole companion?

And then it came to him, as if in answer. *Do not separate yourself from the world.* That it was God who had declared an end to the conversation. Who had heard enough and decreed that it was time for Greenglass to stop talking. That his penitence was done, his atonement over, and that it was time for him to learn new words, a new language. To turn his devotion, his passion, his supplications, and most especially his love, over to the things of this world, this earthly world, and no other.

9

There was a phone message for Aaron, he should come to the shack.

"From your friend Eli Cooper," Shroeder said. Lior passed him the note. Shroeder, at the desk, was tipped back in his chair, hands behind his head. "Seems your father's been calling."

Aaron nodded, stuffed the note into his pocket, turned to go.

"Don't you want to read it?"

"I know what it says." He hadn't made his weekly call home. His father was hounding him—where was he, they wanted to hear from him, he wasn't living up to his end of the bargain. Aaron had given him Eli's phone number in a moment of weakness when his father insisted they have a way to reach him in an emergency.

"I hear your father's a very big name in America," Shroeder

said, bringing the hands down onto the table. "Much bigger than I thought. Not only with the Jews."

Aaron shrugged.

"You ever hear of Aaron's father, Lior?" The other man shook his head. Shroeder turned back to Aaron. "Guess Lior here isn't much of a reader. Tell him about your father, Aaron."

Aaron shrugged again. Lior didn't want to hear about this. Shroeder was just razzing them, like he razzed everybody.

"Don't be modest, Aaron. Tell him how your father is a bestseller in America. Isn't that right? He makes a good living off those Nazis. What's he done—ten books?"

"Twelve."

"Twelve. Impressive." Shroeder made a slow nod. Aaron knew what he was thinking. That his father had made a lot of money off the concentration camps, the built-in drama of the ovens, the starved survivors wandering afterward all over Europe. Shroeder wouldn't have been the first person to say so; Aaron had seen the articles about his father, the ones that pissed his father off. *Twenty-five years sucking the tit of the Holocaust,* one of the worst had said. And this: *Churns out a cloying new melodrama every two years.* Then there were the plots. About his last book someone had written: *Another pity-soaked saga about skeletal martyrs stumbling around Buchenwald or Bergen-Belsen— ludicrously renamed Belsenwald—with staged fake heroics at the end to keep you turning the pages.* Aaron felt bad for his father but had to admit the guy had a point. At the end of the story, an emaciated woman strangled an SS goon and then snuffed the kommandant's girlfriend with rat poison. It was kind of a stretch, the rat poison part especially.

"So you like having a famous father?" Shroeder asked.

Another shrug. "It's okay."

"Mine was also famous." Shroeder looked over at Lior. "Did I ever tell you about him?"

Lior nodded and folded his arms. Aaron wanted to go. He

didn't want to talk about his father or anyone else's. But he could tell Shroeder expected an audience.

"Oh yes," Shroeder said. "Not a writer. Something else. Military wing of the Irgun. You know about them, Aaron? Nineteen forty-six, my father and Menachem Begin blew up the King David Hotel. Headquarters of the British government in Palestine. Best day of his life. He told me once that if he'd been granted only a single day on earth, he'd have chosen that one." He sat back, eyed Aaron carefully, as if gauging his reaction. Lior lit up a cigarette, blew smoke at the ceiling. "He went to prison, but when he got out he was a hero. Everyone in the country worshipped him."

"Is he still alive?" Aaron asked because a response seemed required.

"No. He died when I was ten. Heart attack." Shroeder kept his eyes on Aaron, pinning him into place. "Not what anyone would have predicted. Hard to live up to such a father. Especially once he's dead." Shroeder turned to Lior, releasing Aaron from his visual grip. "How about your father, Lior? He still walking this earth?"

"Sure is." Lior tossed the cigarette pack to Shroeder, who struck a match against the desk and lit up. "Lives in Hadera. School custodian. Likes to play shesh-besh in his spare time."

"You're a lucky man," Shroeder said. "With a father like that, you're free." He looked back at Aaron. "Unlike some of us, right, Aaron? We carry our fathers on our backs wherever we go."

So, yes, the rumors were true, Aaron told the six kids crammed into his claustrophobic cell of a room that night. His father was a famous writer.

Very famous, he added, even if some of them out there—he pointed with his chin to the shoebox-sized window—hadn't heard of him. But the people in the room had, hadn't they? They knew who he was.

Oh, they certainly did, Emily, one of the Australian seminary girls, said, passing Ben-Ami the joint. They'd all piled in a couple of hours after dinner and were sitting on the hard floor—Emily and one of her friends, plus Ben-Ami, Davidson, and a short, practically mute South African kid with a bad facial twitch who'd managed to weasel in. Isaac or Yitz, something like that. The weed was Ben-Ami's, but Aaron had had to buy it off him because the little get-together was Aaron's idea. *These two girls want to hang out. They're leaving tomorrow, the four of us can have a party.* He told Ben-Ami it would be fun, but Ben-Ami wasn't interested, and Aaron knew the girls wouldn't come if it was only him, so he told Ben-Ami he'd buy the stuff from him and anyone else who wanted could come too.

"Everyone reads your dad in Australia," Emily said. *Austraya*. That's how she said it. She was twenty and wore a tight T-shirt over big breasts. Aaron knew the type, religious girls in long skirts who wore close-fitting tops. It was like they secretly wanted you to take them off; otherwise they'd wear baggy sweatshirts like what Emily's skinny friend beside her was wearing, the other girl leaning against the wall sipping a lukewarm citrus soda Aaron had managed to pilfer from the tent. Not this Emily, though; she was showing herself, wanting him to notice. He'd watched her turn her fleshy lips into an O when she exhaled and wondered if she was wearing lipstick, if she'd put it on after supper, before coming over. "Not that I've read any myself, I should admit. My mum has, though. She told me about the one where the survivors of a camp get sent to Sweden to recover from the TB? How hard it is for them to find work and learn the language? She loved that story, it made her cry."

"Yep. My father's been milking the Holocaust for twenty-five years," Aaron said, accepting the joint from Ben-Ami. Ben-Ami closed his eyes and leaned against the wall next to Davidson, who was already stretched out, asleep. "Some of the stories are kind of a reach, though. Like in his last one? Someone kills the kommandant's girlfriend with rat poison." He took a long inhale, held it, then let two streams out his nostrils, like a dragon. "Like they actually had rat poison available."

"How do you know they didn't?" Emily said, flexing an ankle. Her legs were extended in front of her, her bare feet maybe eight, ten inches from his.

Aaron gave the joint to the South African. He hadn't much noticed girls since he'd quit the useless semester abroad, but lately ones like Emily seemed all over the place, demanding his attention. The other girl's eyes were closing, she was practically comatose; obviously she'd come to be the chaperone. "It's one of those things you just know," he said. "Anyway, it doesn't matter because his stupid American readers lap it up. It's this whole guilt thing because they weren't there. And the guy who writes the blurbs on the back? Mr. I-Am-the-Holocaust? *Lest we forget! We must not forget!* He writes the same thing on every damn book." Emily flexed the other ankle. Her legs were on the thick side, all of her was on the thick side, fleshy and round, and it both repelled him and turned him on. He didn't like girls who were fat—though she wasn't exactly *fat fat*—but there was something about them that made them impossible to ignore. You couldn't forget that they were *female*. All that pillowy roundness. Unlike the skinny ones, where you could overlook it. Girls like Emily didn't let you overlook it; they were always reminding you of what you wanted and couldn't have.

The South African was holding out the joint. Aaron didn't think he knew how to smoke it. The kid had shown up that day and Aaron had felt sorry for him, all by himself, oddly short and with a nervous twitch that made him blink nonstop. Emily leaned over to take the lit cigarette, and Aaron could see the outline of her bra. *Jugs*, his friends in high school used to say. *Fun bags. Racks. Sweater cows.* It had bothered him, the way they talked, but now he understood. They put themselves in your face all the time, these girls. Emily sat back, took the joint into her mouth. "But you know what's really lame?" Aaron said, watching her. She was puffing out her lips. "They think he was there. In the camps. Like he was born in one, or is really old. Or that at least his parents were." Emily blew out smoke. "He gets his so-called 'devastating details'"—he made quotation marks in the air—"from the library. From the New York Public fucking Library. Then he gives these pompous interviews and makes his big pronouncements." He put on a fake British accent. *"After the monumental tragedy of the Holocaust, there's nothing left for a Jew to write about."* The accent fit his father, though Emanuel Blinder and the whole pretentious Blinder clan had practically never set foot out of Brooklyn. Or at least had never lived in England. Even the Emanuel part was pretense, since his father's real name was Eliot. "That's one way to keep out the competition," Aaron said, closing his eyes.

"But does he actually say he was there? You know, interned?"

"He lets the assumption stand. Same thing."

A few beats passed. "Do you also want to be a writer?"

His eyes flashed open. "Hell no. Are you kidding? My grammar sucks and I can't spell. Though my father probably would've wanted that. He was always on me to take writing classes, as if I could actually write. It was stupid. Anyway, back at my college I was interested in animals. You know, livestock. They called it animal husbandry. I took a couple courses. It was awesome. But my father and his terrified wife, who does whatever he says, Madame Skinny Professor Anne, wouldn't allow it." He did the British accent again. *"What, Aaron a shepherd? A cowboy? Raising goats and cows and horses? This is the Blinder family! We're novelists! We're historians! We don't do animals."*

"What about your mum?"

Mum. Like he had a mum. "My mother took off when I was three. That's why my father loves me so much. He had to take care of me all by himself. Interfered with his precious writing time, you can be sure."

"And you don't see your mum?"

"No. No one even knows where she is. Probably couldn't stand my father so she fucking vanished."

Emily leaned her head drunkenly against the wall. The used-up joint smoldered in the ashtray beside her. "Bummer, not having a mum. What's her name?"

"JoAnne. Or maybe it's Joanna." A slightly sickening rumbling started up in his gut. The weed and bad food. His sensitive stomach. He surveyed the room. The South African was asleep, propped up in a corner. Ben-Ami had curled up on his side, close to Davidson. Too close. There was something about them. Aaron had seen them arguing in the dining tent like a married couple fighting about something other than the dishes.

He looked away. He never talked about his mother. Neither did his father, who refused to tell Aaron anything about her. Like she'd never existed. Like Emanuel Blinder had succeeded in wiping her off the planet. The night before the big Anne wedding, when Aaron was fourteen, he and his father had had a big fight because he wanted to hear the truth, find out once and for all why his mother had left. His father refused to say until Aaron provoked and provoked, badgering him in the kitchen, all the party stuff piled up and ready to go, bottles of champagne and little place cards with white ribbons, the lightbulb everyone thought was a wineglass wrapped in a cloth napkin that they'd step on and break, until his father finally screamed, *Because she didn't want us! Neither of us!* She had gone off for half a year to some hippie commune *to find herself!* his father shouted, red-faced, and when she came back, he refused to let her have visitation because she didn't deserve it. *That's right! Didn't deserve it!* After fighting him in court at the beginning, pathetic little attempts to make a show like it really mattered, she gave up and stopped trying, and now, he said, he didn't know where she was and didn't care.

Emily was taking a sloppy sip of her friend's soda. It was dribbling down her chin.

"I don't care about my mother," Aaron said, watching her. "She can live wherever she wants. And my father, well, he's way out of date. Forget the Nazis. They're old news. They were just a warm-up,

a rehearsal. The next big chapter for the Jews hasn't yet been written."
Noises outside, someone talking. Patrol. It was past midnight. He'd
told Emily he'd originally planned to join the Israeli army but now
had something different going, something better, there at Adamah,
where the real action was. Enough of this wimpy Jewish shtetl mentality, depending on everyone else to protect you. You had to be pro-
active, take care of things yourself. "The real enemy is here," he said,
jabbing a finger into the floor. "Right here, right now."

The voices were just outside. What did he mean? Emily said.
Them? she said, gesturing at the doorway. Did he mean them?

Of course not. She should wake up and smell the horse manure.
The A-rabs, that's who. He said it the way certain Southerners said
niggers. *Aye-rabs.* The new Nazis. The latest incarnation of the eternal haters of the Jews. And he had it all over his famous father on this
one, had it over him in spades. Because he was there, in the thick of
it. And his father was not.

She wanted to wait for everyone else to wake up and leave but Aaron
was afraid she would change her mind, so he told her no one would
be able to see them if they were up on the bed, even if by some lunatic
chance one of them came out of his dead sleep.

"I don't know," she said, tipping her head.

"C'mon," he said, patting the sheet, an urgency leaking out that
he didn't want her to hear. "It's no big deal. Just sit down. You don't
have to lie next to me or anything."

She just stood there, looking at her feet. Her tits were big and
ripe, and he knew she wanted him to take her top off, that she wanted
him to see them and touch them. That's how these girls were. They
advertised them and had them out front all night and were just
waiting.

"I need to go, Aaron. I could get in trouble for this."

Trouble? Trouble? So maybe she wasn't twenty like she said;

maybe all those Australian girls were in high school. Or maybe their school was super-strict. Well, so what. She was here of her own volition with those great knockers, and he had a hard-on like a tree limb and she was leaving tomorrow. Fucking tomorrow. He reached up and pulled her toward him.

She yanked her hand away. "I want to go. I could get expelled for this."

"No one's going to know."

"I don't care." She turned but she was slow-footed and woozy and he was faster. He sprang from the bed and grabbed her, pushed her onto her back on the mattress, then climbed on top and said she better be quiet or else she was going to get into deep shit. Because if she made noise, she'd wake her stupid friend and everyone else. And then she'd really be up the creek. Then he shoved a hand under her T-shirt and felt them. Two soft globes, spilling out of the stiff bra, two pillows he could bury himself in like a little boy. God, he wanted so much to lay his cheek there and feel them. He yanked up the shirt so he could see, but as he lifted it he caught her eyes, the terror in them, the silent hot tears streaming out, and he stopped. Just like that. Stopped. His gut churned, and he couldn't do it. He couldn't. He could never do anything. He got off her fast, the hard-on gone, drooped into nothing, dead, and quickly moved to the wall, his back to her, and closed his eyes. He couldn't look at her. She'd come to his room and acted all gushy and willing, those big eyes and that red smiling mouth, but then it'd all gone wrong and he didn't know why. He heard her gasping, trying not to cry, that fast staccato panting, catching her breath. Then the slurry murmur of her friend, Emily's *Get up! Now!* commanding the other girl to stand, then the door opening and they were gone.

He waited. He wasn't going to turn around, wasn't going to go out into the hot night to see them running, the friend staggering beside her, or maybe alert now, alarmed, debating who to tell, except they wouldn't tell anyone because what they'd done was against the rules, going to a boy's room, and they wouldn't want anyone to know, a stain on their reputations. Stupid messed-up girls. She'd come to his room and acted like she knew what was going to happen, like she wanted it to happen, and then she'd fled. He felt sick; he wanted to throw up; he wanted to hit someone. She'd come in all gaga over his famous father and his stories of wanting to join the army, and then she'd turned into a child, Red Riding Hood afraid of the wolf, like he was some monster or rodent or worse. She was just like Julie, like all of them, acting as if he was some untouchable. He pulled himself away from the wall, stepping over the motionless bodies, and went back to the bed and lay down. The flowery scent of her was still on the sheets, and he curled himself into a ball, sniffing the pillowcase, wishing to bury himself in the smell of it, to lay himself on those pillowy breasts, curling himself tighter and tighter, the churning in his gut coursing through him like a wave.

All night and the next day he ran to the bathroom every five minutes and had fevers and chills. By the second evening, someone bundled him in a blanket, and Lior drove him to a clinic in the nearby village where they gave him medicine and left him to sleep in a cool clean room. He slept, woke, threw off the blankets, took more medicine, then slept and woke and slept some more.

And then, suddenly, he was awake. And hungry. Starving. He pulled himself up. There was a curtain around his bed, and he could see a window through the opening and that it was daytime.

"*Ata b'seder?*" A nurse, middle-aged and all business, swept aside the curtain with a single swift motion. Was he feeling better?

"Much better."

"Good. Now go to the toilet and we see what comes out, and if it's all right you can go home."

"Someone's going to look in the bathroom?" He couldn't bring himself to say the word *toilet*.

"That's right. And that someone is me. Don't flush, leave every-thing there, then come back to the bed."

He swung his feet over the side and stood, then, wobbly, grabbed the bed rail. He steadied himself, shuffled to the bathroom. When he came out, Lior was next to the bed, sitting on a low twirling stool.

"So. Feeling better, Mr. Blinder?" It was the first time Lior had talked to him alone. And in English.

Aaron nodded. The nurse was already in the bathroom, inspect-ing. He crawled into the bed, pulled up the covers.

"That's good," Lior said, rubbing his hands together. Ben-Ami said he'd been a paratrooper. Someone else said he was an expert sharpshooter who'd done undercover work for the Mossad. Unlike Shroeder, he didn't talk much.

The toilet flushed. "Everything's okay, you can leave now," the nurse boomed. She came out, drying her hands on a paper towel. "A parasite, a bug, anyway it's passed. Pick up the medication at the desk," she told Lior. "You pay on the way out."

"So, his shit is clean?" Lior smiled at the woman.

"Cleaner than a baby's bottom."

Aaron thought he'd die of embarrassment. He wanted to bury himself in the covers and never come out.

Adamah would pay for the medicine, Lior said at the desk, but the clinic bill should be covered by Aaron's health plan from home. He did have a health plan, didn't he? The university programs required it, they assumed his was still good.

Actually, Aaron said, he didn't want his parents to know.

About the bug? Lior asked.

No, Aaron said. Where the clinic was.

They didn't know he was there? At Adamah?

Aaron shook his head. They thought he was in Jerusalem taking classes at a free yeshiva. They thought he was living on Gad Street off Bethlehem Road and working at a pizza place.

And if they knew?

Aaron shook his head again. Lior handed him back his insurance card, paid the clinic in cash.

They stopped in the village for supplies. Lior went to the hardware store. At a falafel place sandwiched between a grocery and a florist, Aaron ordered one with everything—tehina, eggplant, pickles, salad, fries. The guy stuffed the pita to overflowing, then slipped the whole thing into a paper V and handed it over.

"Charif?" Aaron asked. Did he give him the hot stuff? Because he wanted the hot stuff, the fiery chopped things that burned all the other Americans' eyes and noses and left them gasping for lemonade and Coke.

Of course, the guy said. He asked for everything, he got everything. Just like an Israeli.

Right, Aaron told him. Just like an Israeli. He sat at the counter and ate. It was the best food he'd had in weeks. He felt purged, cleansed; his body had been purified. He was glad he'd had to go to the clinic. Sometimes you had to go through something and were transformed. Like Jonah in the belly of the fish. It was a test. The old aimless Aaron was gone. Forget about girls and weed and wasting time. This was his new life, he was going to take charge.

He wiped his mouth with a napkin, checked his watch. Three o'clock. Morning in America. There was a post office across the street with a pay phone. He was supposed to call his parents. That was the deal. Once a week, collect. Lior told him he'd been at the clinic for two days. He'd already been at Adamah for eight. Which meant his last call to Brooklyn had been more than two weeks before.

He started across the street. Then he stopped. He hated those calls. Hated the excruciating silences, Anne's strangled voice, afraid to say anything nice, his father's barely disguised disgust dripping off every syllable. And then, finally, the interrogation. What was he doing. What were his plans. He was like a yo-yo, his father said, bouncing from unproductive thing to unproductive thing. He should come home, go to Brooklyn College or City if they'd have him, his father certainly wasn't going to spend good money for him to live upstate in a dormitory when he could just as well live at home and go to school nearby, for all he seemed invested in it. If he balked and didn't want to answer, his father said he was still supporting him, young man, he'd better not take that tone with them.

Lior was coming out of the hardware store. He saw Aaron, pointed in the direction of the grocery, then the car: one more stop, and they would go. Aaron waved, nodded. Well, he didn't need his father anymore. Or bony, timid Anne, who buried herself in her books and had talked to him a total of maybe fifteen minutes in the seven years she'd been married to his father. He didn't need them or their money or their miserly, grudging support. Adamah was taking care of him now. Adamah was where he belonged, with Lior and Shroeder and the others.

He walked back toward the grocery. A few doors down, in the shadows, a tiny barbershop with a single chair looked as if it had been scooped out of the concrete. The man inside put down his newspaper when Aaron walked in. Shave it off, Aaron told him, watching in the mirror. All of it. The man placed a plastic smock over him. His face had gotten thinner since he'd gone to the clinic; he had lost some of his American softness, a roundness that had stuck with him since he was a kid.

The barber cut off a thick shank and dropped it on the floor. Piece after piece went down. They lay on the stone like dead mice. The man started up the shaver. First the back, then the sides. Without his hair Aaron looked haunted. His eyes were huge. If someone saw him in a picture, they'd think all that was missing were the striped pajamas.

The barber finished up. He dusted off Aaron's neck with a brush, ran a little oil over his scalp and rubbed it in. It shone like a pale light. Aaron paid and left the shop, headed to the grocery to find Lior, help with the bags.

Lior was at the register; Aaron could see him from the big window. He went inside. He'd been changed, was someone entirely different now. He didn't have to answer to his parents anymore.

If he didn't feel like it, he never had to see them again.

10

Yona walked the streets of Claudia's neighborhood and allowed herself to consider defeat.

I phone. I leave messages, she'd emailed Claudia. *But nothing comes back. If I were to scream into Dena's face demanding an explanation, I'm afraid she'd say finally that it's because she doesn't care.*

She turned down Hebron Road in the direction of Emek Refa'im Street. Valley of the Ghosts Street. Not very ghostly now. It was the least alien of the city's neighborhoods, filled with bagel shops and coffee places with names like the Roasted Bean, even—God help them—a McDonald's. Ten years before, when she was feeling homesick at the university, she went there to console herself with an American hamburger and oily fries. On one side of the street were old three-story Arab-style buildings, their pointed arched windows and faded blue shutters collecting the morning sun, and on the opposite, another of the city's ubiquitous construction sites. Giant yellow cranes moved like crayon-colored dinosaurs, their heads raising and lowering with menacing precision. She stopped to read the sign. A deluxe high-rise promising the ultimate in luxury living: three hundred square meters of space, twenty-four-hour security, American-size kitchens with top-of-the-line European appliances, even an exercise room and a pool on the roof. A smaller placard in French had been posted for the benefit of the latest likely purchasers, Parisian Jews bolstered by a strong euro who were snapping up flats all over the country. Insurance policies in case the French Moslem underclass who hated them took their hatred to new levels.

Under a canopy of filigreed acacia trees she turned left. She'd walked down this road every day since arriving. Three stone mansions built by the local aristocracy after the First World War took up the whole block. Now they housed a science institute, a publishing company, and, the most spectacular because of its lush gardens, a tiny European women's college. She ducked into a shaded bus shelter across from the school's wrought-iron entrance gate and sipped her water bottle. *Olive Branch International College*, the name carved into a metal sculpture tree by the gate. She loved that tree, graceful yet sturdy. Or maybe it was the inscriptions she liked: *founded by His Majesty's Government of Denmark, Her Majesty's Kingdom of Sweden*, royalty that sounded like something out of Shakespeare. And the place did emit a pervasive pastoral, almost Elizabethan, serenity. Tranquil but a little bit grand. You could almost forget where you were. And no wonder: it was an oasis of the arts, according to the groundskeeper for the science institute next door. Music, painting, poetry. Each September, he'd watch the students arriving with their clarinet cases and polished cellos, their smooth leather portfolios, somber-looking women from Sweden and Norway and Finland. They took rooms in the neighborhood and sometimes put on performances, but mostly they kept to themselves.

Two of the women were on the stone veranda now, their easels poised between the pillars. They wore long summer dresses and looked out in the direction of the old German colony with its picturesque stone cottages and churchy windows, feathery green cedars that looked like quills on old-fashioned pens. One wore a white chiffon head scarf that covered her hair and was wrapped neatly around her neck. They looked like a postcard, or a lithograph from the nineteenth century. *Painters of Jerusalem*. If Yona were an artist, she'd be a primitivist—the vivid colors, the lack of pretense, of irony. But of course she was not an artist; no one would mistake what she used to do for art. She'd had her fling with drawing and painting, and then, because she had to be practical and because her talent was small and her confidence even smaller, she'd given it up. Instead she was a gallery assistant in a dead-end job where the snooty owners required everyone to dress in black and treat the customers with attitude, and where no one missed her, no matter how long she was away.

She sipped her water. The painter in the scarf put down her brush, walked to the other end of the veranda. She seemed to be studying the light. Did people in the neighborhood also rent her a room? There were few Arabs in that part of town. Not long before, one had walked into a popular restaurant and, within seconds, blown it up. A father and his about-to-be-married daughter were among the dead. It was the morning of the wedding.

The painter returned to her easel. Yona surveyed the grounds. The gardens were dappled with a surreal golden sunlight, brightening the beds of purple and white flowers, the sculpted topiary, the shimmering emerald lawn. A naked stone cherub lounged in a sparkling fountain. The place was beautiful but there was something off about it. An aching desperation. A longing, in its manicured perfection, to pretend it was anywhere but there, as if it were trying to call forth a more peaceful age, a more civilized location. Like a miniature Oxford. *Only speak English*, the science institute's groundskeeper had told her sadly. *Everybody must to speak English*, which is why his wife couldn't get a job in the college dining room. Very fancy, they served a four-course lunch at midday and tea every afternoon. Very good school, very good food. But you had to speak English, and his wife's command was poor.

The sun had arched higher. Soon it would be the heat of the day. Yona left the shelter. She emerged onto Emek Refa'im and, within moments, in front of the crowded Holy Bagel, nearly collided with her sixth-grade deskmate, Shira Feinbrenner. Finally, a ghost.

"Yona? Yona Stern? Oh my God!"

"Shira? What a surprise." Except it wasn't. Not truly. Every other person in the city seemed to resemble someone Yona had gone to school with. And in fact most of the girls from her school turned up in Jerusalem at some time or another, to study or volunteer or take a job. The more devout would come back to New York talking about getting wigs when they got married and sending future daughters to matchmakers once they reached seventeen. *So backward,* Yona's mother had seethed whenever talk of such trends came up. *They spend their lives in the kitchen and are congratulated for having baby after baby, one a year. Like prize sows.* Yona's father had whipped around and stared at his wife. Sow? Did she say sow? It was the cancer talking, he said. The medication. She would never have spoken like that otherwise. Yona had never forgotten it. She was eleven years old.

"So what are you doing here?" Shira said eagerly. She had on strawberry pink lipstick and neon green eye shadow and bright blue dangling earrings in the shape of stars. Almost, Yona thought, Christmasy stars. She was also wearing a canary yellow cap, only her dark bangs exposed. Yona had heard that Shira had married Ezra Falk, the heartthrob of Yeshiva University High School. Someone had spread a nasty rumor that Ezra was only after Shira's father's money.

"Just visiting. You know. Vacation."

"That's great." Shira nodded a few times too many, and then Yona remembered: the long, sad, we're-so-sorry faces she had to look at every day the year her mother died. The other girls thought it a sin if they smiled around Yona, poor Yona, so they did their laughing behind her back when they thought she wasn't paying attention, and then turned and addressed her as if she were a cripple, or someone with mental retardation. Yona had become a half orphan who shamefully but truthfully was glad—glad!—her mother had died so that maybe life could become a little more normal. Except it didn't. The reverse. Her father crawled into a shell and never came out.

"You have time for a coffee?" Shira said, waving toward the Cup O' Joe on the corner and sounding slightly desperate.

Time? She had more time than she knew what to do with. And because she'd hardly talked to anyone in ten days, and because Shira Feinbrenner's familiar, colorful face was about the most welcome one she'd laid eyes on since arriving, she said yes.

Three small children, an eight-year marriage to, yes, Ezra Falk—after an uninspiring stint at Stern College ostensibly concentrating in education but mostly majoring in getting it over with—and a condo in Riverdale where Ez was assistant rabbi at a synagogue with no possibilities for advancement: this was Shira's story. She told it without humor or cynicism, and it seemed to have the mournful ring of resignation, a low-grade but persistent unhappiness dealt with the way people deal with certain health problems: you learn to cope, to live with it, to lower your expectations. Thirty years old and already giving up.

"So Ez has been studying here for a month," Shira sighed. "The congregation sends the assistant r's over to supposedly keep them fresh and energized, but I think it's to get them out of the way. The senior doesn't like them to get too popular. And the congregation doesn't want to upset the top gun." She twirled a finger in the air. "Big muckety-muck, supposed to have the ear of the president." She shrugged and picked up her soda.

"What about you? What've you been up to?" Yona asked.

"Me? The kids of course." Shira mouthed the straw. "Whole trip kind of sucks, actually. I know I'm supposed to love it. Supposed to be so excited, Jerusalem, all expenses paid. But the truth is it's isolating and boring for me. I have no child care—today's a fluke, Ezra's parents are visiting—Ez is out day and night, and I don't know a soul. Thank God we only have one more week. I envy you."

"You envy me?" In an unexpected fit of confession—maybe it

was the need to unburden herself, maybe she wanted to make what had been brewing in her head more real by uttering it out loud, or maybe it was Shira's breezy friendliness that seemed refreshingly nonjudgmental—Yona had told her about Elias and all his predecessors and her desire to break the habit, and then, while she was at it— what did she have to lose?—tossed in the problem of her numbingly unsatisfying career.

"Yes you. Oh sure, I heard what you said about those married guys and your lousy work, but at least you get to make your own mistakes. And now you can do what you want. You could go to art school. You could find someone who loves you for who you are. It's not that I don't adore Ezra and my kids, but I wish it hadn't been so damn predetermined. The whole thing was prescribed by the time I was ten. Hell, by the time I was born." She sat back, took in a breath, then blew it out, puffing up her nicely rouged cheeks. "And I'll tell you, it only gets worse. Once you start with schools and the community?" She shook her head at that, because of course there would be community, religious life was all about being with others. That was supposed to be the best part. An instant social structure. Friends. Support. Yona's parents' community fed them for years after her mother died. "Then you really have to march in lockstep. Be the good girl." Shira shrugged again. Enough; she didn't want to sound like a complainer. "So did I tell you I saw your sister once? At a rally?"

"No, you didn't say." Yona had kept the Dena part brief. A reunion, she'd told Shira. They hadn't been in touch, lifestyles wildly different, plus the distance, two dead parents. Yona was trying to bridge the chasm but it wasn't easy.

"She's quite a firebrand. I'm not into that stuff, the Gush, the radical settlements. Some of Ezra's friends took us with them." Shira tipped her head. The earring stars fluttered. "I hear she's a big deal in those circles. And fierce. Tough. Was she always like that?"

"Political?"

"No. Righteous. No compromise, no backing down."

Yona picked up her iced coffee. The years of unanswered letters. Dena's stonewalling silence at their father's funeral. Yona's futile efforts to apologize. And now, the one awful visit, the not-ringing telephone. "You could say that," Yona said, looking into the glass, swirling the contents.

"Boy, you just never know with people," Shira said wistfully. She had her chin in her palm and was gazing out at the street. "We all used to admire your family so much. Especially after your mother died. My mother was always saying, 'Look at those Sterns. So much dignity. No one falling apart, no one oozing emotion.' You too, you know? Maybe you got a little rebellious later on but you always looked so great, no one could tell. And your sister, the perfect student, always volunteering and doing charity stuff right and left. And of course your father. A big prestigious dean while mine owned a couple of paint and wallpaper stores. We all thought your family had it so together."

"It looked good from the outside, didn't it."

"Yep."

"And that, it seems," Yona said, lifting her glass, "was all that mattered."

She walked Shira to the bus stop, then kept going. The building was unchanged. The same straggly little garden in front, the same overgrown purple bougainvillea clinging to the stone façade. In the cool entry, she glanced at the names on the mailboxes. Next to the slot for the second-floor-rear flat was a neatly typed label: *Varda Cohen*.

No one answered the buzzer. She went around back, to the covered parking and rear garden, as desolate as the front one, the soil cracked and desert-dry. Two motorcycles were chained to a metal fence. She wandered over. They were serious machines, big and hulking, not like the tinny Vespa David had kept there that summer, an underweight little scooter his friends told him would get him killed on the lunatic Israeli roads. David hadn't cared; he loved it. When

Yona sat behind him, they were like Bonnie and Clyde, he said, steal-
ing something and getting away with it. Now David was in Albany
with a wife and three children and a law office in a wood-frame
building with his name on the glass. Their relationship had survived
a month after they returned to New York, when Yona insisted on the
inevitability of its failure. It was doomed. They were doomed. Nothing good could come of their taboo beginning. David, devastated,
accepted a job upstate and Yona went back to NYU and took up with
the adulterous thirty-six-year-old assistant professor of her under-
subscribed seminar on the Romantic poets. Needing to numb herself
against the possibility of any legitimate entanglements, terrified of
whom she might next destroy, she was glad to take on the role of
professor's worshipful nymph. And so the pattern began, a bad girl
making sure she never got more than what she deserved.

"*Slicha.*" Excuse me. A man in a Reebok T-shirt holding a shiny
black helmet. "I need to take my motorcycle."

She looked down. She was gripping the handles. "Oh. I'm so
sorry. I didn't realize."

"No problem." A broad smile. Jet-black hair, blue eyes. Another
Israeli from central casting. He slipped into English. "You looking
for someone? I can help you?"

She flushed. He smiled more. "Do you know Varda?" she blurted
out. "In apartment three?"

"Of course I know Varda. You want to see her?"

"I want to see her apartment. I once lived there."

"Ah." A shrug. "Pity. Because she's abroad."

Yona waved awkwardly. "Well, what can you do."

"So you come back, that's all. One week, maybe two, she returns."

"I'll be gone by then. Back to the States."

A thoughtful nod. He put on his helmet, buckled the chin strap.
Then he positioned himself on the seat, preparing to go. "Listen," he
said, "write me your number. The guy across the hall from her has
the key. He goes to water the plants and bring her mail." He gestured

with his chin toward the building. "I see him tonight, I'll ask if he will show you. Then I give you a call."

She tipped her head, buying time.

"It's just a telephone call, sweetheart." Another winning smile. "Nothing to worry."

Flustered, she dug in her bag for her notepad, keeping her head down as long as she could so he wouldn't see the crimson burning up her face.

His name was Eyal and he'd lived there for two years. "Varda gets a shitload of mail," he said, handing Yona the stack. The neighbor with the key had to go out so he'd given it to Eyal. "Art magazines, catalogs. A fortune in postage."

They stepped inside. Tomato red walls, wooden masks over the couch, prints and pastels and sketches, an explosion of greenery on the living room balcony. "She's a sculptor, Varda. But she keeps no work here," Eyal said. "Too big. She has a studio in Ein Kerem. Iron, bronze, I don't know what else. Very modern."

He went to the kitchen with a watering can, and Yona moved through the flat, stopping at the bedroom doorway. A neatly made double bed, a teak wardrobe, more colorful art. That summer, she'd walked to the old professor's flat in Rehavia each morning, and in the afternoons strolled the city or swam in the pool at Ramat Rachel. David studied while she was out, his bar review notes covering the little dining table so they ate on the balcony and watched the street, cheap meals of soft pita and fresh hummus and eggplant salad, the best plums and figs she'd ever tasted. They had tried so hard, she to shake the guilt, David to make her love him. He took her on trips to the beach where the misty salt air prickled their faces, and to the little vacation cabins up north for the mountain air and spectacular views and fresh goat milk, where you could get a deal if you showed up at the last minute and spoke to the owners in your American-accented Hebrew; they seemed so moved that you'd taken the trouble to learn their isolated lonely language. She'd wanted desperately to feel what David wanted her to feel, what she also wanted to feel; for it to be a violently inevitable romance, like from a play or a novel, the kind of passion kings gave up their thrones for and heiresses turned away inheritances for. Because that would have made it worth the cost. But she couldn't will any such thing into being. She couldn't love David. She was just a girl, barely out of adolescence, aching for her lost parents, her cold and angry sister, taking whatever affection she could, where she could.

She drifted back into the living room. Eyal was finishing with the plants.

"Seen enough?" he said. He'd swept through the rooms with the watering can, collecting dead leaves, adjusting the shutters, making sure no one had tampered with the window locks, theft, even on the second floor, he'd said, shaking his head, rampant.

"Thank you, quite enough," she said, and followed him out. She was glad to be going. She didn't want to return.

She agreed to coffee. Who wanted to go back alone to Claudia's echoey flat? Plus, she'd extended her stay because Claudia was extending hers. The gallery certainly didn't need her. They'd never needed her. She only had the job because Elias was a client. *Take your time, things are slow,* Mariah, her boss, had written, though of course things weren't slow. Mariah, the mistress of euphemism. And the self-appointed arbiter of taste. *I suppose you'll go see the Chagall windows at that famous hospital in Jerusalem,* Mariah had sniffed, the legendary artist deemed by the gallery crowd to be the painterly equivalent of *Fiddler on the Roof,* all mush and sloppy sentiment, colorful art, like colorful clothes, against the law. Mariah could say that, she announced, because she herself was Jewish. Yona wondered if Mariah would fire her when Elias let slip that he was again on the prowl. No, not if. When. Maybe Mariah had already done it.

"Ach, some of these people in the territories, they're crazy," Eyal said after Yona told him the reason for her visit. He took a bite of an apple torte. "They'd rather kill themselves than give an inch. Like Masada. Which also was full of crazies. We bring all these tourists up there to look and say, Wow, how amazing, three years in a desert holdout against the Romans! But they were a bunch of fanatics. They started a revolt, killed any fellow Jew who didn't agree with them, and murdered their own children rather than surrender. This is how we sell our history? Is this lunacy or what?"

She nursed her espresso. His family, he'd said, were six generations in Israel on his mother's side. Two hundred years. On his father's side they'd come from Austria. Nineteen fifty. A scarred handful after the camps, the DP centers, detention in Cyprus, a tent city outside Tel Aviv. The works. After the army he went to India like everyone else and became so smitten with the handicrafts that he started an import business. Some of Varda's masks had come from there.

"Let me tell you something," he said, tapping the table. "The radical settlers I know, and believe me, I have a few in my family closet, they need black and white. They don't like the gray. I'm not saying they're simple. No. They're very smart. Some of the religious memorize the Talmud inside out. But they like absolutes. And drama. They don't want to be ordinary people thinking about car payments and bank overdraft. They want a big life. Historical, theatrical." He took another forkful of the torte, offered her the plate. She declined. "But it's maddening, you know? They've got this victim mentality: Everyone hates the Jews. Europe hates the Jews, America hates the Jews. Every anti-Semitic incident in every one-horse town in New Hampshire or Arkansas is like the Third Reich. Becomes, how do you call it, a self-fulfilling prophecy. How can you make peace with Syria if you think Assad is Hitler reincarnated? Every time a government here tries to negotiate, someone calls him Chamberlain."

A family had sat down at the table next to them. Tourists in sneakers lugging camera bags and water bottles. The mother began reading to the kids from the menu. *Cheese toast. Fettucini alfredo. You'll like that, Josh. It's noodles with cream.*

Eyal drank his coffee and shook his head glumly. "Sorry to go on like this, it just gets to me. Like they have the monopoly on ideals, you know? I just wish they'd do something else with them. Like go settle the Negev or clean up the Kinneret. And stop slicing up the country-side with all the special roads just for them so they don't have to drive through the Palestinian villages. They're yelling all the time about God's promise of the territories and meantime they're doing a pretty lousy job taking care of the land we already have." He took another bite. "You know how much the government spends on them?" He wiped his mouth with a napkin, took a drink to wash down the cake. "Billions. You ever see these settlements? They're beautiful. Brand-new community centers. State-of-the-art schools. Some of them have villas. Ten rooms, a dunam or two of land. And thousands of soldiers patrolling their roads and fences. The drain on the army is unbeliev-able. Meantime we've got a million and a half Israelis living in poverty in Beersheva and Ashkelon and everywhere else. Not to mention the Arab towns. We don't need to even talk about that."

A waitress had appeared at the next table. She was explaining. Yes, cheese toast was grilled cheese. No, they didn't have the bright orange kind.

"So these cousins of yours," Yona said, "out in the settlements, do they call you a post-Zionist or something?"

He waved, dismissive. "A stupid label. Like if you challenge them, you're ready to throw Israel into the garbage bin." He jabbed the table again. "Look, I'm as patriotic as the next guy. I'll defend this country till the day I drop. I was in the army, I go to reserves every year. You see me running off to America, to Australia?" He shook his head, disgusted. "Would I like us to have sovereignty over Bethlehem? Jericho? Sure. Would my grandparents like to live again on the kib-butz they founded near the Gush on land—land, by the way, sold legally to the Jewish Agency by Arabs—they had to flee in '48 when it was captured by the Jordanians? Sure. But we can't have every-thing we want. That's reality. There are other people living in this place who also have fields and orchards, who've been here for gen-erations, and we can't turn a blind eye anymore. It doesn't matter what happened forty years ago. Or four thousand. The people there have their narrative and we've got ours, and that's that. We have to find a way to move on. Both sides do. They have to stop filling their kids' heads with nonsense about returning to fairy-tale places inside Israel that don't exist anymore, that were destroyed during Indepen-dence, and we have to stop letting the settlers call all the shots and grab the Palestinians' land." He finished the torte and pushed away the plate. "Ach, the whole thing makes me sick. You shouldn't let me get started."

The tourists were staring at them. Eyal finally turned their way.

"Sorry," he said. "Didn't mean to disturb your meal."

"Oh no, no," said the father. "It was fascinating. You're very passionate." He had a British accent, which surprised Yona; the kids had on Boston Red Sox T-shirts, and the wife had sounded a hun-dred percent Ted Kennedy.

"You would be too," Eyal said wearily, "if you lived here."

11

*F*elicia *began bringing home kugels* and cheese blintzes and seven-layer cakes, foods from her childhood that Greenglass had never seen in the house before. He would catch a glimpse of her standing at the kitchen counter sneaking a piece of something ordinar-ily forbidden. A fragment of a rugelach. A corner of cherry danish. A sliver of chocolate almond bark. She'd turn to him with moist eyes and say she'd been thinking of her dead father who worked in a bakery in Sheepshead Bay. Every afternoon he'd come home after his shift, ten or twelve hours that began in the dark, smelling of yeast and lemon and sweat, his shoes floury, and leave on the table an apple strudel or mandelbrot or honey cake before he went to lie down. Maybe it was Mark's visit, she said. Suddenly she felt consumed by the memory of her father. He died when she was fifteen and had left the family penniless.

But hadn't she always said he wasn't a very nice man? Greenglass asked from the doorway. Gruff and difficult, everyone had to tiptoe around him? His seamstress wife had to practically sew by candlelight to accommodate his rigid scheduling. Never available to his daughters, even on weekends, even when he was awake.

"It's true, he wasn't," Felicia said. "But he brought us pastries," she said, looking at the box of butter cookies on the kitchen table, a snowy white square tied with a delicate red string. Later, Greenglass would see the label, an address deep within the hot belly of Brooklyn. It would have taken Felicia half the day just to get there and back. "He couldn't offer much, but it was the best he could do. And he gave it to us."

12

It was *Ben-Ami* who approached Aaron, not the other way around. He was out of his mind, practically suicidal. Davidson was making plans to leave.

Ben-Ami's crying made Aaron sick, but he listened like a social worker and told Ben-Ami they had to do something to get Davidson more involved, more invested. It was like an initiation into a fraternity, he told Ben-Ami. They had to get Davidson to buy in, that's all. Make him feel part of a mission. Then he'd stay.

"What do you mean?" Ben-Ami said, sniffling. Friday afternoon, almost everyone gone home for the sabbath, even Shroeder, who, as far as Aaron knew, didn't have a wife and kids but disappeared almost every weekend anyway. Only a handful of people were on the premises, including Lior, who never left, and the two Israeli painters, who still didn't talk to Aaron. He and Ben-Ami drank lukewarm tea in the dining tent. Davidson was off sending emails home, telling his parents he loved them, he missed them, he wanted to go back to Skokie and start over.

"An action, man," Aaron said, tapping the tabletop.

"What're you talking about?" Ben-Ami wiped his nose with his palm.

"An Arab site. In Jerusalem. It'll be just a warning, no one gets hurt." Aaron pushed aside his tea. He'd been waiting for this, waiting for a chance to do something, and now it had walked over and sat down in front of him.

Ben-Ami waved him off. "You're crazy."

"What do you mean I'm crazy? I thought you were tough, demolitions in basic training. I thought we had to show everyone what's going down in this country, Era of Redemption, remember?"

Ben-Ami turned away.

Aaron grabbed him by the wrist. "You want to wait a hundred years for the Israelis to say a fucking nice word to us?" The friendship with Lior after the clinic visit had been short-lived; as soon as they were back at Adamah, Lior ignored him again. He'd even made a joke in front of Shroeder about Aaron's shaved head, calling him Brooklyn's undernourished answer to Kojak. Shroeder had laughed. Since then, Aaron had taken to wearing an old Atlanta Braves baseball cap someone had found, a big red *A* above the bill. "You know what they think of Americans? What they call us when they think we can't hear?" He leaned toward Ben-Ami. "Cunts. Stupid girls," he hissed. "Even you. Even though you were in the army."

Ben-Ami looked at him a long time. Even Ben-Ami would have

to admit Shroeder favored the Israelis. Everyone knew it; the Israelis lorded it over them constantly. They thought they were so invincible, so smart. The Americans were wimps to them. Aaron and Davidson and Ben-Ami did their jobs and didn't complain, and the Israelis thought they were suckers. Pushovers doing exactly what they were told. Ben-Ami turned away. "Forget it, Blinder. I don't want to get into that kind of trouble."

"What kind of trouble? They'll give us a medal, realize we aren't anyone's grandmas, see we've got initiative. You want to stay here and install toxic ceiling tiles the rest of your life? I sure don't. That's not why I came out here." Ben-Ami looked back at him. "Shroeder will be impressed. He'll see we've got what it takes. You know how many actions have gone on since I got here? Four, five, I'm sure of it. That guy Tal and his pal Dror? Where do you think they go all the time with those duffel bags? To the gym? They're scoping places and planting explosives. I know it."

Ben-Ami shook his head.

"I'm telling you," Aaron said. "I overheard them."

"You did not."

"I did." He was pushing things, he should be careful, Ben-Ami wasn't stupid. "At least I'm pretty sure that's what they said."

"Don't give me any bullshit, Blinder."

Aaron leaned closer. Ben-Ami reeked of weed. He must be smoking all day, every day. "Okay, okay, I didn't hear exactly that. But I know they're doing it. Who else is blowing up those cars in East Jerusalem everybody's always whispering about? In Ramallah? Causing those 'sudden malfunctions'? Come on, Ben-Ami, wake up. Everyone's doing stuff. This is how to make the right things happen, just like Shroeder says. Scare the Arabs off. Let them see we aren't giving up. Let the government see." He waved around the dining tent. "Why else are we out here?"

Ben-Ami reached for his packet of Marlboros. "How's this going to do anything for Davidson?"

"You'll see, it'll excite him. Get him to realize what's going on in this country."

Ben-Ami lit a cigarette, blew smoke off to the side. "He doesn't give a shit about politics. He doesn't even hate the Arabs. He wants to go home, go back to college, see his family." He took a long drag, blew a tower of smoke rings, then watched them feather into nothing. "Probably wants to go off and fucking marry the girl next door."

Aaron took a sip of cold tea and studied Ben-Ami. Ben-Ami would never get Davidson to agree to an action. Which meant Ben-Ami would never do one either. "He have a Holocaust history in his family?" Aaron said.

Ben-Ami turned back. "What the hell are you asking that for?"

"Just answer."

"Christ, yes. Everyone in Skokie does."

"Good. I'll work on him."

Davidson's grandfather survived Dachau after leaving his then twelve-year-old brother with the wife of a Polish grain dealer who sold provisions to the family before the war. The brother spent three years hiding in a well on the Polish people's property, contracting lifelong respiratory disease in the process. After the war the brothers found each other in a DP camp in France and hobbled, broken, all that remained of their extended family, to America, where Davidson's grandfather met Davidson's grandmother, a battered survivor of Majdanek. Davidson's father was born in 1951; he married and had two children, Davidson and his sister Lucy. Lucy was mildly retarded and lived in a special supervised residence fifteen minutes from home. Until he came to Israel, Davidson, whose aborted college career had been at University of Illinois, had never been more than two hundred miles from his family or separated from them for longer than a week.

"That's rough, man," Aaron said after Davidson told him his

grandparents' history. They lay on their backs blowing smoke from Ben-Ami's precious supply of Moroccan hash. The stuff was expensive but necessary, a lubricant to get the otherwise close-mouthed Davidson to talk. That, and the mention of Aaron's father and his books. Because of course Davidson had heard of Aaron's father; everyone in Skokie had.

"What those people went through for the survival of the Jewish people," Aaron said. He took another pull. "You know, if it weren't for them, there wouldn't even be an Israel."

"What are you talking about? The first Zionist Congress was in 1900 or something. Eighteen nineties maybe. Decades before Hitler."

Aaron waved at the night sky. Ben-Ami was off somewhere biting his nails. Aaron had told him to calm down, that if there was one thing he knew how to talk about it was the Third Reich. "Those did nothing. It was because of the war, the gas chambers, that the British had to relent and give us our state. World opinion. They all felt so guilty. Without the camps it would've dragged on for decades. Or we'd have been given Uganda or some loser piece of Argentina." He passed Davidson the joint. "It's on the backs of people like your grandparents that this country was built. It's because of their sacrifice."

Davidson sucked in, held the smoke in his lungs, murmured something unintelligible.

"But now," Aaron said, staring at the stars, "we could lose it all. The Arabs. They could take it away from us, every inch. And the world wouldn't even blink. Like it didn't blink before. Roosevelt, the great big progressive American government, did it do anything to stop the Nazi machine? Did Churchill? Did they bomb Auschwitz when they could have? Or let in those refugee ships off the coast of Florida? Like the SS *St. Louis*, 1939. The American government refused to admit them, sent them back to Germany. Nine hundred people straight to the ovens. Fucking Cuba took in more Jewish refugees than the United States. No one cares about the Jews except the Jews."

Davidson said nothing. Aaron let the words hang there. He was doing great. The names and facts and dates, stuff he could recite by heart. And the somber mood. Davidson wasn't arguing. He loved his family, his parents, his grandparents, loved them more than anything. More, even, than Ben-Ami.

"They can destroy our last safe haven," Aaron said softly. "All that suffering—your grandparents, your father's uncle, their whole murdered family. Hell, even my father's family. It'll all have been in vain."

Aaron took the joint back from Davidson, heard a faint sniffle. Davidson welling up. *Thank you, God,* Aaron thought, closing his eyes and putting the magical glowing cigarette between his lips.

He told Shroeder and Lior on Sunday that relatives from the States were visiting and wanted to take him out, and since he couldn't let on where he was living—an unwritten rule at Adamah, the place not exactly legal so you didn't broadcast it to the whole world—he had to stay in Jerusalem for three nights. They told him to have a good time and eat a lot of restaurant food, and where the hostels were. Shroeder gave him three hundred shekels to cover the cost, then threw in an extra hundred to be generous. Aaron took the bus and walked the city for hours, his pack like a weight of bricks on his back, looking for a promising site. East Jerusalem would have been good but he attracted too much attention, so he gave up, got himself a hot meal and rented a bed at the hostel down the street from the King David. It was there that he got an idea. A pimply kid from Pittsburgh talked to him over breakfast about how all the Scandinavian countries were disgustingly pro-Arab, supporting all sorts of institutions that were really covers for Hamas and the Al-Aqsa Brigades and Islamic Jihad. Cultural organizations. Community centers. Schools.

"They even have this college. Right here in the western part of the city. Right under our noses."

"Oh? Where's that?" Aaron said.

They were in the hostel cafeteria. For the equivalent of four dollars you could get all-you-could-eat. Hard-boiled eggs, three kinds of cheese, yogurt, fresh rolls, cucumber and tomato salad, vegetables, fruit, juice, coffee, pastry. Some women's college supported by Denmark or maybe Norway, the kid told Aaron, loading up his plate for the second time. Supposed to look legit but it's really a hotbed.

He found it that afternoon, sat across the street in a bus shelter pretending to read. A big metal sculpture tree stood at the entrance, the words *Her Majesty's Kingdom of Sweden, His Majesty's Government of Denmark* engraved on shiny silver leaves. The place was surrounded by a fancy wrought-iron fence, and women speaking weird languages moved through the courtyard carrying leather portfolios and instrument cases in the shapes of cellos and violins; one on wheels looked like a harp. So-called instrument cases anyway. They could be concealing anything—weapons, explosives. Some of them were huge, probably weighed a ton. And the place. It certainly didn't look like any college Aaron had ever seen. It was quiet and seemed empty much of the time, and when he ventured inside, after telling the half-asleep guard in his best Hebrew that he was an architecture student studying the building's history, there were no packs of giggling students, no flyers on the walls, no smells of institutional food wafting through. He didn't even see classrooms. It was like a giant private mansion; in fact, it probably was some rich person's mansion, probably some Danish benefactor in Hamas's pocket. That's how those Europeans were. In the Palestinians' pocket. The place practically reeked of fakery. What college had only a few dozen women, some of them almost as old as his stepmother, tiptoeing around like they were in a nunnery and wheeling those enormous cases that could be hiding anything? And those portfolios: they could be filled with blueprints, plans, diagrams of the country's power plants, the nuclear reactor at Dimona. It was a perfect ruse. Timid-looking women nobody would suspect. A handful even wore Arab head scarves. A cover, absolutely.

He returned that night and the next day, and again the next night. Shuttered and locked by eight o'clock, the place was dark except for a big spotlight on the building's front corner. He came back one last morning and drew a detailed sketch of the outside—the lawn, the gardens, the fountain with a chubby stone cherub, the front terrace. Then the pitch of the roof, where the windows were, the doors, external supports, electrical wires. Then what he remembered of the interior.

By Wednesday afternoon he was showing Ben-Ami the drawings in his bug-infested room. Davidson was getting cold feet, Ben-Ami told him; he was talking about buying his plane ticket now and going home next week. Ben-Ami was starting to think it wasn't a good idea either. Too dangerous. He didn't like that Shroeder wouldn't know. What if something went wrong?

"What's going to go wrong?" Aaron snapped. "You know explosives. You said you could do them with your eyes shut."

"How the hell do I know what might go wrong? The street might be closed off. The building might be having repairs. Soldiers could be crawling all over the neighborhood." He bit a cuticle. His nails were ragged shreds.

"So then we call it off, that's all. We don't do it. We come back and tell Shroeder we had a terrific night of R & R in Jerusalem."

"I don't know."

Aaron had to control himself. He couldn't afford for these guys to bail. "Look, I'll talk to Davidson. It'll be fine." He watched Ben-Ami gnaw his lip. "We'll do it on Sunday, okay? Sunday night. That gives you four days to get it together, including Saturday when nobody's here. We'll tell Shroeder you're going nuts, weeks without a break, that you and Davidson need a night out. I'll tell him my relatives are still visiting and want to treat us. We come back the next day, we're a little late, that's all. We'll say we missed the last bus."

Ben-Ami stuck half his hand into his mouth, chewing four nails at once.

"Davidson's going to love it," Aaron said, trying to ignore what Ben-Ami was doing. "You'll see. One of these, and he'll be hooked. He'll want to stay here forever." Ben-Ami changed hands, looked at Aaron with hopeless, beseeching eyes. He so desperately wanted to hear what he wanted to hear. "And then," Aaron said, "he'll never want to marry the girl next door."

13

They called themselves a fact-finding mission, Yona heard someone say. Thirty middle-aged Americans crowding into the first four rows of the synagogue down the street from Dena's apartment on a Wednesday evening listening, rapt, to a grizzled man named Shroeder who was introduced as one of the movement's living legends, a visionary dedicated to the cause, without whom the whole enterprise would have collapsed decades ago. A man who nearly single-handedly spearheaded the opposition to Oslo, those dreadful, best-forgotten so-called accords championed by Israel's spineless left that would have given away the store to Arafat and his corrupt and lying minions. The man who, Yona now remembered, was Aryeh Ben-Tzion's mentor and guru, according to Dena's little girls. His *rav.* Yona sat in the back of the room trying to be inconspicuous. Once more, she had pressed; once more, Dena had relented under duress.

You're not calling me. I've extended my stay, I'd like to see you. Please.

A pause. *I don't really see the point.*

The point? Yona wanted to reach through the phone lines and shake her, yell into her face *Who are you?* But it would get her nowhere. Instead she said, *I'd like to at least see your children. What about that?*

And so, a strangled invitation. Because maybe Hila had asked. Or because in a country where a hundred relatives turned out for every birthday party and baby's bris, Dena's children looked at their mother's paltry lineage and saw a black hole.

Or maybe because the current pregnancy was sapping Dena's iron resolve.

A mission from Cleveland will be here. A lecture, then open houses so they can meet us. You can come. You'll have to stay over, there's no bus that late.

From the next question Yona refrained—*Will I meet your husband?*—for obvious reasons. But then, at the lecture, she saw him. He was up front, next to the one named Shroeder, Aryeh Ben-Tzion, a short but sturdy man with a trim dark beard and intense blue eyes, thick feet encased in Roman-looking sandals. He was presiding over the map, a topographical blowup propped on an easel, the biblical names Samaria and Judea in black marker on the bottom because you didn't use the despised Anglicized term West Bank, names, like so much in this country, the bearers of destiny-altering meaning. Unlike Shroeder, Aryeh Ben-Tzion had been introduced without fanfare, nodding at the assembled, saying little. His English was good enough but he tended to spit out the words, as if to get them over with. As if he found the language tainted.

"By this time next year," Shroeder was saying in accented but unashamed English, pointing at a shaded ridge on the map above the Arab city of Nablus, "three hundred new Jewish families could be living on these hills. We've got a list, commitments, they're ready to go. All we need is money." For trailers and generators and pipes, for trucks and construction crews. For a media campaign to mobilize support and keep morale high.

In the rows, heads nodding. The men stroked their chins as if they were at work; the women folded their hands and concentrated.

They were part of the *We*. The fact that they would never live there themselves, would never want to live there, was irrelevant. They knew what they were being asked. They'd brought their checkbooks. And they were glad to do it. American dollars had built that country; there were commemorative plaques on every university classroom and hospital coatroom, and they would continue the tradition now. The fact that the new plaques would be affixed to the walls of a violently disputed building in Hebron taken over by Jewish squatters, or on a caravan of pre-fab trailers deep in Samaria on land whose ownership had been recorded in the name of a Palestinian family since Ottoman times, only added to the appeal. If the U.S. government was pushing Israel to tear down these outposts, the good Jews of Cleveland would pay to make sure they stayed up.

"Okay, we're tight on time," Shroeder said after consulting with a third man who seemed to be his assistant. "You have questions, come up and ask. Meantime there are refreshments. In half hour we go to the homes."

They got up, stretched, milled around. A spread of fruit and cold drinks had been laid out on a folding table. Someone opened the doors for air. The charter that had brought them, a luxury coach with a small placard on the windshield reading *Chovevei Tzion*, Lovers of Zion Tours, idled noisily, the driver keeping himself cool by running the A/C nonstop.

"Terrific speaker," said a fiftyish-year-old man wearing shorts with two dozen pockets as if he were a fly fisherman from Maine. He held out a handful of grapes. Yona declined. "I was here for six months in '73, arrived two weeks before the war. Supposed to be at the university but they put us to work instead. I delivered the mail." He took a grape and sighed. "Best six months of my life. Never felt so alive before or since. Part of something important, you know what I mean? Just don't have that at home." He popped another grape. "Parents made me come back. I'm a developer in Shaker Heights. You new to the group? Haven't seen you before."

Yona made a perfunctory smile. "No, I'm just visiting. My sister lives here."

"Ahh, your sister lives here." The words were drawn out slowly, reverently. *Ahh. Your sister lives here.* "She been here a long time? Can we meet her?"

"She's preparing at the house. Or so I'm told. I just got here myself. She's on your list."

He pulled out a folded sheet from one of the many pockets. A pen and a wad of tissues fell onto the floor. He left them there. The mission members could stop in at any of the addresses during the evening to talk to actual settlers. One movement spokesman would be posted at each house. Dena's husband, fielding questions up front from the crowd, would be the spokesman at his. "Which one is she?"

"Ben-Tzion. Hanevi'im Street."

"Don't you love it?" the man said, reading the names. "Ben-Tzion. Son of Zion. And Hanevi'im Street. Street of the Prophets. As if Isaiah and Jeremiah and all the rest of them were right here with us in this room." He nodded sagely. "And indeed they are. You must be so proud of your sister. Raising a family out here where life is lived on the edge, dangerous, prepared to do whatever is necessary to safeguard our holy ancestral lands."

"Do you have kids?"

"Pardon?"

"I asked if you have kids."

"Certainly. Three wonderful boys. Twenty, eighteen, and fifteen. All went through Ida Crown. Yeshiva in Chicago. Excellent school. Oldest is prelaw at Harvard."

"Why isn't he here, protecting our holy ancestral lands? Why aren't they all here?"

He looked at her a long minute. "That's a preposterous question." Then he glared. "You have a very big and insolent mouth."

. . .

It seemed crazy to be in the same room with her brother-in-law and not say anything. She waited behind the crush of people peppering him with questions, exhibiting their familiarity with the geography and politics so as not to appear like mere walking bank accounts. They dropped names of people and settlements, tossed in dates and events as if they'd been there, authenticating themselves, ratcheting up the We—*We're all on the same team!*—a familiarity that elicited nothing from the other one, Shroeder, not even a nod. He seemed to Yona to be profoundly bored. Or not to like them very much. He glanced at the clock and tapped his thumb into the opposing palm. Aryeh Ben-Tzion, on the other hand, was listening intently. Focused, earnest, committed. In another life he might have been a union organizer. Or a very hardworking therapist.

Shroeder stepped away from the circle, heading to the drinks. He knocked into Yona's elbow as he passed, uttered an apology in English.

"None needed," Yona said.

Shroeder stopped, took a step back. "You have a question? I see you standing here a long time."

"That's all right. I'm waiting to talk to Aryeh Ben-Tzion."

"I can answer everything."

"Not really. I want to introduce myself. I'm his wife's sister."

A slow nod. Shroeder stroked the gray beard. "His wife's sister. I was not aware she had a sister." A considered appraisal. The eyes went up and down, covering all. He was not shy. "You are from where?"

"New York."

"First time in Israel?"

"No."

"But Aryeh you don't know."

"That's correct."

"Well." He looked her over again, as if sizing her up for auction. "Well." Then he glanced at the crowd still pressing for Ben-Tzion's attention. "Guess you'll just have to wait your turn."

· · ·

At Dena's apartment Yona hung back in a corner. She was introduced to Aryeh when they all arrived—there had been no time
at the synagogue—an apparently distasteful task to be dispatched
as quickly as possible. *My sister Yona.* There was no handshake, no
smile, instead a nod like a salute and a stiff *Welcome to Givat Baruch.*
Yona would sleep, Dena instructed, in Anat and Hila's room; all the
children were in bed except Hila, who was staying at a friend's. On
the dining table was a more sumptuous spread, coffee and tea and
homemade cakes, dried fruits and nuts, lending the otherwise spartan surroundings an almost discordant air of festivity. Again Yona
was struck by the deliberate austerity of the rooms, as if Dena, like
the Soviet apparatchiks who built the drab apartment blocks in Eastern Europe in the darkest days of Communism, was determined on
principle to keep things as colorlessly utilitarian as possible. There
weren't even cacti on the balcony, a gesture that, judging from the
neighboring porches, was more or less standard and effort-free.

The Cleveland women had gathered in folding chairs around
Dena, politely asking questions. Yona listened from the periphery.
How did she manage to keep a job while raising such a large family? Was she ever afraid to drive the roads through the Palestinian
villages? Did she fear for her children's safety as they got older and
ventured out on their own?

Dena gave brisk, unapologetic answers. No, she was not afraid
to drive anywhere. Five kids plus a job was not unusual there, children learned early that they were required to help. She was not fear-
ful for them; they were part of something bigger, a higher purpose.
What will happen, will happen. What mattered was having a life
with meaning. Sometimes sacrifices had to be made.

A silence. "What kind of sacrifices?" one of the more timid
women said. The others looked over at her. They seemed surprised
to hear her voice. She was dressed head to toe in beige—beige skirt,

beige blouse, beige stockings, despite the heat, that came to their sad conclusion in a pair of orthopedic beige sandals. The kind of woman Yona used to see at school helping out in the library or the lunchroom. The type the girls, and everyone else, ignored. A spoon rattled in a glass. *Ping!* They all knew what the woman was asking. Had Dena said what they thought she'd said?

"What kind of sacrifices?" Dena repeated, looking around at the assembled, taking her time, letting the question sink in. "Did Abraham question God when He told him to bring Isaac up to Mount Moriah and bind him to the altar? This is how it is. Being ready to give up life for the sanctification of the Holy Name. Even if the life you have to give up is more precious than your own."

The beige woman turned ashen. A pale apparition become paler. The spoon *ping*ed again. For a long time no one spoke.

By eleven o'clock the Americans were gone, carried off in their air-conditioned coach to the Dead Sea for two days of recreation until their next stop, a planned Jewish development in Arab East Jerusalem. The first. A handful of chain-smoking locals from the nearby apartments let themselves out after finishing up the coffee and remains of a poppy seed cake, leaving Shroeder, a man named Tzviki who lived next door, and the quiet third organizer, Lior, Shroeder's right hand, who'd hardly spoken all night. They sat around the coffee table in a tight square with Aryeh. Yona and Dena wordlessly cleared plates and glasses, folded chairs. When they were done, Dena went to the back to check on the children. Yona sat at the dining table on the other side of the room with a copy of the *Jerusalem Post* left by one of the Americans and allowed herself to be ignored. From the way they spoke to her, it was clear the men assumed she had no Hebrew.

"*Laila lo ra, nachon?*" Tzviki said, his back to Yona. Not a bad night, eh?

Shroeder shrugged. It was okay. They could use another twenty grand. But for the size of the group it wasn't bad. "Tell them how much in the checks, Lior."

Seventy-five thousand, Lior told them. About five thousand a couple.

Murmurs of approval. It was a good showing, Aryeh said. They weren't all rich. Yona turned a page, glanced at the headlines. Lake Kinneret at an all-time low. *"Nu, v'mah im ha-sh'ayla?"* Tzviki asked. What about that question? The guy in the first row, Tzviki said, asking about the actions?

"Eediot," Aryeh said, disgusted, and lit a cigarette. Idiot. The same word in Hebrew and English. "A big-mouth Kahanist. *Terror Neged Terror.* Expecting us to comment." Yona stared at the page. Terror Against Terror. Meir Kahane's rallying cry in the '80s to get Jews to blow up Arabs. Arab buses, Arab schools, municipal buildings in Arab towns. Because if Arabs were killing Jews at random, Jews should do the same back. A horror of moral corruption, Yona's father used to say. *This is where it breaks down. If we start killing innocents, we've already lost.* Aryeh blew out smoke. Like any of them was going to endorse such a thing in front of a crowd, he said. What did the guy want, public political suicide?

Maybe he was Shabak, Tzviki offered. Shin Bet. Maybe he was looking for an easy tip.

Shroeder waved him off. Shin Bet was not so stupid. They wouldn't try to extract an admission in front of a bunch of salivating Americans remembering their glorious lost youth. No, Shin Bet had nothing to do with that guy. He was just another parasite sitting in a six-hundred-thousand-dollar suburban house dreaming of killing Arabs while he built more shopping malls for his wife.

"Maybe he knows about something," Lior said, a tone of concern. Yona glanced up. She'd been studying him all night. Another generically handsome Israeli, dark-haired and fit, neck veins taut as cello strings. Lior looked over at her, and she quickly went back to the paper, stared at a photo of the depleted lake. "Maybe he was fish-ing, maybe he knew something was up."

"What's to know?" Shroeder said, irritable. "That a couple of hotheaded American kids like to talk about blowing up a few Arabs of their own? *Nu*, so let them. I gave one money this week to go to Jerusalem, probably told his friends he was off looking for targets. I don't ask and they don't tell. Just like Mr. Barney Frank, the faggot senator from Massachusetts, his explanation for the U.S. Army." He picked up a coffee cup. "No wonder they're losing in Iraq."

"You're worried about something, Lior?" Tzviki said.

Silence. Yona turned a page.

"*Tir-ey,*" Aryeh said. Look here. Yona glanced up. Aryeh made an impatient O with his fingers, thumb and forefinger joined, an upturned palm. "The kids in these places, they get excited. It's part of the adjustment. So they talk."

"And if they want to do something," Shroeder said, "we should let them. Let them feel their oats; it's good training. If we stay out of it, don't let them spill their plans, we're fine. If they succeed, good. If not, okay, so they don't succeed. Meantime someone's been made afraid. What, every car that explodes in East Jerusalem has a faulty transmission? It's the loose cannons. So who cares? Let them." He drained his coffee cup. "Some of these Americans, though—pains in the neck. The one I gave the money to, he has a famous father. A writer. Kid has delusions of grandeur."

"You take the chaff with the wheat," Aryeh said, tapping ashes into an ashtray.

"This one's looking at a school," Shroeder said. "That's what I hear anyway. Some women's college. Jerusalem."

"Forget about it, Naftali," Aryeh said sharply. Yona kept her eyes on the paper. Aryeh was uneasy, Shroeder should shut up, he was saying too much. "You don't want to know."

An awkward silence. Dena came in, sat on the arm of Aryeh's chair. Tzviki yawned loudly.

"Go home, Tzviki," Shroeder said. "Go be with your beautiful wife." He slapped him on the shoulder. "Make yourself another baby tonight."

Tzviki laughed and got up.

"You too, Aryeh, go to bed," Shroeder said, pulling himself up. "Your wife here works all day, then again all night, very devoted though she's exhausted. Look how her eyes are closing. Lior and I will go."

"It's okay, Naftali," Dena said, sounding sleepy. "You don't have to rush."

"*Zman, motek*," Shroeder said. It's time, sweetheart. Yona felt his searing gaze on her and looked up. He switched into thickly saturated English. "Plus you want to be conscious tomorrow for your honorable sister visiting from the great United States. The country that holds the purse strings of the world, whose presidents send over all sorts of important underlings to tell us what to do. And whose Jewish diaspora loves to come to the rescue of its primitive brethren in the East."

"*Maspik, Naftali.*" Lior to Shroeder, his tone harsh. Enough. It's not necessary. "You must ignore Naftali," Lior said to Yona in labored English. "At this hour he turns into a werewolf." Tzviki made a little laugh.

"That's all right," Yona said. "Same thing happens to me. Eleven o'clock, midnight, I too start to bare my fangs."

Lior smiled. Touché. Aryeh got up, began collecting the remaining glasses and cups. Shroeder patted Lior on the cheek and said, in English, "Stop flirting with the tourists, Lior. Your wife won't be happy."

"No?" Yona said to Shroeder. "And what about yours?"

A broad smile, cynical and insincere. "I don't keep a wife myself. A man can have only one mistress, and mine is the cause. This is how it goes for me." A shrug, exaggerated helplessness. "A pity, yes? I'm sure I would make beautiful children." Then he turned to the door, Lior and Tzviki behind him, and the three of them went out into the hot night.

14

Regina's door was ajar. The folding table, the dishes and glasses, her clothes were there, but she was not. Greenglass looked for clues, signs, a note. He sat in the lone kitchen chair and waited an hour, left to get something to eat, then came back. The rooms felt uninhabited, ghostly, a presence there he refused to name. He remembered the calls he used to get, from the police, the EMTs, the emergency rooms, and dialed the hospitals, the nearest precinct, finally the morgue. When she didn't appear by two o'clock, he tried information for her mother in Rockaway, her sister in Virginia, and got dead ends. He reminded himself that she could be anywhere, that he had no right to expect her to hang around just so he could play the hero, the deliverer.

Still, he left the apartment, got on a train. He hadn't done the ride in years. The landscape was a blur of used car dealers, scrapyards, industrial parks. When he got off, it hit him all at once: the salt air, the low-hanging mist, the squawking gulls. He found a cab. The driver had never heard of the place. Greenglass directed him, working by feel. A right here, a left there.

The building was boarded up. He stared at a faded triangular spot on the clapboard where the Star of David had been. The driver asked if he wanted to go back to the station but Greenglass declined and paid him, watched him drive away. The big white birds hovered, expectant. He went up the wide steps and tried to see in through a space between the plywood windows. The boards rattled with the wind. The first time he'd climbed those steps he'd been so terribly young. Young and needy. Oskar Kleinfeld waved him into the shadowy study, the big books already laid out on the table. Hebrew, Aramaic. Kleinfeld said, in his thick accent, *Come, let's read.* As if Greenglass could read. As if Greenglass had the slightest notion how to look at any of those sacred books. He was a lost and damaged soul, and Kleinfeld took him in. Week after week, the old man would urge him on, Greenglass's Hebrew awkward and halting, and Kleinfeld would praise him, then parse the sentences and translate, commenting if Greenglass made even the most tentative observation. *Excellent. I hadn't thought of that.* Then Kleinfeld would run his bony finger down the page until he reached the next significant passage. From the Ethics of the Fathers: *Where there are no men, strive to be a man.* And: *Do not judge your fellow until you have been in his place.* And this: *Do not be sure of yourself until the day of your death.* The old man would pause, his mind on another continent, in another decade, with his vanished family, his vanished village, then look again at Greenglass, a flicker of recognition. *For next time. Think on this, a very important paragraph. For next time.*

He walked down the steps. Across the street, an elderly black man was watching him from in front of a pharmacy.

Greenglass crossed over. "Excuse me, do you know anything about that building?"

"Them Jews passed on. Some died, some went down to Florida. The rest is all living now on the other side of Rockaway. Another temple over there. Gateway to Something. Farther out."

"What about the rabbi? Kleinfeld. Oskar Kleinfeld."

The man scratched his cheek. "Don't know nothing about him. Old fella?"

"He was old." How old, Greenglass couldn't guess. He could be seventy or a hundred. Greenglass had never heard Kleinfeld's story. *Some memories are not meant to be kept alive.* Greenglass had last spoken to him the previous September. The call was brief, Kleinfeld on his way to an appointment. The man shook his head and said he was sorry and Greenglass thanked him and crossed the road. He walked around to the back, past the weedy patches of dirt along the sides, through the broken-up parking lot. The asphalt was littered with candy wrappers and beer bottles and dented cans. The big white birds hopped across the trash, pecking hopefully. What could he do for Regina now? He would call all the retirement homes in Rockaway, the social service agencies, but he would not find her mother, her sister. He would not find anyone. He looked at the back of the old synagogue, at the boarded-up door, corroded by salt and water and wind, and it came to him, a line he'd studied with Kleinfeld for weeks. It had tormented him, its meaning elusive, frustrating. He became fed up with these riddles. Impatient, even disgusted. Why couldn't the rabbis be more straightforward? It was driving him crazy. What did they want from him? How would he ever learn? Why did Kleinfeld even bother? He would never grasp any of it. He was twenty-five years old, learning what the smallest child learned at six. It was too late.

Then one afternoon at the pit of his despair, he read the line again and a light broke over him. It was about hope. About holding on to even the most fragile possibility, about believing there was always one more chance. *The day is short, the task is great, the workers are lazy, and the Master is insistent.*

That night his mother put a challah on the table.

"You don't have to do that, Mom," he said as she set out plates and glasses, a pitcher of water. His course was finished and his father was due home any minute; they would eat together. The ritual items infuriated Lenny. In ten years of religious practice Greenglass had never seen a challah on his parents' table.

"I don't care what he thinks," Felicia said, chin high, walking around the chairs distributing silverware. An hour earlier, Greenglass had shaved off the beard, put on a gray-striped shirt from the closet, a pair of new tan chinos. His mother had nodded and told him he looked nice. "You're leaving in two days," Felicia said, placing a fork in its rightful position. "Your father needs to grow up."

15

*L*ior *was stretched out* on a lawn chaise in front of the shack, a towel draped around his neck, a pair of Ray-Bans covering a quarter of his face. He looked like he'd gone for a run. Friday afternoon, everything slowing down. Aaron stood beside the lounger, his Atlanta Braves big *A* baseball cap pulled low over his forehead, and asked Lior if he'd help him get Shroeder's permission so that he and his two American buddies could go to Jerusalem after the weekend, on Sunday.

"Again to the city, Mr. Blinder," Lior said, moving the glasses an inch and squinting up at him. A bottle of lemonade was propped up on the dirt.

"It's not for me, it's for my friends. They need a break, need to get out of the routine."

"That's what the sabbath is for." Lior waved grandly. "The sunset comes and the world is quiet. Nobody working, time to relax. Take leftovers from the tent whenever you feel like it, also cookies, a piece of cake, indulge in Shimi's wonderful cooking." He smiled. No one would call Shimi's cooking wonderful.

"C'mon, Lior, you're a good guy, you could help me out here." Aaron was afraid of annoying Shroeder; everyone said he had a temper, you didn't want to get on his wrong side.

Lior took off the glasses, hoisted himself up, and leaned on an elbow. The towel slid off his shoulder. "Let me ask you something, Aaron. What are you doing here? You don't look so happy to me."

"What are you talking about? It's great."

"And your friends? Also happy?"

"They're fine. Is it because we're Americans that you're asking? Because we need a breather now and then? We're just as tough as the Israelis."

Lior waved away the question. "No, no, not because you're American. Because maybe this is not for you, that's all. Maybe you want to go back to Jerusalem and work at the pizza place, take your free classes." A shrug. "You don't have to stay here if you don't want to."

"Who says I don't want to?"

"I'm just saying. People come and go, like the South African kid, Yitz. It's no shame to leave."

"Yitz was a putz. I don't want to leave, I like it here."

Another shrug, and Lior let himself back down, closed his eyes, the towel under his head. He put the glasses back on. A sunbather at the beach. "Well, your friends don't look too happy to me. The big guy, Davidson, I hear he wants to go home. And Ben-Ami seems pretty on edge. And you. You look too skinny. You got that hat to cover things up, but I can see your face. What's the matter, don't like the food here?"

Aaron glanced around, agitated. Could Lior tell? Did he suspect something? Did everyone? Though Davidson's homesickness was no secret. "Just because Davidson might leave doesn't mean I want to. We're not joined at the hip, you know."

Lior smiled.

"And Ben-Ami, that's just his personality. He's a nail-biter, a nervous type. Doesn't mean anything." He tugged at the cap, pulled it lower. "And I'm trimming down, getting lean. No law against that, is there?"

Another shrug.

"So are you going to help me, Lior? I don't want to piss Shroeder off. But my friends really need to get away, and my relatives are still in Jerusalem. They want to take us out. It's just overnight."

"What kind of relatives?"

Aaron ran a hand across his forehead. What kind of a question was that? "Just relatives. Regular relatives."

"Which side? Your father's or your mother's?"

"What difference does it make?"

Lior took off the sunglasses. "Just asking. You never mentioned your mother. She famous too?"

"No. She's dead."

"Oh. I'm sorry to hear it." A pause. "What happened to her?"

Aaron looked away. Why was Lior asking so many questions? "I don't want to talk about it. Anyway, it was a long time ago." He turned back to the chaise. "So are you going to help me, Lior, or what?"

Lior regarded him. He felt like a bug under glass. "What?" Aaron said. "What're you looking at?"

Lior tipped his head. "You don't look good to me. You look sick. Pale. Maybe you should take it easy for a few days."

"I feel fine. I always look this way. Stomach stuff, it's my life. I chew Tums. You know what they are? Chalky little tablets, I've got them in a million flavors. Look, my friends really need to get away. And my relatives want to pay for everything. I'll rest up in Jerusalem, I'll eat well." He wiped his forehead again. "So what do you say, Lior, you going to help me?"

Lior put the sunglasses back on. "When you want to go? Remind me."

"Sunday."

"What time?"

"I don't know. Late afternoon? We can work the whole day and catch the bus when we're done. Just need to be in the city for the evening."

"What do you need overnight for? Return bus runs till midnight."

Aaron looked away again. He'd told Ben-Ami they'd get tripped up on that. Shroeder didn't like people traipsing around on Adamah's dime. It wasn't summer camp. They had a job to do. But Ben-Ami had insisted: What if something went wrong and they had to do it really late? Like if the car he was borrowing wasn't available, or there was an alert in the city, or one of them ran into someone they knew? They had to be prepared, have a backup plan. You always had to have a backup plan.

"The other guys are burned out, Lior. I'm only telling this to you. Confidentially. They're totally committed to this place but they need to get away. It's just one lousy night, we'll be back Monday morning."

Lior moved the glasses a notch, squinted open his eyes again, reached for the lemonade. He watched Aaron while he took a drink, then put the bottle back on the dirt. "I'll mention it to Naftali when he returns. Probably Sunday morning. But if I were you? I'd wait to ask him about it after lunch, when he's in a good mood. He's nicer when he's not hungry."

16

In *Liberty Bell Park* in central Jerusalem, which had near its entrance an exact replica of the Benjamin Franklin ringer in Philadelphia, Eyal told Yona about the end of his abortive love affair with a Dutch woman who'd gone back to Holland six months before. He had called Yona the morning after she'd gotten back from the Cleveland mission's visit to Dena's: how about a picnic Friday afternoon?

Eyal? Picnic? Date? She was not ready for this. The glittery leggy idol watched from the coffee table while Yona told him she thought she might be busy.

You think? You don't know? Friday is tomorrow.

She went blank. He answered for her. *What are you afraid of? That someone might like to talk to you? Meet me there at two, okay? You like shawarma?*

"We should never have dragged on so long," Eyal said. He was propped up on his side on a flowered sheet that held the crumbs of their demolished lunch. "It was the sex that messed it up. Because she was so ambivalent. Yes, no, yes, no. But basically always no. And at our age too. Can you imagine? Like high school."

"Why wouldn't she sleep with you?" Yona said. She lay on her back watching the cloudless blue, afraid to roll over and look at him while uttering the question because she couldn't imagine anyone not wanting to sleep with him. Just saying the words to his face would come out as an invitation. Was there something about him she was missing? Was the Dutch person blind?

"You promise not to laugh?"

"Laugh?" She turned her head. His mouth was fifteen inches above hers. He looked worried.

"I won't laugh."

"I don't believe you."

"Really. I won't. Honest."

"All right." A pause. "She said she was thinking of becoming a nun."

"A nun? I thought you said she was Jewish. Inspired by Anne Frank, the plight of the Dutch Jews in the war, the whole nine yards."

He waved away her question. "No, no, she was going to *become* Jewish. Hadn't yet. Was in this country two years, and yes, in love with Anne Frank, the whole sad story. Probably why she came here. But just when I meet her"—he snapped his fingers—*"poof,* she's thinking to enter a convent. Turning back to whatever she was before. What kind of luck is that? An entire year we drag on like this." He tipped his head back and forth, imitation Ping-Pong match.

"Yes. No. Me. Jesus. She couldn't make up her mind who she likes better."

Yona had to suppress the laugh. It really was funny.

"Don't smile, it drove me crazy. She was completely fucked up. I was too stupid to see it. I thought these European women who came here and wanted to join the Jews were great. Why not? The more the merrier. Like in my parents' day, when they came from Finland and Sweden to volunteer on kibbutz and all the Israelis went berserk, had never seen so many tall *blondinis*. But now I know better. I'm finished being someone's Holocaust fantasy. I think she only wanted an Israeli guy so she could produce a pack of little Anne Franks who'd live past age twelve."

"Fifteen."

"Okay, fifteen." He paused, studying her. "You know all the details? The horny boyfriend, the depressed sister, the frigid mother?"

"Of course. Required reading in my school. Practically every year. So how'd it finally end with the Flying Dutchwoman? When she left the country?"

"No. I got strong for a minute. Told her she couldn't have it both ways—be with me like her best friend but not really be with me. I didn't want to fall in love with Mother Teresa." He picked at a crumb on the sheet, tossed it away. "I told her to go home and figure it out and send me a postcard in a few years to tell me what happened."

Yona turned away and looked at the sky. A plane moved soundlessly overhead. She watched it dissolve into a speck. "That was brave of you. I stayed in messed-up relationships long past when I should have. No nuns but married men. Married men who lied to their wives. Or purposely told their wives just to torment them. Men who bought me vacations and jewelry and got me jobs."

"Did they deceive you?"

She looked at him. "Deceive?"

"Tell you they'd leave their marriages for you."

"No."

"Okay, so you weren't being taken. You weren't being a fool."

"This is true," she said. "How did you know that?"

A shrug.

"You're right, they never betrayed me like that. I never wanted them to leave their families. Or marry me. I suppose I got something from each of them. I suppose it wasn't all bad." She turned back to the sky. "But now I don't want that anymore."

17

Greenglass went to Regina's one last time. She wasn't there. He put down his suitcases, placed a note on the card table, thought twice and walked to the back to put it on the bed.

He stopped in the doorway and looked at the narrow cot. There was no box spring, just a mattress and rumpled sheets on a metal frame. He walked over and slowly sat down. It creaked with his weight. He put his face on the terrible pillow that smelled of smoke and sour milk, and closed his eyes and knew he would never see her again. That his youth, and all that raging love and pain, were finally over. He had loved her with all the passion he'd had, and then, with that same passion, he had tried to save her, and now it was done, and all he felt was a great ocean of sadness. Sadness for the boy he'd been and the girl she once was, and for that pure and perfect love that was pure because it was the first. That piece of yourself that you can give only once, the heart that loves wholly and without reservation. *You're different,* she'd said to him the first time he saw her, a cigarette poised between two fingers like an actress in the movies. She had that long dark hair and seemed to stand taller than any other girl in the room, one of those awkward freshman mixers where everyone tried so hard to be suave and aloof, eighteen years old, thinking they were all grown up and that they knew anything. He'd been leaning against a wall with two or three others, everyone talking about their summer because they didn't know what else to talk about. He had worked on a construction crew for one of Lenny's properties, hauling fifty-pound bags of concrete and breaking his fingernails and inhaling cement dust because he wanted to do something with his hands. *You're smarter,* she said when the others had drifted off. *Not in the book way. Worldly. Sharp. You see through things. I like that.* She was so beautiful and brilliant and fine he felt he'd been anointed. That for one shining moment maybe he really was smart and worldly and sharp. For the first time, he began to think of himself as a man.

A wind rattled the glass at the window. He pulled himself up. Her clothes were on the floor, her books scattered, as if someone had kicked them. Slowly, he picked up each garment, the forlorn shirts and battered jeans and balled-up socks, straightened them out and carefully folded each one and laid it on top of the dresser. He gathered up the books and neatly put them in a pile, then found a plastic bag and emptied the ashtrays and collected the old sandwich wrappers, the greasy napkins, the cans sticky with sugary congealed soda and dead ants.

He turned back to the terrible bed. It looked like the bed of a prisoner, the brutal metal frame, the cheap narrow mattress. He straightened the sheets, smoothed the thin blanket, tried to fluff up the sorrowful pillow, making it up as best he could so that if she ever came back, she would know that someone had been there who had loved her and cared for her and hoped that she would be all right.

18

On Sunday neither Shroeder nor Lior was around. No one at Adamah knew why. It wasn't like them to both be off the grounds. Aaron told Ben-Ami and Davidson to calm down; he'd talk to Shroeder the following day and they'd do it Monday night instead. The man couldn't possibly stay away for two days.

At four o'clock on Monday, Aaron went to the shack and told Shroeder that his buddies were going stir-crazy and needed to go to Jerusalem to get some decent food and entertainment, that Aaron's relatives were still in the city and wanted to take them out. They'd sleep over and be back in the morning. His friends hadn't left Adamah in four weeks, he said; they weren't used to that kind of hardship. Even the army gave you regular furloughs.

"Yeah? What do you know about armies?" a guy named Omer asked Aaron. Shroeder looked at papers on his desk and laughed.

"From books," Aaron said. "I read books. Every army gives their soldiers a break. Even during the Civil War, the Union recruits got to take a hot bath and eat a real meal once a month."

"Oh? You comparing this to a civil war, Blinder?" Omer said. "So, *nu*, which side are you on?"

"Cut us some slack, will you, Omer? We're just soft Americans. We need a little recreation." Aaron glanced around. "Hey, where's Lior? Haven't seen him in a couple days."

"Away," Shroeder said, not looking up from the desk.

It was odd. Lior never left. He was Shroeder's right hand, it was his job to be there. And now there was this Omer, with his arms crossed. A replacement.

"Is he okay?" Aaron asked.

"What are you, his mother?" Omer said. "His brother? Your brother's keeper?"

"Just asking."

"You here to talk about Lior," Omer said, "or about Jerusalem?"

"Let them go, let them go," Shroeder said, not looking up, waving. Pharoah, agreeing to liberate the slaves. "Drive them to the bus stop, Omer. Assuming, of course, they're coming back."

"Oh, we'll be back," Aaron said.

Shroeder kept his eyes on his papers. Omer gestured to the door, Aaron should go first. "Give them some spending money," Shroeder called out after them. "Wouldn't want them stranded in Jerusalem without the bus fare to return."

They had hid the two biggest gym bags early that morning in an abandoned irrigation shed a quarter kilometer from the bus shelter, Aaron and Ben-Ami creeping out at first light, the air cool, the roosters from the neighboring collectives shrieking like they couldn't stand the silence. Ben-Ami was a mess. He told Aaron he'd decided he had to let Davidson go. That if you really cared for someone, maybe you had to put their wishes before your own, even if their wishes hurt you. *I'm thinking I should just stop pressuring him and let him leave. Let him go back to Chicago. Maybe even accept that he might, you know, one day get married or something.*

It was the frankest Ben-Ami had ever been. He really loved Davidson. It was sort of beautiful in a way. But it was also sickening. It made Ben-Ami weak. A fool.

Why don't you wait and see what happens after tonight? Aaron had said, though the truth was he didn't care if Davidson left. Davidson would have served his purpose, which was to get Ben-Ami in. In fact, his leaving might be good. The whole business had been one royal pain in the neck, holding their hands every other day so they wouldn't back out, getting Davidson to buy in. If Aaron played his cards right, he might even be able to get Ben-Ami to teach him what he knew, and then Aaron wouldn't need Ben-Ami anymore either.

Yeah, well, the crazy thing is, Ben-Ami said, the roosters maniacal, *I know he's doing this tonight for me. To make me happy. He thinks this is what I want. And then he'll be freer to leave. Like he did something for me before he left.*

Now Aaron walked back up the road with the two big duffels. He could see Ben-Ami and Davidson talking in the bus shelter where Omer had dropped the three of them twenty minutes before. A nagging thought flitted through Aaron's mind, an irritant, like a pebble that shifted around in your shoe. Lior. Maybe that whole conversation on Friday had been about Lior leaving, not Aaron; maybe Lior was the one who wanted out. But that didn't feel right.

He walked up to the shelter, put down the bags. The blood red graffiti on the concrete screamed *Am Yisrael Chai! The Nation of Israel Lives!* Ben-Ami and Davidson fell silent. Whatever it was they were talking about, they didn't want Aaron to hear. Which was fine with him. He didn't want to know about their sorrows, their twisted back-door love. Ben-Ami nodded at him, acknowledging the duffels. In the far distance something loomed like a mirage. A vision, like a prophet's. The bus, coming up over the rise. Aaron stepped out to watch, the huge front grille, the massive tires, the big window, like a shield, climbing up toward the ridge. A messenger from another world rumbling toward them in a great cloud of dust and smoke. Off to the side, when he thought Aaron couldn't see, Ben-Ami took Davidson's hand in his and held it for a long time before finally letting it go.

19

Under a tangerine dusk, Eyal and Yona made another picnic on the flowered sheet. She had gone with him and a dozen of his friends to the beach in Tel Aviv on Saturday and for a hike in the Jerusalem hills on Sunday, but when he'd called from work that morning, Monday, to suggest dinner in the park, she told herself it didn't mean anything, that he was simply a social animal who didn't like to be alone. Because she was leaving in little more than a week and to imagine anything else was out of the question.

He was smiling at her. Grinning, really. It was embarrassing. They had each polished off a shawarma with fries and a bottle of beer, and he'd vociferously marveled at her appetite. He was sick of all the emaciated women who starved themselves in order to have a couple of spoonfuls of ice cream and didn't have the strength to walk up a set of stairs. It was such a relief to be with a person who ate. Not that she had to worry about that sort of thing, he added, waving at her lean outstretched form.

"How old are you?" she said.

"Thirty."

"Me too."

"Good." He leaned down and kissed her forehead. "We won't fuck this up."

"'This'? What makes you think there's a 'this'?" Though she wasn't entirely oblivious; they'd been out together four days running. Still.

"There's always a 'this.' Friends. Or something else. We'll go slow. See if we like each other. What's the rush? I'm not sixteen, I can control myself. You can too."

She hoisted herself up on her elbows. "That's ridiculous. I'm here only another nine days."

"So? Israel won a whole war in six."

"But then I go back to America."

"So?"

"So that's far away! Very far away."

A shrug. "Nothing's forever. Not even America. You'd fit in very well here. My family loves Americans, mixes up the gene pool. We could use a little diversity in our line."

She collapsed back onto the sheet. He lay down beside her. "So tell me about your parents," he said.

She composed practice emails to her boss.

Dear Mariah, Though I'm still away, I am herewith resigning my position at the gallery. I know what you always said about gallery assistants foolishly being wannabe artists, but in my case it's really true. Not sure how or where, but I plan to pursue painting full-time.

Dear Mariah, If you haven't already fired me, I quit. I want to paint, even if you think that's laughable.
P.S. I am very interested in the expressive potential of primary colors.

Dear Mariah, Sometimes it takes getting away to figure out one's priorities. I am leaving my job at the gallery to take art classes and become a painter. Thanks for all your support and inspiration. They've been immeasurably helpful, even if it doesn't appear that way on the surface.

Dear Mariah, I won't be returning to the gallery after all. Thanks for the experience. I now own a wardrobe full of scary black clothes, which I suppose will come in handy someday.

20

*T*he thick *Tel Aviv heat*, the earthy smell of it, the noisy Israelis: Greenglass was so glad to be back. He exited the terminal area, pulling his suitcases behind him, found the Jerusalem-bound van in the airport lot, and wedged himself into the second row.

"Lo oved," the driver barked when he tried to open the window. It doesn't work, don't bother. Greenglass gave up. Who cared? He was so tired he could sleep in a furnace. He settled in, closed his eyes.

And then he was there. At his apartment. He unfolded himself, stepped over his seatmates, retrieved his bags, and paid the driver. He stood on the sidewalk and gazed at his building. The white stone was bathed in a lush, spreading rose. He loved this building, loved the very street name. *Chopin Street.* Sometimes he imagined the tubercular composer playing a plaintive nocturne on a piano high in the air above them, floating over the sidewalk like one of Chagall's yearning fiddlers. He took a long, deep inhale—there was sage and rosemary nearby, a brisk chaser of wild mint—then stepped into the darkened entry. He bypassed the postal boxes—Rachel had his mail—climbed the two flights to his flat, let himself in and went out onto the balcony and let the mountain breeze embrace him. *Home.* He loved this city, his first true home. Chosen home. Even if the choice felt at first more like chance, an unsolicited job offer three years before. A teacher from his yeshiva had moved to Jerusalem to start a program for American boys looking to test the waters of religion, did Greenglass want to come work there? The decision had taken him ten minutes, so ready was he to leave New York. Though the program folded within six months, Greenglass, even when unemployed, even when nearly broke, never stopped believing the opportunity had been a gift.

He closed his eyes, the breeze ruffling his shirt. More than ever, he felt the city welcoming him out here on his balcony. Perhaps it had said a prayer for him, a silent traveler's prayer on his behalf. He had uttered so many prayers for Jerusalem, maybe it had said one for him in return. *May it be Thy will that he return safely to me.*

He went back into the living room. He was suddenly famished. Starving! He got to the kitchen, reversed course, nothing there, and anyway he should go out. Celebrate. He showered, opened his suitcase. The old pink madras shirt lay on top. It was such a loud, preposterous shirt, and yet he liked it, a piece of his past that was beyond memory, beyond association. He had no idea when he'd bought it or where, but there was something enthusiastic about it. A wholesome cheer. *Take me!* it seemed to beg when he was packing, and he did, as if wanting to introduce the city to a cherished old companion. *And this, my friend, is Jerusalem.*

Dressed, combed, he grabbed a plastic water bottle, left his apartment, started down the stairs. Rachel's door. He stopped. He could call her, tell her he was back, but his mobile was upstairs, still in his desk drawer, not charged. He took a brave step, knocked, rang the buzzer.

"Mark. You're home! How are you?" She squinted at him. "Wait a sec. You shaved. And—" She stepped back. "Changed your clothes."

He had what felt like a grin on his face. A probably too-big, probably stupid grin. Did he look like a jerk?

"And you certainly look happy," she said.

"I am. I'm so glad to be here. Want to go out for a sandwich, a piece of cake? I'm starving! What do you say? I'll probably be up all night with jet lag, so a little more coffee won't matter. How about it?"

Where did this courage come from? He hadn't asked a woman to get a sandwich or a coffee in ten years. But here he was, in his old loud shirt, and here she was, smiling, her cropped dark hair sweet-smelling and shiny in the hallway light.

"Great, I'll get my bag. Be right back."

He waited in her little vestibule, astonished. *Great. I'll get my bag.* Maybe the city was praying for him after all.

21

Aaron knelt beneath a shaky tree and slid his two gym bags off his shoulders, then looked back. He could hear them murmuring in the dark, Ben-Ami's nasal whispers, Davidson's reluctant grunts. He wished they'd hurry up, wished they'd stop arguing so he could forget about their big teary drama and concentrate on what he was meant to do and let God or Shroeder or whoever else be the judge.

He waited on the sidewalk by the wrought-iron railing, looking out across the darkened lawn at the sculpture tree and the fountain with the naked stone baby, a sliver of silvery light glistening on the water. A shadow stretched over it, as if something was slowly floating by the face of the moon. Once, at his college, he spent a whole night outside by himself in the perfect blackness, a velvety spring night at the end of his first year before he had to go home for the summer. It was the first time he'd ever been in such blackness, and though he was a little afraid, it had given him a feeling of peace. A place to forget all the noise in his head, and his father and Anne, and all his failures. He'd slept out under a tree and watched the stars. Maybe it was a mistake not to go back to college. Maybe he should have gone there after the kibbutz or the weeks at Eli Cooper's, back to the barns and the goats and cows. He used to look out his dorm window on the tenth floor of the awful tower and see in all directions, the acres of fields and the flame-colored trees that bordered them in the fall, reds and golds and oranges, and watch the horses standing there with their flicking tails. He liked that. It would calm him down and take his mind off himself. Maybe he should have gone back.

"Blinder, wait up," Ben-Ami hissed.

A pair of gleaming eyes emerged out of the shadows. Aaron shoved away the trees and the barns and the horses. Ben-Ami's eyes shone like white stones in a dark river. They had put on ski caps and blackened their faces just as Ben-Ami had learned to do in the army, and it gave them all a rodent look, like raccoon. Or skunk.

"You're moving too fast," Ben-Ami said. "We've got to time this exactly. Synchronize. Davidson's gone to the other side. You're rushing, not paying attention, losing focus. You're going to screw it up."

Aaron said nothing, let Ben-Ami's nagging-grandma voice rant. From the minute they'd arrived in the city he'd let the kid spout off, because if he said anything he was afraid they would bolt. Even up to the very end. All evening Ben-Ami had been saying they should call it off, that they weren't ready. When Ben-Ami and Davidson had gone to pick up Ben-Ami's friend's car, Aaron wasn't sure they'd return. Now Ben-Ami's eye whites were three inches from Aaron's face, and Aaron could smell dope on his breath. He couldn't believe the guy was doing this stoned, but again he kept silent because who was he to tell anyone what was needed under the circumstances.

"Your bags," Ben-Ami said, "you want to wedge them in right up against the wall, one at each end, where I showed you on the diagram." His breath was pungent, sour. Fear mixed with marijuana and the greasy falafel he and Davidson had wolfed down hours ago. Aaron hadn't been able to eat a thing, his stomach tied tight like a fist. "You've got three minutes. Sixty seconds later they blow, just like Davidson's on the other side. No looking around any corners, no dawdling, use the flashlight only when absolutely necessary. Walk slow so you don't trip, all kinds of crap on the ground to fall over. When you're done, you run to the car. Same deal for Davidson. Jump the fence when you leave. The main gate is too lit up. We drive away and watch from a distance. And if I see any lights going on and off inside, I'll fucking kill you."

"I told you," Aaron said, "there won't be any lights. There's no one in there. The building's empty. Nada. It's a front for fucking Arabs. It's midnight. They're all out diddling their girlfriends or making plans to kill the Jews."

Ben-Ami exhaled, showering Aaron with a foul mist of oily, weed-tinged spit, and Aaron climbed over the metal fence and skulked across the hushed lawn toward the building. He passed the big sculpture tree, the silver leaves reflecting the moonlight. *Olive Tree International. Zeit,* the pimply kid at the hostel had said, pointing to the olives on the buffet. *For olive. Same word in Hebrew and Arabic, zeit, zayit. Hey, it sounds like Birzeit, the militant university near Ramallah.*

Yeah, Aaron had said. *It's probably a branch, probably the same thing.*

Probably is.

He fell over something in the garden, hitting his forehead, a thin trickle of blood, got to his feet and walked along the edges to avoid crushing more flowers. When he got to the building he crept along the perimeter, away from the giant spotlight on the front corner, groping across the wall to the other end. A gasp of icy wind ruffled his sweatshirt. All day it had been threatening to rain, a bizarrely unseasonable chill though the clouds had finally lifted. Still, he'd thought he'd be sweaty, nervous. But he wasn't; it was going to be great. A statement. Shroeder would be surprised, impressed; he'd say he'd underestimated Aaron. He found the end of the building, got down and crawled on his knees, the ground cold and rocky, felt for the little rise where the water pipes were, then shoved the first bag up against the stone. Supports would be there, Ben-Ami had said. Structural supports. For maximum damage.

He stood up and hugged the wall, inched to the left one step at a time like a partner in a dance. One-two. Two-two. Three-two. At fifty-two, he slid down and pushed in the second bag, then shined the flashlight onto his watch. Two minutes gone. He was near the building's front corner. He scanned the ground with the narrow beam, surveying his work. Good. Very good. He'd had enough of their stinking bombs going off all over the city, their nauseating rhetoric about the Israelite son of the monkey, the filthy Zionist dog. He was sick of being passive, sheep to the slaughter. A meek, timid, shtetl Jew walking docilely to the ovens murmuring Psalms.

A noise in the courtyard, footsteps on stone. He snapped off the light and froze. *Clack clack clack.* Someone was approaching the main entrance, nearing the spotlight.

His chest pounded wildly. He leaned around to look. A man wearing glasses and a screaming pink plaid hippie-type shirt, holding a plastic water bottle. He was heading toward the doors. He looked like a tourist, someone who'd mistakenly wandered over.

"Stop!" Aaron shouted in English, running out under the glare. "You've got to get out of here! Now!"

The man halted, stared at him. His face turned to chalk.

"It's going to blow! Do you understand? Do you speak English? You've got to run!"

The bottle slid from the man's hand. Bounced on the stone. "What are you talking about?"

He was an American. Aaron waved frantically. "It's going to blow up! You've got to run!"

"What about you? Let me help you!"

The man took a step forward, under the light, and for an instant

Aaron thought he knew him, that he'd met him somewhere, or someone just like him, a well-meaning teacher or guidance counselor or
social worker, someone who cared. A fool, a bleeding heart, just
like all the other bleeding hearts who thought they could save you
with words. Who thought that behind every evil deed was just a hurt
and damaged child, and that all anyone needed was a little love and
understanding. They were so naïve, so hopelessly naïve. It was too
late for that.

"You've got to go!" Aaron yelled, backing away, "You've got to
get out of here! We all do!"

"All? Who else is here?"

"No one!" Davidson. He had to get to Davidson. The man was
looking at the entrance doors, making up his mind. Aaron couldn't
wait another second. "There's nobody in there, I swear! You've got
to run! Please!" Surely the doors would be locked, surely the man
would discover that and flee. "Please go!" Aaron screamed before
turning and running off into the darkness to the other side. "Davidson! Where are you? Davidson!"

He found him crouched by the wall next to one of the bags.
Except he should have been finished by now. He should have been
on his way to the car, on his way to safety, to Ben-Ami. He shouldn't
have been huddling there, paralyzed.

"There's someone here! We've got to stop this! Can we defuse
these things?" They had sixty, maybe ninety seconds. Ben-Ami was
out there in the blackness looking at his watch, walking to the car.
"Where are the timers? Where are the fucking timers!"

Davidson shook his head. In the shadows he looked like a lost
bear, a big man now tiny, stranded, helpless. An odorous stream
trickled out near his shoes. He was peeing in his pants. It was no
good. Only Ben-Ami knew how to make the things work. Even if
they could unzip the bags and see inside, Aaron wouldn't know what
he was looking at. Neither of them would.

"Okay, we'll call him! Get out your phone!"

Davidson didn't move.

"The phone, Davidson!"

A hoarse whisper scraped out. "I . . . I don't have it."

"You don't have it? All right, forget it! We've got to run, they're going to blow!"

Davidson's eyes were clouded and rheumy, like a frightened child's.

Aaron tugged on his arm. He was sure the front doors were locked. That the man couldn't possibly have gone inside. Didn't they lock them every night? Davidson wasn't moving. "C'mon, Davidson, you've got to get up!"

A foul stench rose up. Davidson was losing it, he had no control. He looked like he was going to pass out. Aaron slapped him across the face. "Wake up, Davidson! Snap out of it!" Again he pulled on the thick arm. "Grab onto my neck! Get on my back, I'll carry you out!" He leaned down. He was going to vomit, the stink enveloping him like a putrid cloud. "Grab on, I'll get us out! It's going to blow!"

Davidson crouched by the wall, an animal whimper coming from somewhere deep in his throat. Aaron wheeled around, tried to lift him. He reached under his armpits, screamed that they had to run, had to get away, but Davidson recoiled and Aaron slid in the reeking puddle and lost his grip. Again and again, Aaron tried to pull Davidson up but the man refused, and finally, when Aaron saw in Davidson's face that he would never get him out of the fetal crouch, never get him to understand what was about to happen, never get him to see that this was his life, that this was all there was ever going to be, he let go and lit off into the brutal night. And when, seconds later, a blast ripped open the sky and the stinging smell of burning seared his nostrils and he saw in the eerie glow of the flames the silhouette of Ben-Ami running toward the fire, he didn't look back, the curdling sounds of Ben-Ami shrieking *Davidson! Davidson!* from somewhere in the darkness ringing in his ears for what felt like miles.

PART
2

22

At a concrete playground studded with miniature metal ponies Aaron stopped running. He took hold of a cold post, felt his heart racing. The sirens. Shrill and accusing, as if they were inside his skull. He pulled down his ski cap and put his hands over his ears like a child or a retarded person, squeezed his eyes shut. If anyone saw him, they'd feel sorry for him, his hands up on the sides of his head like someone who couldn't handle things. Who couldn't cope.

The sirens were shrieking and he opened his eyes. His sweatshirt was filthy, also his pants, his shoes. He was shivering. He hugged himself, looked at the playground. From the light of a streetlamp he could see that the ponies were faded, once upon a time painted sky blue and cherry red and pumpkin orange, to be cheerful. Their small curved bodies were perched on fat springs so that when you sat on the chipped saddles you could pretend you were riding, galloping off into the sunset like in the final scene where the cowboys ride off to *The End*.

He went over to a dull yellow one, its big painted eye coal black, its head and mane pale in the glow of the streetlight, the color of butter, of a girl's hair, and grabbed onto the handles, swung one leg over, and sat. The pony wobbled. He clutched it tighter, pushed forward, closed his eyes. The pony began to rock. He held on and let himself be carried by the rhythm of it, a child being lulled to sleep, his dirty hands wrapped around the handles, his muddy shoes positioned in

the metal stirrups. Up down, up down. A small, frightened boy rock-
ing on a toy pony on a starless night with the siren roar and shrieking
howls, endless, in the distance.

23

*L*ater, *Yona would tell herself* that she'd heard it, a crackling
like lightning around midnight, but that it didn't register, the
music in Eyal's apartment too loud, too many people crammed into
his living room eating, drinking, arguing. But then the cell phones
began to ring. And then everyone knew. A friend of Eyal's drove her
there. She had to go see, she told him. She knew the place, had passed
it every day.

A crowd was massed on the sidewalk, dozens of soldiers milling
around, everyone murmuring and gaping at what used to be the roof,
a crater smoldering in the glare of the police lights. The veranda lay
crushed under a mountain of broken stone and glass; one of its pillars
looked crippled at the midpoint, as if it had been hit in the knee, a
giant's leg about to crumble. Swaths of lawn had been scorched black.
The cherub in the fountain was gone. The air was choked with soot.

"What happened? Was anyone injured?" Yona asked an elderly
woman in slippers and a bathrobe who was holding tightly on to the
iron railing, safeguarding her place like a refugee. All around them,
people were snapping pictures and making calls. *Terrible. Huge. Is it
on the news yet?* "Was anyone in the building? Do you know?"

The old lady shook her head, pointed to the ambulances clus-
tered by the ruined structure, red tube lights twirling. Who would
want to blow this nice place up? she said. Musicians, painters, poets,
such talented young women. What did they ever do to anybody?

Yona moved through the throng. Had there been any word? What about the perpetrators? Shaking heads, clucking tongues. No one knew anything. Sometimes a group claimed responsibility immediately, someone said. Hamas or Al-Aqsa, Islamic Jihad; there'd be rhetoric, proclamations, a cell leader in Damascus announcing on Al-Jazeera that it was in retaliation for an Israeli raid or to show the Jews who's boss, teach the Zionist dog a lesson, footage of people dancing in the streets in Gaza City and masked men shooting rifles in the air. But other times it took days for anyone to speak up. You could never know.

More jeeps screamed up. Policemen jumped out and strung red plastic tape along the railing. Nobody allowed on the premises, one of the officers—arms spread, blocking the gate—barked at a reporter and his photographer who were pushing to get through. But a crew from Channel One had just jumped the fence on the other side, the reporter insisted. The policeman told him to move back and shut his trap. Did he want to get himself killed? He didn't care what any idiots were doing on the other side. It was too dangerous. Possibility of collapse, rogue electrical fire, even another bomb. Everyone knew how it went. A first explosion that drew a crowd, then a second, to finish everyone off.

Yona pushed herself away from the crush, suddenly in need of air—the smoke, the giant klieg lights of the television crews, the hundreds of bodies jockeying for position. In an instant, her spot was swallowed up. At the edge of the crowd a short teenage boy motioned to her, she should step away, out of earshot of the others.

"I heard you asking questions," he whispered in British-tinged English. She had to bend down to hear him. South African. Eighteen, nineteen. He had a nervous twitch, an unstoppable blinking. "The victims by the ambulances? Americans, I'll bet you."

"Americans?" she said, incredulous. "I thought the only women studying here were from Scandinavia. Europe."

"They weren't students," the boy said. He paused to suffer the contortions of his face. His mouth became a Munch painting, a silent, twisted scream. It was hard to look at. When he was finally done, he said, "And they weren't women either," then turned and hurried away, vanishing into the stand of bodies before she had the wits to think of following him.

24

It was only the finest pinpoint of light.

But it was all that mattered. And Greenglass so wanted to go there. So wanted to swim up the long, dark shaft and go through that tiny opening and be bathed in the warm glow of it, let himself merge with it. He felt it like a magnet's pull, so beautiful and complete, all he would ever need. All he had to do was let himself.

But there was something, or someone, pushing him back, keeping him anchored where he was. Denying him. *Mark*. A voice, then an invisible hand stopping him, grinding him back into the terrible now, the terrible now of his body. The tunnel beckoned but the voice was refusing. It was coming from the end of the shaft, where the light was, a whispered command telling him, though there were no words: *No*. That he could not come, that it was not yet time. That he was not yet finished with this life. That despite the brokenness of his body and the pain that awaited him, he could not depart. That he could not yet leave this world, that he would not yet be released.

25

Aaron woke, freezing. It was getting light, the sky a vacant white-gray that always looked to him like death. This would be what the world looked like if the sun ever cooled. No color, no sound, silent and numb and bleached of life.

He pulled himself up. Sometime in the night he must have moved to a bench and lain down. His clothing was foul, everything about him reeked; his ski hat was on the dirt. He picked it up, pulled it on. An acrid smell hovered. He glanced at the playground. Candy wrappers were scattered across the cement; cellophane Bisli bags were trapped among the tree roots like deflated party balloons. Chipped blue monkey bars stood like a prison cell in a desolate corner of the lot, rust peeling the edges. They would never allow monkey bars like that in America; everyone would sue. The ponies were still, their big black eyes staring at nothing.

Lights shone in a few windows of the apartment buildings. He stood up, then, suddenly dizzy, grabbed the back of the bench to steady himself. He wanted to vomit. But he was empty; he hadn't eaten in a day. His stomach seized, a dart of pain shooting across his abdomen. He left the playground. His head pounded. A corner market was opening, a man pulling up the big metal grate. A slow, loud grinding. *Click. Click. Click. Click. Click.* Aaron put his hand in his pocket and drew out change. When the man saw him, Aaron pointed to a shelf, mumbled something about a Coca-Cola, but the man waved him away, too early, not open yet, come back in an hour.

He walked on. His legs were rubber. He thought he might faint.

He imagined Ben-Ami suddenly rounding a corner, the two of them staring at each other like ghosts. He wished it were yesterday, or the day before. Or last year.

At the next market, he waited on the sidewalk while the man finished turning on the lights, unlocking the register.

Coke, could I buy a Coke? Aaron murmured, adding, *I'm not feeling well.*

The man gestured with his chin to the cooler. *Take. Go ahead.*

Aaron removed a bottle, reached into his pocket.

Forget it, the man told him, waving. *I don't take money from a sick person. Go. Take.*

He sat on a low wall outside an apartment and sipped. The sky was deepening into blue, the colorless void receding. Another living day. The birds were out. *Caw! Caw! Caw!* He finished off the Coke, carefully put the bottle in a trash can, kept walking.

Jaffa Road. This he knew. The buses were starting. He had to sleep. Had to get out of his terrible clothes and wash and sleep. He turned left, toward the Old City, toward the windmill. He bought a second Coke. The city was coughing itself awake, sputtering car exhaust, the store grates rising, *click! click! click! click!* huge mouths opening. A *whoosh!* of laundry water was tossed out a back window; a woman on a balcony beat a rug with a wooden paddle. Merchants were putting out their wares, people buying bread, heading for work. Children carried thick schoolbags, garish backpacks, *My Little Pony* stenciled on pink nylon in front of him, a baby blue creature with flowing purple hair winking coyly. Two men in black hats hurried past, heads down. Off to pray. Could he stop one of them, ask them to pray for him? What would he want them to say? *O God, Master of the Universe, do not let me see what I have done.* He turned onto King David Street. Passing a bakery, he thought to go in, to buy a hard roll or pastry, but his stomach revolted and he went on, the buttery yeasty smell behind him mocking, taunting. A wave of nausea rose up and he took another drink from the bottle to silence it, and kept moving.

At the path to the hostel he stopped, tried to smooth out his pants, scrape the mud off his shoes. He had no bag with him, not even a toothbrush, his pack in Ben-Ami's friend's car. Where was that car? Where was Ben-Ami? At the thought of the car and of Ben-Ami waiting there in the dark, hunched in the driver's seat, looking at his watch, waiting for him, for Davidson—*Davidson! Davidson!*—he felt his stomach heave, felt the Coke moving back up into his throat, and swallowed hard, a metallic taste, slick and viscous. He willed it to go back down, waited for the upsurge to pass. He could do this. He could walk inside and ask for a bed. He had a wallet. Money. Maybe they'd remember him; he'd been there just a week before, three nights, they might still even know his name.

Hey, Aaron, they'd say. *What happened to you?*

Oh, out all night, got a little wrecked. Friend coming later with my stuff.

He moved up the stone walkway past the straggly garden, the dying summer flowers. He opened the heavy door. A small dark man he'd not seen before was behind the reception desk, his gaze down, looking at something Aaron couldn't see. The newspaper, a list of the day's guests. The lobby was empty. There was a faint smell of toast and burnt coffee.

He went to the desk. The man looked up. Aaron asked for a bed. The man turned to a bank of tiny cubbies on the wall behind him, began searching for a key. Two hands came down onto Aaron's shoulders, clasping him hard.

26

Eyal called at seven in the morning. Had Yona heard? One death confirmed, no name given, no nationality. Another unidentified person was in the hospital. Was she okay? It could be traumatic seeing it so soon afterward. Even just hearing about it could be traumatic.

She lay in bed, eyes still closed. This was how it always went, everyone calling everyone else. Checking in. Comparing information. One day you're walking down a pleasant sunny street, and the next, it goes up in flames.

"I'm fine," she said.

"Good. I'm going to work. Call you later."

She closed the phone. Leaned back into the pillows.

Another ring. "Hello?"

"Did I wake you?" Shira Feinbrenner.

"No." She looked at the clock. Nine-thirty. She propped up the pillows, made herself upright.

"So have you heard?" Shira said. One death so far, one in critical condition, nobody claiming responsibility. Shira and her family were flying home tomorrow. Not a moment too soon, in her opinion. "Who would want to destroy a nothing little college?" Shira said. Yona could make out the jangly singsong of children's TV in the background. Shira's kids, planted in front of a video. "And what a weird name. Olive Branch International. Like it was some Middle East peace center. Not very peaceful, if you ask me."

Yona pulled herself up higher. What did Shira just say? A college?

And, according to the twitching phantom in last night's crowd, American casualties.

Of course. The loose cannons. The kids the man at Dena's was murmuring about. Naftali Shroeder, lynchpin of the movement. One of them at his—what was it anyway? not a settlement exactly; a hothouse, an incubator—one was looking to blow up an Arab school, he'd said. A women's college. Jerusalem. His words. The boy had gone scouting. He could have seen the painter in the head scarf and assumed. The nasal drone of a neutered television dinosaur floated through the phone line.

"Hello? Yona? You still there?"

"Sorry." What could she say? Nothing to Shira, nothing to anybody. She waved, distracted. "I'm just, you know, upset."

"Of course you are," Shira said. "It's a shock. The place isn't that far from you. You could've been walking past there yourself last night. God forbid."

She dressed quickly, left the flat. At the corner she flagged down a cab.

"Hospital, please."

"Which one?"

Which one. How many were there? She had no idea. "Hadassah. The university." Because it was the most famous, the one she'd seen in every Jewish magazine in her parents' house, pictures of EMTs and high-tech laboratories and state-of-the-art burn units. And those famous Chagall windows.

"The bombing victim," she said in breathless, purposeful English at the information desk in the lobby. She tried for calm. Control. She had to be there; she couldn't just sit in Claudia's apartment on her hands. She knew who was responsible. And that made her responsible too. "I'm a relative, I'm here to see him."

The woman had brassy dyed hair and was wearing too much

rouge. She looked at Yona with hooded eyes. "You have a permission? A paper? You must to have a permission. From the authorities."

"Please," Yona said. She was near tears, genuine, if for reasons other than what they seemed. But at least she'd come to the right place. "Can't you see I'm his family? From America? Please."

The woman glanced around, then looked at her computer screen. This was Israel; no one went by the rules. "Go. Second floor, critical care."

But Yona didn't know the name.

"Where?" she said, waving her arms, semihysterical. It wasn't all an act. "I don't understand! Where?"

"Miss, you must to behave yourself. Now listen. Second floor. Critical unit. You'll see the room, his name on the chart. Mark Greenglass. That's it. Okay? You can make it there?"

Yona exhaled, nodded. "Yes. Thank you. I can make it."

Was it wrong to deceive? She allowed herself fifteen seconds to dwell on the question as she walked to the elevators. If anyone stopped her, she would claim emotional distress and leave, say she had an irrational fear it was someone she knew. No one was going to arrest her.

But if she was right, if this was the work of Shroeder's bloodthirsty boy, then she had to go upstairs. Because someone had to keep vigil. To atone.

She walked down the circular corridor. No one gave her a second glance. The room was hushed, the other bed empty, the chairs empty. He was sleeping, a maze of tubes and drips snaked to his arms, a battery of machines and monitors behind him, part of his face and scalp and hands wrapped in gauze. She took one of the plastic chairs against the back wall, tried not to make noise. He filled the length of the bed, an average-size man. Mark Greenglass. Whoever he was. She watched him breathe. If she could have prayed, she would have.

"Hello."

She startled, turned.

"I didn't mean to frighten you." A small pretty woman with short dark hair put a cool hand on Yona's. She spoke in American English. "You looked almost asleep."

"I'm sorry. I didn't realize."

The woman sat in the adjoining chair. "Are you a relative?"

Yona searched her face. "Yes. Yes, I am."

"Oh thank God. Finally. I'm Rachel Craft, Mark's downstairs neighbor. We're, well, friends. I was with him last night, before it happened." Her eyes welled up.

"Yona. Yona . . ." She trailed off. She couldn't give a last name. Because they would trace her to Dena, there'd be immediate arrests, a total stranger lying her way into the hospital room of a bombing victim. She'd raise red flags all over the place.

"From New York?"

"Yes, New York, I was here on vacation." She turned to the bed. "How is he?"

"Not good. In a coma. One of the doctors said that's a useful response, shuts down the body to preserve the organs. Minimal activity to help survive. But who knows."

"And the injuries?"

"Burns. Broken bones. But internally? The brain? They have no idea. He must have been very close to the building. That's what they're saying." She reached for a tissue. Behind them, outside in the corridor, a cell phone rang. *Abba. Lo tov. Dad, it's not good.*

A maternal-looking nurse in a pink smock padded in, followed by a young doctor in blue scrubs. The doctor was already pulling the curtain around the bed.

"You will please excuse us, all right, *motek*?" the nurse said to Rachel, putting a soft arm around her shoulders. *Motek.* Sweetheart. "Half an hour, you and your friend can return. You feeling okay? Maybe you can eat something." She turned to Yona. "You help each other, all right?"

"We'll go to the coffee shop," Rachel said to Yona. The nurse disappeared behind the curtain. "You must be so worried. Had you just seen him, when he was teaching?"

"Teaching?"

"In New York. When he was in the States."

"No, I was traveling. I haven't seen him in a long time."

He was a popular instructor for programs all over the city for newly devout types, those coming to learn after a bad phase with drugs or school problems or because something was missing. He'd taught at yeshivas, at the free classes offered to scruffy backpackers who were sightseeing or showed up, curious, at the Wall, and for college groups from America who wanted to bring in someone the kids could relate to. His own history, he'd told Rachel, was a lot like some of his students'; the religion had rescued him. But he'd lost the passion, the ability to cleave, connect. The *kavannah*. He didn't know why. He'd walked to the Olive Branch college that night because he was to start teaching there in a week and had never seen the place. It had been arranged long distance, by email and phone.

"He had jet lag," Rachel said, not touching her coffee. "So hard to sleep when you first arrive. I have that every time I come back from Canada. That's where my family is. Toronto."

She was trying valiantly not to cry, though it was obvious Mark Greenglass was not just a neighbor. "I was bringing in his mail, watering his plants," she said, looking off toward the cafeteria windows. She hadn't slept all night. She'd rushed to the site and confirmed his identity when she heard the news, then rode in the ambulance with him to the hospital. "As soon as he got back from New York, he rang my bell. We went to the Aroma down our street, had a sandwich, shared a piece of cake." She went for another tissue. "I'm sorry I'm so weepy. The crazy thing is I only got to know him in the few weeks before he left. We'd never even been out together before. But he's very nice. Very special. Well, you must already know that."

Yona pretended to be interested in her coffee. How was she going to keep up the charade?

Rachel stuffed the tissue into her pocket. "I had the feeling before he went to the States that he was going through something big. I don't know why. Maybe it was because he'd lived in the building for two years and I'd had almost nothing to do with him, just an occasional nod on the stairs. But then, right before his trip, we started talking. A few words at the mailboxes. A conversation at the bus stop."

"And was he? Going through something?"

"He was. It was about his religious practice. He gave up the Orthodox clothing while he was away, shaved off the beard. I almost didn't recognize him." Rachel looked down at her coffee but didn't pick it up. Yona pushed a roll in her direction. She ignored it. "He told me last night that he needed to change his life. Like really change it." She looked off again in the direction of the windows. "Everyone who comes here does that eventually. Sometimes it's why you come in the first place. To fix something that isn't working."

Yona picked up her own cup. "Was that true for you?" she asked.

Rachel turned back, glanced once more at her untouched coffee, then at Yona. "I was twenty-seven years old, working in Toronto for a high-tech company, saving up for a condo, when a man broke my heart. Said he wasn't ready for a commitment. Two months later he married someone else. So I came here, got a job teaching English in a high school. That was five years ago."

"Obviously you'd been here before."

"Sure. The usual conscientious Jewish upbringing. Usual for Toronto Jews anyway. A few trips with my family, then again with a high school youth group, a summer during college volunteering at a school for the disabled." She allowed herself a small smile. "All the things nice Jewish girls are supposed to do."

"So you like it here."

"Yes. But if you'd asked me five years ago if I wanted to do something radically different with my life, I'd have said no. Back then I thought I just needed time to get over the boyfriend. No one ever thinks they've come here to reinvent themselves. It's only after-wards that you realize. You tell yourself you're here just to get over a breakup. Or because you're between jobs. Or to take a little time before graduate school. Or to get away from the family for a little while. You say it's for six months, a year. Later, you see things weren't working out at home for a reason. That your life needed shaking up. Coming here, you get that shake-up. Sometimes it succeeds, some-times it doesn't."

An elderly couple inched past their table. The man leaned heav-ily on a cane; the woman held his elbow. "And now," Rachel said, watching the old people, "Mark wants to start over too. Make a new life. New work. New friends . . ." She trailed off, watching the cou-ple's torturous progress.

"And maybe start something with you?"

Rachel turned to Yona. She was very pretty, even prettier when she smiled. But now she only looked sad. "We talked for five hours last night. I don't usually do that. But who knows if he'll make it?"

Yona left the hospital, went to the school again. The sidewalk had been cordoned off. Beyond the iron railing, police and fire and army people were sweeping across the grounds and through the ruined building, examining the wreckage, collecting debris in special bags, calling on walkie-talkies. Every now and then one of them would look back at the crowd on the sidewalk. An audience, riveted.

"Mamash no'ra," said a man next to Yona, shaking his head. Truly awful. Not a place in the country was safe, not even a quiet lit-tle street like this one. What did the Arabs want from them? They'd given up Gaza, they'd give up all the rest if they'd just stop sending

over bombers and launching rockets into their cities. If they would only leave the Jews alone.

"What makes you think this is the work of Arabs?" Yona asked.

He stared at her like she was crazy. He was in his sixties, old enough to have been in two or three wars. What, he said, did she think the Danes did it to collect the insurance? Or maybe the neighbors because they didn't like the landscaping? What was the matter with her?

She went back to Claudia's, sat on the balcony with a glass of juice. A warm haze floated over the city; she could hear a muezzin in the distance. The call to the noon prayers. The news was still being coy on the subject of Olive Branch; the investigation was continuing, no one was claiming responsibility. He'd been so lucky to secure the teaching post, Mark Greenglass had told Rachel the night before; he owed the guy at the New York institute big-time for getting him the job, a fellow named Wasserstein or Wasserfall or Wasserman, Rachel couldn't remember. Things were starting to fall into place, he told her over their shared pastry. He had a good feeling about it.

But now Mark Greenglass's hopes hung by a thread, as did his life, and those culpable were—where? Celebrating? Shrugging? To Naftali Shroeder, to Aryeh Ben-Tzion, the truth didn't matter. What counted was the perception of truth. If the Jews of Jerusalem, of all the world, believed that this unobtrusive little college, this oasis of the arts that wanted so much to be a refuge, had been blown up by Arabs—an implication that would be left to stand if there was nothing in the press to contradict it—so be it. Less chance of another territorial withdrawal. Of more concessions. Of any despicable so-called peace talks. More justification for their cause. *This is what we pray for*, Dena told the stunned women from Cleveland in her living room. *The privilege to resist, to fight. To liberate the land in God's holy name. Whatever the cost.*

The muezzin was finishing his chant. First to the east, then the west, then north and south. It seemed to Yona to be a live human voice, though she'd heard they were often recordings now. In some cities, the honor used to go to a man who was blind so that when he ascended the minaret to sing out his cries, he wouldn't be able to see into the courtyards of his fellow citizens and violate their privacy.

But listening now—*Allah u Akbar! Allah u Akbar! God is great! God is great!*—Yona wondered if perhaps only a blind man could bear to do it. If maybe all calls to the faithful, of all religions, were made by those who were blind. The trumpet charge to the Crusades, the whipped-up cries for jihad, the pumped-up settler rallies in Zion Square refusing to withdraw, to *Never forgive! Never forget!* Because that way they would never have to see what it was they were calling for.

27

They had Ben-Ami. He was down the hall in another room crying his eyes out like a girl. He had told them everything.

The bare bulb hurt Aaron's eyes, and his head throbbed. Was it a special bulb, supposed to look normal but really designed for interrogation? Infrared rays that seared you and made you blind if you looked too close, like watching an eclipse without protective glasses? He tried to keep his eyes open but the light kept making them want to close. He wanted so much to sleep.

"We don't need to lay a hand on you because you are an American and are going to tell us the truth, isn't that right, Aaron," the man behind the desk said, his big hands folded in front of him, his English thick and guttural and harsh, the *r*'s stuck in the back of his throat. He looked like someone's overworked father. "Just like your friend Barney down the hall."

Aaron blinked wide, tried to keep his head up, his gaze steady. A floor fan whirred pointlessly in a corner, oscillating left, right. Left, right. Everything looked hazy, blurry.

"You need coffee? Something to stay awake?" the man said, and didn't wait for an answer, instead lifted a finger, pointed past Aaron's shoulder. Behind Aaron, someone walked to the door, opened it, and went out. He didn't dare turn around. The man refolded his hands. Aaron tried to watch him, then felt his head droop, his eyelids go heavy.

An icy torrent. He jerked his head up. He was drenched. Footsteps behind him, the sound of a dropped metal pail. The man at the desk moved a cup and saucer in his direction. "Drink."

He didn't want to drink. Coffee upset his stomach, gave him cramps. He was sensitive to acidic foods. The man moved the saucer another half inch. Some of his fingers were gnarled, one of the nails a deep bruised purple.

Aaron picked up the cup, his hand shaking. Black, scalding. And thick, like mud. If he didn't drink it, it would end up in his lap. He took a tiny sip. Bitter, the taste of ash.

"So. Why don't you start at the beginning."

Aaron brought the cup down, spilling onto the saucer. He was freezing. Behind him someone lit a match. He didn't know how many were back there. Two maybe. The smell of cigarettes floated up. Maybe three.

Something was off.

"Don't you have to do this with a lawyer present? Or don't I at least get to make a phone call?"

A footstep behind him. The man at the desk shot up a hand. *Stop.* Another step, retreating.

"A lawyer, you say?" the man said. He had gray-black hair, dark pouches under his eyes. "You believe you get a lawyer?"

"I just thought, well, I mean, I thought, before you question someone—"

The man leaned across the desk. His shoulders bulged under

his shirt. He wasn't wearing a uniform. None of them had. The bulb made his skin ghostly. "This is not a television show, you understand? This is not a movie. This is also not the United States and you have not been picked up for snatching a lady's purse." He sat up straight. His face was flushed. He paused, as if waiting for the color to drain. "Of course, we can move you to prison if you'd rather. People ready to take you right now. Then you'll get your lawyer. Eventually."

Aaron's head felt light. He was afraid he might pee. He squeezed his knees together. His pants were sodden from the ice water. He made a quick nod. "I understand." His voice came out small. "No lawyer."

The man folded the hands again. The purple nail shone in the monster light. His face was stone. The room was a tomb. Another match was struck, a sizzling, then a faint inhale.

The man waited.

"I had this idea to just . . . just, you know, do a little thing to try to scare them. No one was supposed to get hurt. Set off a little explosion, that's all. When no one was there."

"Scare who?"

"The Arabs of course."

The man glanced at one of them behind Aaron, then looked back. "And how would blowing up this building scare the Arabs?"

"It's a cover for one of their colleges, their terrorist college in the West Bank. Birzeit. Because it's called Olive Branch, you know, *zeit, zayit?* It means olive. It's supposed to look like a regular school but really it's a cover. For Fatah or Hamas or Islamic Jihad."

"Someone told you this?"

"No, I figured it out myself."

A cough in the back, then a snicker. The hand shot up again. *Stop.* Silence.

"So you thought of this place alone?"

"No, wait, I forgot. Another kid told me about it."

A second look past him. "What kid, tell me about the kid."

Something was beginning to assemble itself in Aaron's brain.

There'd been a terrible mistake, something very bad had happened. Worse than he'd thought. His seat was an icy puddle.

The man leaned forward, tapped the gruesome nail. "I asked you a question. What kid?"

"Sorry. Sorry." Panic gripped Aaron's chest, it was hard to breathe. Davidson. Was Davidson really dead? And the other guy. Surely he ran away. How could he not have run away? He was shivering.

"You need something to refresh your memory?" The coffee cup was sliding closer, like a little animal crawling on the man's desk. It moved six inches, stopped.

He had to pick it up. He didn't want to. Trembling, he reached for it. It spilled onto the saucer again, onto the table, then his legs, his shirt. He couldn't get the cup near his mouth. He used both hands, dribbled onto his chin. Nobody moved. He made himself drink. Bitter as tar. His gut contracted; pain shot through his middle.

"So?"

He got the cup back onto the saucer. "He was . . . I met . . . I met . . . I ate breakfast with him at the hostel. Last week. He's the one who told me about the school."

"What did this kid look like?"

"I don't remember."

The metal pail clattered behind him.

"He was, wait, let me think." He closed his eyes. "My age. Skinny. Acne." He opened his eyes. "He said he was from Pittsburgh. He ate a lot of breakfast."

The man tapped the table. Someone lit another cigarette.

"Who did you tell about this plan?"

"No one. Just the two guys who did it with me."

"No one else you were living with?"

"No. We kept it a secret. Nobody knew."

A pause. The man rearranged his hands. "Except the boy from the hostel."

The hostel. The word rattled. How had they known to look for him there? Had he told Ben-Ami he'd stayed there? He didn't think so. How did they find him? Who was that kid, the one from Pittsburgh?

"So this boy told you about the school. Then what?"

"Then I scoped it out."

"You went to see it?"

"Yes. I watched it for three nights. And twice during the day."

"And what did you see?"

"A big building. Like a mansion. Students. Women students."

"Doing what?"

"Walking around. They had big instrument cases. At least they looked like instrument cases. But they could have had anything inside them."

"What else?"

What else. What else. He was shivering and needed to wipe his nose. He used his wet sleeve. "Some of them were carrying leather cases. Like for blueprints. And they weren't all young, some were old, in their thirties, older."

"Did you go into the building?"

"Once. It was quiet, I didn't stay long."

"Did you see Arabs there?"

"A few."

"A few?"

"Two."

"How did you know they were Arabs?"

"They wore those scarves on their heads."

"I see. Did you hear Arabic?"

"Arabic?"

"Yes, Arabic. The language of the Arabs. Did you hear Arabic?"

"No."

"Did you see a mosque for their prayers? Did you see Arab

instructors?" The man's voice was rising. He was getting angry. "Did you hear Arabic music and see signs in Arabic advertising lessons and flats for rent and part-time jobs and all the other hundreds of things you'd see at an Arab college? Did you? Did you?"

Aaron's hands were shaking. "It's . . . it's a cover," he stammered. "That's why it looks that way."

The man leaned forward. "Cover?" His speech came out as a hiss. "Birzeit is the name of a village, not a fruit! That's where the university started, in 1953, that's how it got its name. Olive Branch is a European women's conservatory. Students come to study music, art, dance, it's been here since 1925. The two have nothing to do with each other!"

The air was thick with smoke. Aaron was having trouble breathing. The man forced himself to straighten up. "You expect me to believe this?" he said. "That any person who'd watched that place for three days, for even one day, half a day, would conclude it was an Arab college, a cover for what—Al-Aqsa Brigades? Is this what you expect me to swallow? Do you think I'm an idiot?"

"No, of course not. It's just . . . it's just . . . that's what I really thought. That kid who told me about it, he said that was probably true."

Footsteps behind him. They stopped just short of his chair, just beyond his vision, three huge men like trees. Were they going to hit him? Burn him with the cigarettes? Something worse? The man leaned over the desk again. He was perspiring. He spoke slowly, as if to a child. "Now you tell me the truth, Aaron. Because no one would mistake this place for an Arab institution. Who really put you up to this? Who's behind it?"

"I'm telling you the truth! It was just me. Me and my friends. I thought it was a cover for militants. I did."

A finger beckoned. The three men crowded Aaron's chair. The ash of one of their cigarettes was an inch long.

"The truth, Aaron. Who put you up to it? Which group?"

"No group, I swear!" A hot, humiliating stream leaked into his pants.

"Palestinian Islamic Jihad? PIJ? The Popular Front? Kutla Al-Islammiya?"

A heavy hand fell onto his shoulder. It could break his neck with a single twist. "No! None! I swear!"

"Anglican Students United? Friends of Palestine Abroad? What about those, Aaron? What about those?"

"No! I'm telling you the truth! Anyway, those are Arab groups!" He started to cry, salty mucus above his lip. "Why would I be working for an Arab group? Why would they send someone like me to do this?"

"To make it look like Jewish terror! To confuse us! To anger the Europeans, gain sympathy! To make us look like animals who blow up schoolchildren! What do you think—that this is some game? That everything is exactly as it appears? That you're in an adventure fantasy where the good guys wear cowboy hats and the bad guys have black mustaches and capes? Is that what you think? Is it? Is it? You stupid boy! You stupid, foolish boy!"

Aaron was gasping for air, heaving uncontrollably. His face was a watery mess, his clothes soaked, even his shoes. The man got up from the desk, made a disgusted wave, went to the door and told the others to take him to a bathroom and give him a towel and clean clothes, lock him in a room and let him go to sleep.

They knew everything about him. Adamah. Shroeder. The Overseas Program. His stint on kibbutz. Eli Cooper and the apartment on Gad Street. Even his two years at college upstate.

What about Ben-Ami? Aaron asked. Could he see him, talk to him?

No answer. They had brought him back into the room after he'd slept. He had no idea what time it was, how long he'd been there, what city he was in. If it was a city. The room had no window. They'd blindfolded him in the car outside the hostel, then driven off, and he'd had no idea of how far they'd come.

"You're a lucky boy," the man behind the desk said, rubbing his eyes. He looked like he got no sleep. A sandwich and a ginger ale were on his desk beside a glass of stale-looking tea. Aaron's stomach rumbled. They'd given him hummus and pita earlier but he was still hungry. He was afraid to ask if the food was for him. He ran a hand along his thighs. He wore someone's black sweatpants, a green sweatshirt that said *Jewish Federation of Milwaukee* in big gold letters. They had let him take a shower, and he saw in the mirror cuts on his face from when he'd fallen, a gash that ran across his forehead like a line drawn by a pen. "You're getting a visitor. In a few days."

"A visitor?" Aaron felt a thin ray of hope, a dim light in the bleakness. "Is it Shroeder?" Was Shroeder coming to rescue him, to bail him out, explain? A couple of kids who got carried away, he'd say, but otherwise they were good boys, helping to build the Jewish State, they were on the right side.

"Shroeder?" The man spat out the name like it was Hitler. "You think Shroeder's going to come help you?" He laughed, a chilling, terrible laugh. "Shroeder doesn't give a shit about you. Shroeder would deny even knowing you except he can't because we have too much proof. But Shroeder isn't going to come within a hundred kilometers of you. And if he ever did, he'd say he knew nothing about what you were doing."

"But he didn't, it was all a secret! We didn't tell Shroeder a thing!"

Another laugh, this time shrill, even vicious. "You think Shroeder didn't know what was going on? Who gave you money to stay in Jerusalem last week? Who gave you bus fare two days ago and ordered that you get a lift to the stop? You think for one second Shroeder didn't know what you were up to, your friend Barney making bombs in gym bags inside Shroeder's private little fiefdom, his personal little nation-state? You think he doesn't know what's going on in every square inch of that place?"

Aaron felt himself go cold. Shroeder knew? Everything?

The man leaned across the desk. The bulb seemed to shrink into the ceiling, in defense. "And Davidson. You think Shroeder didn't know that that poor *frier* who got fucked over by every one of you was a weak link? You think he gave a shit about the life of that boy? A life he could have saved but instead let you sacrifice for the sake of his megalomaniac visions?"

Aaron's stomach curdled. The man ran a hand over his face, the gruesome nail black in the fierce light. He seemed to Aaron suddenly old, worn, and it occurred to him that the sandwich was probably for him, that he was the one who hadn't eaten in days. What was his name? Aaron would have liked to have known it, would like to be able to remember him. Did he have any children? Did he have any sons? Had his sons ever done anything bad?

"But why?" Aaron said, and heard his voice coming out tiny and faint, distant. "Why would Shroeder let us go to Olive Branch if it's not an Arab school? What would he have to gain by us going after the wrong target?"

"Gain? Gain? Chaos! Mayhem! You think it's an accident that you met up with that pimply-faced kid at the hostel? Shroeder has them all over the city—at the youth villages, the yeshivas, anyplace people like you show up. He wants violence! It's like a drug, a fix! He needs to keep stoking the fire. An explosion happens, and everyone's afraid, and then they blame. The Jews blame the Arabs, the Arabs blame the Jews, the two sides hate each other more, and Shroeder watches from the sidelines paring his fingernails. Why do you think we let him keep running that whorehouse out there? That's right, you heard me! Whorehouse! Because he lures in weaklings like you and seduces them with his visions of apocalypse, and then, like a pimp, he sends you out to do the dirty work! But we let him stay there because one day he's going to fuck up, fuck up big-time, and then we'll get him."

The man sat back, exhausted, picked up the glass. So they knew all about Adamah. They were probably watching it. Of course. Someone there was probably a spy.

But then why didn't anyone stop him and Ben-Ami before it was too late? Did their intelligence not get out? Aaron, trembling, squeaked out the question.

No answer.

"Did Shroeder intercept the information? Figure out who it was, who was inside?"

More silence. The man sipped the tea, looked away.

Lior. It had to be. Lior! He had disappeared. What had Shroeder done to him? Aaron's chest pounded. "Were there any more, more . . . you know, casualties? Besides, you know, Davidson?"

The man turned to him, looked at him a long time. He no longer wanted the sandwich, the ginger ale, would never want another sandwich or ginger ale in his life. Because of course there were more casualties. Davidson. Lior. And the other one, the tourist out for a walk. He had just appeared, shown up by accident, Aaron had told the man behind the desk. Thirty, thirty-five, a regular guy dressed like anyone else except for the hippie pink shirt. American. He had wanted to help, but Aaron told him there was no time, that it was too late, that he should run.

But now. Davidson. Lior. This other one. Who knew how many casualties there were? Oh God. He was responsible for not one death but maybe two, maybe more. He was a murderer. A real murderer. For the rest of his life this is how he would think of himself.

"How many casualties, you ask?" the man echoed, looking at him over the glass. "We'll tell you when we know."

When they know? Aaron closed his eyes, began to shiver. His life was over. From now on, wherever he was, in this country or somewhere else, imprisoned or free, with a thousand others just like him or all by himself, his life would consist only of small, unlit places where he would be alone with the horrific, unchangeable truth. He had killed people.

"Don't you want to know about your visitor?"

He opened his eyes. Visitor?

"A few days. Someone comes to see you."

"Who?" His voice came out small. High-pitched, like a child's.

"Who else. From the States. Your father."

He lay on the hard cot under a thin blanket and stared at the green ceiling.

His father.

And Shroeder.

Was it true what the man had said? If Shroeder knew, why didn't he warn them, tell them it was a bad idea, a stupid target? Even if he didn't like Americans, he couldn't have been that cruel, that callous. They had been hard workers, he and Ben-Ami. Davidson too. They spoke only Hebrew, did their jobs, didn't complain. All he wanted was for Shroeder to see that he was worthwhile, someone Shroeder could respect. For Shroeder to just once look at him, notice him.

He pulled the blanket up to his chin. What if Shroeder or his pimply operative had been the one to turn them in? To make an anonymous call and get rid of them because what were they going to do with them now, Davidson dead, maybe someone else, Aaron and Ben-Ami on the run, Ben-Ami never able to keep quiet, probably a wreck?

But no. Shroeder couldn't have. They had to have found Aaron, found Ben-Ami, on their own. They were the police, the army, whoever the man in the bare-bulb room was, Mossad or Shin Bet, the most sophisticated intelligence in the world. They picked him up at the hostel because they'd been watching Adamah and watching him, because they were sharp and they knew. Because Lior got information out even if it was too late to stop them. It had to be. This was the Israeli military, the strongest, the smartest there was. The people who stormed Entebbe. Who tracked down Nazi criminals in every country on earth. Who won three wars despite the odds, a hundred million Arabs against three million Jews, and who took out Yassin and Rantisi and every other Hezbollah and Hamas mastermind they could find. They didn't need Naftali Shroeder or his skinny stooge to make an anonymous call to tell them where to find someone like Aaron.

And Shroeder would never have done that. No matter how brusque he was, how cynical, he wouldn't have turned his back on Aaron like that. Wouldn't have tricked him into believing that one day he might matter, would one day be tapped for important things. Shroeder wouldn't be glad to be done with them, the pesky, annoying Americans, wouldn't be sitting now at his grimy metal desk in the claustrophobic shed, lighting up another cigarette, surly Omer by his side, the two of them smiling, *those stupid kids*, Shroeder's feet up on the dented surface next to the overflowing ashtray, *those dumb, stupid American kids. Nothing but problems. Parasites wanting a taste of glory, he was better off without them, they didn't have what it took, would never have what it took.*

He squeezed his eyes shut. Darts of pain rocketed through his abdomen. He curled himself up like a baby, his hand by his chin, gripping the rough blanket hard.

And now his father was coming.

His father.

Voices in another room. Footsteps. The interrogators. The police. He pulled the blanket higher. When he was a little boy, he'd lie in bed at night and hear his father in the study down the hall, typing or listening to music, something quiet and calming. Sometimes his father would get up and walk to the kitchen for a glass of water, a cup of coffee, then go back to the study, and Aaron would listen, tracing his father's journey through the apartment and not be frightened because although he was alone in his room, he wasn't really alone. He'd hear the tapping of the keys, his father's desk chair scraping the floor, just the two of them in the apartment, his father typing and Aaron safe in his bed down the hall. *Tap tap tap. Tap tap tap.* The endless tapping all night long.

He squeezed his eyes tighter. He moved his hand up and put his thumb in his mouth, pulled the blanket over his head and listened for the long-ago sounds of his father in his study. A lullaby all night where his father worked, *tap tap tap, tap tap tap,* urging him to sleep, his father, *tap tap tap tap,* reassuring, right down the hall.

28

*F*elicia was holding Greenglass's hand, showing him how to cross the street. They were in a beach town, the slapping surf behind them, the salty air ripe with anticipation: there'd be cups of lemonade and butter cookies in a box with a red string, sand like velvet between his toes. He was a child, five or six, old enough to cross alone.

You look left, then right. Like this.

He watched her, then turned his head in both directions.

No, silly. You must really look. See if cars are coming and wait.

Again, a look each way, the gulls swooping overhead, the *vruum vruum vruum* of the traffic. The street was huge, wide and endless, an asphalt sea. Days and days on the curb, practicing, the birds hovering like vultures, the giant cars, shiny patent leather black and minty green and taxicab yellow, convertibles like boats, great white fish with glinting silver fins. Left, right, left, right. Felicia's hand was buttery soft and smelled of apple pastries and dark chocolate. Then one day she wasn't there. He was on the curb alone. On the other side was a carousel, children playing, a boarded-up synagogue where the wind rattled the flimsy wood. Oh, how he wanted to go there!

But the street was a black ocean and the cars kept coming, one after another after another, leviathans roaring down the tar, eating the road, teenagers yelling from the backseats, tailfins monstrous in the blinding sun. He stood on the curb, paralyzed, exiled, while the children across the way paid no attention and the carousel kept turning, and the winds battered the boards, leaving him standing alone on the opposite shore.

A moving shadow. Muted sounds, as if coming from a great distance. Greenglass opened his eyes. No salt air, no speeding cars. A dark room, the *whrrr* and *bzzzz* of instruments, machines. He felt something pulling him downward, felt himself as a great weight. His breathing seemed heroic, defying gravity. He listened. An intake of breath, a faint exhale. Then again. And again. And still again.

So he could breathe. And see. And hear. He considered moving his head but the effort seemed herculean, his skull a block of stone, impossible to lift. Even the thought of it exhausted him, and he closed his eyes. He had surfaced too soon. He felt himself drifting down, folded once again into the warm cotton-wool of sleep, waiting to be carried back to the wide rushing boulevard and the raptorous swoop of the gulls and the sweetness of his mother's hand, for the crash and roll of the faraway waves. A small, failing planet that any moment could drop away and be gone.

29

Yona opted for a string of half-truths with Eyal.

"A friend is freaked out by the bombing," she told him on the phone. "That's why I haven't been able to see you. I've had to be with her, she needs my help."

"Sure. I understand." He sounded deflated, hurt. Why wasn't she suggesting he help too? He was the one who lived in the country, who had experience with these things.

She pulled a container of juice from the refrigerator. "It's really true, Eyal. I'm not avoiding you."

A pause. "So I can't see you at all? This is 24-7?"

"She's in bad shape."

"She knows one of the victims?" Unofficial word was out that an American had been injured. Possibly a bystander, someone just passing on the street.

"Yes," she said, carrying a glass to Claudia's computer, the cursor blinking, insistent, demanding. *What have you heard?* Claudia had written. *Who did it? No news getting through here. Are you okay?*

"Well, who's your friend? I thought you said you didn't know anybody here except your sister."

More half-truths. "Someone I went to school with. I happened to run into her by chance. She hardly knows a soul, she's relying on me."

A sigh at the other end. She was losing him, pushing him away. But she couldn't tell the truth; he'd run to the newspapers, the authorities, Givat Baruch. Why wouldn't he? He had no sympathy for people like Dena.

"I'll call you later," she said, sitting down at the screen. *No better news here,* she'd begun, then stopped. She couldn't tell Claudia anything either. "Maybe we can get a beer or a coffee."

"Yeah, sure."

"It's not you, Eyal, you have to believe me. Something big is going on here and my friend needs my help."

"Whatever."

Rachel was in the hospital lobby. Her eyes were red-rimmed. Yona led her to two chairs by a window and an enormous potted plant. "What happened? Mark, did he—?"

"No, no, he's the same. But I was just questioned. Two men." She waved at the revolving doors. "They left not five minutes ago. They found me upstairs, asked me to come down here. They wanted to know everything I knew about Mark. His family, his jobs, the trip to New York. As if I would even have that information. I think they're Shabak or Shin Bet or whatever they call themselves. Internal Security."

"And?"

"They're treating him as a suspect."

"Him? A suspect in the explosion?" It was unbelievable. "They think he orchestrated his own maiming?"

"I know. It's like some horrible Hollywood thriller. Things just keep getting worse." Rachel ran her hands over her face. She looked terrible. "I'm sorry to drag you into this, I don't know who else to talk to. They'll probably find you next." She waved at the doors again. "They just left. Literally two minutes ago."

Yona glanced at the entrance. If they talked to her, they'd be at Givat Baruch in half an hour arresting Dena. Probably arresting her too, God knew her behavior was suspicious enough. They could be waiting outside right now.

"It was terrifying," Rachel said. "They had a thousand questions. Why he'd shaved the beard, given up the yarmulke. As if it

were criminal to have a change of heart. Like he was a fraud or a con
artist. They even asked if I thought he used drugs. Drugs! Can you
imagine? Like he was part of the Israeli mafia! Like he was using the
school grounds to score heroin!" Her eyes welled up. She shook her
head. "God, all I do is weep."

Yona reached into her bag, handed over a tissue.

Rachel dabbed at her eyes. "And there was so much innuendo.
Did I know if he associated with extremist groups. Had I seen any
American kids hanging around the apartment building. Did he say
why he wasn't interested in teaching that crowd anymore, was dis-
tancing himself from them." She paused to wipe her nose. A regal-
looking woman sporting an elaborate blond chignon walked past,
staring at them as she clicked by on impossibly high heels. Yona
glared at her. *It's a hospital, lady. What did you expect?* Rachel snif-
fled, went on, unaware. "Then it was about the new job: Was he
happy with the terms, the pay. Did he ever express anti-European
sentiments. And his parents. What kind of relationship did they
have. Did he seem angry when he returned, depressed, or stressed.
Did he mention any other people he visited in New York. You
could almost see them reading a psychiatric manual in their heads,
checking off the criteria to make a diagnosis. Spiritual turmoil:
check. Parental issues: check. Marijuana use ever in your lifetime:
check." She wiped her nose again. "They were relentless. Jack-
hammers. They were trying to be polite, but I could see they were
taking in every move I made. Every twitch or blink. It was like
being under glass."

"Let me get you some water," Yona said, and went to the hospital
kiosk. They were building a case. Trying to link Mark Greenglass to
a salivating kid with a lust for destruction. Motive, means, opportunity; anyone who'd watched a dumb police procedural on TV could
see that. For motive, they'd say he was unstable. And if he had access
to American boys like those in Shroeder's group, he had the means
and the opportunity.

It was almost too easy. He could've eaten at a restaurant where one of those boys had a job, or taught a class with one of them sitting in the back row.

30

When they weren't questioning him, Aaron tried to sleep. He lay on the cot under the thin blanket, the sweatpants and sweatshirt like soft pajamas, and willed himself to drift, wander, anything to escape, because to be awake and alert was unbearable, the same thought flooding him the instant he opened his eyes, a mantra that never ceased, rushing into any available aperture of consciousness: He had killed. Davidson was dead. Maybe Lior. Maybe another. He was responsible.

But Sleep was being coy, playing hard-to-get. It hovered on the sidelines watching Aaron stare at the endless ceiling, every speck a piece of a face, and taunted: *Try and make me.* Because Sleep knew. It knew that, more than anything, Aaron desperately wanted it to come and cast its milky stupor over him. Let him slide into oblivion where even his nightmares couldn't reach him. Where he could be as near as possible to dead.

Except that he didn't want to be dead. That was the terrible thing. He was going to have to face his father and the shame, the loneliness, the suffocation that would become his life, and yet he wanted to live. It would have been so much simpler if he hadn't. One, two, three, *gamarnu.* Finished, over, done. He could have found a way; there were a million things lying around in this room alone. Invitations. Hints. Bedsheets, a box full of old shoes with shoelaces, electrical outlets, a metal fork from his meal. If he'd asked for a razor blade for the bathroom, they'd probably have given it to him. *Let him. One less headache.* He probably could have asked to borrow a gun.

And yet here he was, wanting to live. But did he have to remember everything? Everything? Did he have to keep seeing Davidson's terrified eyes, the scream that wanted to come out of his frozen mouth, the last thing he would ever say? Did he have to keep replaying Ben-Ami's shrieking as he ran into the fire? The pleas of the stranger who'd wandered over, asking Aaron to let him help, the dread knowledge that the man hadn't fled but had been caught in the flames because why else would they be questioning him about him? And his own insistence until the bitter end that they go through with it? After they'd gotten to Jerusalem, Ben-Ami wanted to scrap the plan, ditch it, go to the movies, get drunk, anything—*anything!*—but Aaron refused. *Too late, Ben-Ami, I won't let you quit now.* And then there was Davidson's choked-up voice when he told Aaron about his father's uncle who'd survived the war by living in the Polish grain dealer's well. When Aaron had returned from his scouting mission, he'd gone to Davidson's room because Davidson was chickening out.

Tell me more, Aaron had coaxed. *About your family, your great-uncle. Couldn't get it out of my mind. What a story.*

They named me after him, Davidson said. *He was a huge hero. You know what he told everyone when he was dying? That the bastard son of the grain dealer used to rape him whenever he showed up at his parents' property. Imagine that? Some scumbag Polish teenager raping a twelve-year-old Jewish kid whenever he felt like.* Davidson stared at the ceiling. *He didn't tell anyone till the day he died. They named me after him.*

And did Aaron then ask the names? The great-uncle's? Davidson's? No. Not then, not ever.

You want to live, Aaron? Sleep said. *This is the price. You will never forget. Anything.* He'd glance over at the box of shoes and try to imagine death; try to picture the laces and the sheet and where he could hang it from, how to make it work, and he'd see it and be afraid.

Because he was scared to die. Dying meant he would have to be alone. No one, not even those who despised him, would be with him. He used to see movies where they showed executions, the doomed man in a black hood strapped to a chair, and he would feel himself start to panic, not because death was coming or because it might hurt but because no one was holding the doomed man's hand. How could they let him go like that? All alone into that eternal night?

And so he lay there on the hard cot, his eyes closed, unable to know the time, whether it was day or night, how long he'd been there, what was going to happen to him, Sleep standing on the periphery, mocking: Look. See. Listen. *Here is Davidson crying in his slippery shit. Here is Ben-Ami chewing his nails and begging you to call it off. Here is Shroeder laughing at you from the infernal shed.* And always this: *Here is the sound of the blast, that moment that split your life in two. Before and After. Hear it again and again and again, the instant when you knew it was all a terrible mistake and there was nothing you could do about it. Absolutely nothing. Listen. Listen and listen and listen.*

31

*G*reenglass dreamed.

Rav Eliezer says: A man may of his own free will offer a guilt-offering on any day and at any time, and this is called the Guilt Offering of the Pious. Kadoshim, Keritot 6.3.

From this we learn: One may atone and be forgiven for anything, anytime. Even for that of which we are not aware. Even for that which we do not remember. Also for that for which we may not be responsible. And for that for which we may. Yes, it's true.

From this we learn: One is obligated to seek relief from the sufferings of the heart. Because why else would it be available to us? This is not a trick question with a trick answer. Was it fashioned for the angels, who have no hearts? It was not.

From this we learn further: To live is to make mistakes! To accumulate regrets! We should welcome our mistakes like flowers, collect our regrets and care for them, for they too sprout from good soil.

Learn from this: Listen to Me: I know! Is anything we fashion—a song, a painting, a life, a world—possible without risk? Listen to Me, I know! Do you want to give a slap in the face to Me? Do I make mistakes? Do you even need to ask the question?

From this we must learn: You try, you stumble, then you pick up and try again! You fail, then you fail better! If you don't try, who will do it? Who will live in My creation? Who, if not you? Who!

32

The state investigator was waiting for her on a bench in Independence Park. Fair-haired, forties, in jeans and a blue-checked sport shirt. He stood up and took off his sunglasses as she approached.

"Doron Klein," he said, shaking her hand. He hadn't been hard to find; one call to Internal Security, and she was put through. He'd had excellent English on the phone. She hadn't told him her full name, but now, taking a seat next to him on the hard bench, she had the feeling he knew exactly who she was.

"I'll be blunt," she said. "My goal is to get you to drop the investigation against Mark Greenglass. I believe he's innocent and that you're engaged in a fishing expedition."

A tip of the head. He waited, unreadable, poker-faced. Practiced.

She went on. "What I have to say is not easy. It involves risk for me and others. I have a sister living in Givat Baruch. We hadn't seen each other for ten years until I came two weeks ago to try to make amends. She hasn't been receptive. But she allowed me to come see her twice, and on the second visit I overheard certain settlement leaders talking about American kids from a place called Adamah. They were looking to blow up Arab sites. Kahanists. Like Meir Kahane. *Terror neged terror.*"

Nothing. He watched her. The blue of his shirt matched the blue of his eyes. Someone could easily mistake him for a European tourist. Austrian. German. They were all over the country, second- and third-generation, curious, or burdened.

"They didn't think I understood because they spoke in Hebrew, but my comprehension is very good. I heard them say they gave these kids money to go to Jerusalem to look for targets. And that one of them, one of the kids, said something about a school. So now it occurs to me they probably knew about the plans to blow up the Olive Branch college and did nothing to stop it. That the idea was conceived with their tacit approval."

She put her hands in her lap.

"That's it?"

She nodded.

He folded and unfolded the sunglasses. "Look, Yona, I appreciate your wanting to help, but we know all about Naftali Shroeder and your sister and her husband Ben-Tzion and Adamah. All about the trigger-happy American kids. We've known about these groups for years."

"You have?" She flushed. But of course. What had she been thinking? Of course they knew.

"And what's more," he said, "your evidence is not credible. You have a motive for implicating the settlement people."

She stared at him. "What do you mean? What possible motive could I have?"

"Your sister," he said softly. "You said it yourself. Estranged ten years, she isn't interested in you now." A shrug. "Of course you'd want to get back at her."

"But I don't! I don't want to get back at Dena! That's why I'm here, now, talking to you. I don't want you to arrest her, I don't want anyone to hurt her at all!"

He waved a hand. "Calm down, don't worry, we're not going to arrest her. It would be useless. She's not going to say anything against Naftali Shroeder, her husband's idol, his mentor. She's not going to talk. Or if she did, it would be your word against hers, and you'd lose. You're not a native speaker and you don't live here; they'd claim you misunderstood. They'd say you're out for revenge. Personal. Political. A left-wing Palestinian sympathizer out to get them." He snapped his fingers. "Simple as that."

She turned away. Two Arab women in long tunics and tight black scarves were spreading a blanket on the grass across from them; a clutch of small children pulled juice bottles and tubes of Pringles out of a pile of cloth bags. She'd been so foolish. What was she thinking? That she could save Mark Greenglass by orchestrating a dramatic undercover meeting in a park? "But if you know all this," she said, "why are you investigating Mark Greenglass?"

"We don't know anything about Shroeder's role in this one." He watched the activity on the blanket. "Maybe it's nothing. Maybe he just overheard one boy bragging to his friends. Giving them money to go to Jerusalem doesn't make him guilty. Greenglass could still have been the mastermind. We have to follow all leads, find out who's pulling the strings. We may have the marionettes but we don't have the puppeteers."

"But how could Greenglass be the puppeteer? He wasn't even in the country before that night."

"He knew one of the boys," Klein said. "Or could have. The kid had come to his classes. The yeshivas, they have free lessons around the city. Greenglass was a regular on that circuit. The kid had attended."

Just what she'd feared. A connection. Means. Opportunity. Two of the children on the grass glanced at them, giggled, and quickly turned away, shoving their small hands into the Pringles tubes.

"What's more," Klein said, "we have reason to believe Mark Greenglass had a conversation with one of the American boys minutes before the explosion, on the school's grounds. And that he had time to flee, but didn't. His injuries, and where he was found, suggest he was close to the building when it went up." He shifted his position, recrossed his legs. "This isn't consistent with bystander behavior. Anyone else would have run for his life."

It was crazy. Rachel said he'd been walking off jet lag, had even invited her to join him but she was tired and declined. Surely she had told the investigators this. What did they think, that she'd made it up to provide an alibi for him? Or that he'd invited her along to be a cover? It was Kafkaesque. She put the questions to Klein.

"This is not out of the realm of possibility," he said, looking over at her. He was not unattractive, but his face had the kind of cool impassivity that kept you at arm's length. Maybe that was the point. "Rachel Craft provides an excellent cover." He held up his hand, raised a thumb, as if to tick off the indisputable facts. "First, he returns to the country the night of the explosion, not a day sooner or a day later. This allows him to be out of sight during the planning but back in time to see the execution. Because it's too tempting to miss the fireworks." He raised the index finger. "Next, the jet lag. A perfect excuse, reason to walk there. Backed up"—a third finger in the air—"by his friend Rachel, assuming she's telling the truth, who can confirm the excuse because he invited her to join him on the walk." A shrug. "Had he ever asked her out before? No. One must wonder: why this night?"

"Maybe he liked her! Maybe he just wanted to see her when he returned! Isn't that also possible?"

Another tip of the head.

"Are you saying he was prepared to put her life in jeopardy just to be his cover? That he'd knowingly expose her to this kind of danger?"

He turned and addressed the grass. "He was there in plenty of time to flee. He would have told her to run. She'd have gotten away."

"Then why didn't he run? Why didn't he flee also?"

"This is the question. Perhaps he was trying to call it off. Or there was a malfunction."

It made no sense. Who dreamed this up? "But what possible motive could he have had? He was about to start a job there. A job he wanted."

He kept his eyes on the blanket. The women across from them were expertly slicing fruit and handing out pieces. "That's one version. Who knows what the truth is? He may have been angry. Depressed. He'd been going through some big changes. These can unbalance a person." Another shrug. "His religious life, for instance. It was, how shall I say it? Not very normal. First he embraces religion, then he gives it up. Why all the yo-yoing back and forth? This is a sign of instability."

"You can't be serious. Religion? In this city? A person is allowed to change his mind about God or whatever and not be considered unhinged. Every other college kid who comes here on junior year abroad tries out the religion and eventually gives it up. You can't tell me they're all mentally disturbed."

"Look," Klein said, not unkindly, "you may not like what I'm saying, Yona, but I'm not making it up. There are well-established psychological profiles for people who commit these acts. Not every violent event here is political. Sometimes it's strictly a personal problem. We have to be thorough." The women glanced up, noticing them, then went back to slicing fruit. Pringles tubes lay on the grass like abandoned grenades. "And I'm not unsympathetic," Klein said. "But to implicate Shroeder's people we need more credible evidence than what you have. Voluntary evidence that would be watertight."

"Voluntary? Like what?"

"Like directly from your sister, for example. What she heard

Shroeder say that night. Because her testimony would be against her self-interest. She too loves and admires Naftali Shroeder. To give evidence against him would be quite persuasive."

Two of the children inched in their direction. The younger one, four or five, tipped his head, studying them. Klein smiled, made a little wave. The older boy punched the younger one on the arm, and the little one punched him back, unleashing a tidal wave of Arabic from the mothers. The boys ran back to the blanket.

"I can't imagine getting my sister to speak to you," Yona said.

"No, I wouldn't think so," Klein said. "You'd have a great deal to lose just by trying. And who knows? Maybe next year she'll be more receptive to your overtures. She has kids, after all, she may want them to get to know their only American relative. Maybe even let the girls visit you one day in your Manhattan flat, come to the gallery where you work."

Yona glanced over at him. He probably knew her shoe size and SAT scores too. And about Elias. And of course Eyal, lefty Eyal.

"On the other hand," Klein said, "if she chose to speak to us of her own volition, we would make it entirely confidential. No one would ever know, including her husband. The fact is, even her evidence is not sufficient to close down Naftali Shroeder tomorrow. But it will contribute to building a case, showing a pattern. He incites anti-Arab attacks, then retreats and keeps himself squeaky clean. If we can develop proof of his foreknowledge, it will help."

The women were packing up. A brief picnic. The two little boys carried empty juice bottles to the trash cans.

"Frankly," Klein said, watching them, "I don't mind saying we've had some setbacks recently. One of our best operatives barely escaped with his life. Naftali Shroeder is a dangerous man. I'm not sure his closest associates even know how dangerous." The women folded the blanket and the whole group trooped past. Klein smiled at the children, who grinned and hurried to their mothers. "But this is a personal decision for you alone. I don't envy your choices."

The park was quiet. Behind them, a Beatles song trailed from a car radio, told them love was all they needed.

"There's one more thing," she said. "I've been lying to Rachel Craft, telling her I'm Mark's relative. Which means I can't go back to the hospital to see her anymore because I'm going to get found out; they're trying to locate his parents. I'm worried she'll try to find me, and then she'll connect me to my sister, and then—"

"We'll take care of her."

She turned to him, alarmed. "What do you mean?"

He smiled. "Relax. You watch too many mafia movies. We'll tell her you work for us. That you're helping. She won't go looking." Another shrug. "And if she does, it won't matter. A lot of our people have relatives in the territories. That's what makes them valuable."

Valuable. It was chilling. "And Mark Greenglass? What about him?"

"This evidence from your sister—if it's good, I'll recommend dropping the investigation. I'm confident my superiors will agree."

"And if it's not? Or if she refuses to talk?"

"What can I say? The inquiry goes on. We can't afford to leave a single stone unturned. Painful for his family. Painful for his acquaintances. But what can we do. This is life in Israel. We all make sacrifices."

33

Aaron lay on the cot in the silent room watching the ceiling. He missed Adamah. That was the terrible part. Not the lectures. Or the awful meals. Or the people.

But the quiet. The night sky, big and full of light. You never saw skies like that in Brooklyn. And the cool mornings. The sounds from the moshavs down the road. Even the cows in their pens. He'd felt sorry for the cows, chained and crowded like that. Sometimes, when he was falling asleep, he'd imagine going over there in the pitch black and tiptoeing up and opening the gates and setting them free. He'd watch them step out into the moonlight like children in a fairy tale kept too long in a dark cruel basement, needing time for their eyes to adjust to the light. He imagined the cows looking around at all the open space, and stepping lightly, carefully, not sure if it was real, but then feeling their way, spreading out and dispersing all over the countryside.

Hundreds of cows wandering the land, free and unchained, back in the pastures and fields and open spaces where they belonged.

34

E yal was at the door, motorcycle helmet under his arm.

"I've come to make a speech," he said, and pulled a water bottle from his back pocket and took a long drink.

"Okay," Yona said. "Do you want to come in or do it here?"

No smile. He walked inside, stepping around the water pipes and jungle of plants, and sank into the overstuffed couch. The gold tassels of the pole lamp shimmied. First, he said, was all this about her sister? He had that feeling. She didn't have to tell him everything, or even anything, but he didn't want to be lied to, and he didn't want to be shut out. Because he liked her. A lot. *Ka-cha zeh.* That was that. He might as well let her know. Sometimes it was necessary to be up-front. Direct. Israelis were often faulted for this—it's true, they could be over-the-top—but they were honest and didn't dance around and this was a good thing. In his opinion.

He also didn't want some secret operation—because this was

Israel, every other foreigner was an operative for the Mossad or Sha-bak or the CIA or even the *New York Times*—ruining a good thing. If she was working for one of those outfits, fine. She didn't have to tell him about it, he could wait until it was over, but he wanted her to know he was aware. Not a fool.

The next thing: he realized she was leaving soon, but that didn't mean she'd never come back or that the whole business between them was doomed. The fact is you didn't meet people you connected with every day. But. If she wasn't interested in him, if this wasn't for her, okay, plenty of fish in the sea, he could take it. She needed to just tell him straight-out. He didn't want a repeat of his Dutch lady. So if she's been saying it's a friend in trouble or something to do with the sister when really it's about him and she can't tell the truth, well, here was her chance to speak up. No hurt feelings. Say the word and he'd be out of her face. Done. *Gamarnu.*

He stopped, took a drink of water.

"Are you finished?"

"Yes."

"Okay." He was so terrific. How had she gotten so lucky? "Do you want a better drink? Your water bottle looks warm. Orange juice or something?"

"No."

"A fruit? I have an excess of plums that are about to rot. I can't help myself, I overbuy."

"No." Then an afterthought: "Thank you." He noticed the leggy goddess on the brass table and picked it up and examined it. The narrow waist, the kumquat breasts, the glints of gold. He probably thought it was Claudia's. Probably thought it matched the Toulouse-Lautrec décor. One notch shy of French brothel.

"Okay," she said as he put the statue back. "Well, I have nothing to say except please don't get out of my face."

He nodded at the table, slapped his thighs, got up and went to the door, put on the helmet.

She followed him. "One day I hope I'll be able to tell you what's going on."

"All right. Me too."

"But until then." She took him by the shoulders, pulled him close, and kissed him hard on the mouth. He tasted of mint and cherries. It was not easy to pull herself away.

He did the pulling away for both of them. "I'm off, *habibi*," he said, and flashed her that beautiful smile. *Habibi*. She loved it. Maybe she was starting to love him. "Call me when you're ready." He went out, and she stepped into the hallway and watched him hurry down the stairs.

35

A shiver passed through him. Greenglass stirred in blackness. Regina. Regina had died. It was finally over. The long struggle had ended and she had been released, loosened of the fetters of her body, a droplet of shimmering light moving past him in the darkness, floating up up up, and he knew. He just knew. He felt himself reaching, calling for her without words—*Regina! Regina!*—the light swimming by him like a minnow. It was just beyond his grasp, then over his head, then joined by another and another and another until together they became a pool of perfect radiance. She was traveling. At last, she was traveling, pure and happy. He wanted to call to her again—*Regina!*—but it was too late, the pool of golden light moving far away from him fast, too fast, and he knew that it was she, and that it had ended, that finally she was done with it, and was free.

36

They brought Aaron into a room he'd not been in before, sat him down at the end of a long table. The man from behind the bare-bulb desk wasn't there. Instead there were four men in suits from the American embassy, three Israelis, two military police in uniform, a woman typing on a small silent machine, and his father. Bottles of water marked the places. His father didn't look at him; three people sat between them, blocking the view.

It didn't take more than an hour. His father was to take Aaron home directly, no stops on the way to the airport, not even at his father's hotel—his bags had been delivered by the military police—and Aaron was never to set foot in the country again. He was to remain with his parents under their supervision indefinitely; he would not return to college upstate but would attend school in Brooklyn, if he qualified for admission; alternatively, he would take a job near home, subject to the American government's approval. He would not be allowed to travel outside the United States. He would not be allowed to make overseas telephone calls; all electronic communications would be monitored. If the Israelis were to discover any violations, one of them warned, his thick accent unapologetic—he seemed irritated that he had to use English, had to deal with these spit-and-polish Americans—there would be consequences, swift action, everyone understood what that meant. Neither Aaron nor any member of his family, including his writer father, was to divulge the facts about the incident to anybody, including other family members, in perpetuity. Forever. Neither government could allow the full nature of the event, including the identities of the perpetrators

or their motives, to be made public, as such information would criti-
cally damage Israeli-American relations, not to mention those with
the Scandinavian countries. Plus there was the matter of Jewish terror against the Palestinians, the political ramifications of which could
not be overstated. Any leakage about the persons involved would
drastically hinder the Israeli government's ongoing efforts to rein in
such terror groups—groups which, they would like to stress, have
been outlawed by the Israeli government in no uncertain terms—
and would compromise years of painstaking work. Indeed, right now
they were zeroing in on the very group to which Aaron had belonged.
A public prosecution of Aaron and his co-conspirators would griev-
ously undermine that investigation. Aaron's father, they presumed,
understood. Because, Aaron's father must also understand, someone
in Aaron's position would ordinarily be dealt with far more severely.
Far more.

As for the casualties, the situation was most tragic, one of the
other Israelis said, his English easier to follow, a little British, Aaron
thought as he stared at the plastic water bottle in front of him. His
father was eight feet away, only his folded hands visible, the plain
gold band from his wedding to Anne glinting in the harsh light.
When was his father going to look at him? They had let Aaron wear
the black ski cap so his father wouldn't be horrified by his shaved
head. *Dad*, Aaron wanted to whisper, to reach over and touch those
hands. *I'm sorry. For everything. Look at me. Please. Dad.* As for those
unfortunate victims, the Israeli said, their government would be pro-
viding compensation, as it did for all victims of such acts, to the family of Andrew Davidson, which would also receive a personal visit
from the Israeli ambassador to the United States extending the con-
dolences of the entire Israeli public, indeed, the entire Jewish people,
to Andrew's parents Judith and Joel, his loving sister Lucy, his grandparents, and all his relations. The Americans were likewise doing
their part, the Israeli said, gesturing at the suited-up men across the
table. The deputy American ambassador to Israel had already left,

accompanying the body, or what remained of it, to Chicago for burial. Short of directly saying so, the consular messengers would do their best to keep the Davidson family from concluding that the violence that caused Andrew's death was an act of Arab arson and murder, but, to be honest, they could not make any such promises, especially if the family had access to the Israeli media, which, naturally, was allowing such assumptions to stand since the press had not been given any information to the contrary for reasons of national security just explained. They hoped the incident would soon disappear from the papers as these things tended to do. Meanwhile they were very, very sorry to have to count this young man among the losses to the country's ongoing violence, a young man who had planned to return to college and pursue his dream of becoming a high school biology teacher, according to his grieving family.

The throaty first Israeli started to speak again, harsh and choppy, and Aaron turned to look at the wall, unable to concentrate, to listen, to even keep himself in the room, though of course his body had to stay even if his mind did not. The paint was a pale minty green like the place where he slept, like hospital paint or the color of the hallways in his high school. The kids had all made fun of the green hallways, puke green, they called it, though, really, what color could you paint the inside of a high school? These other victims, the choppy Israeli was saying as Aaron inspected a crack in the minty wall that ran from the floor to the ceiling like a great meandering river, included another man found at the scene who was still alive, hanging on to life by a thread in a Jerusalem hospital. What rivers did Aaron remember? The Hudson. The East River. The Delaware, from a famous painting of George Washington his class went to see at the Metropolitan Museum of Art. One kid had to wait outside with one of the chaperones because he was being a jerk, standing way too close to the million-dollar pictures on the walls. This particular hospital, the Israeli said, was known for its state-of-the-art trauma unit and its expertise, unfortunately fine-tuned in recent years, in internal-organ damage due to explosions of just this sort, blasts that caused heart failure or lung collapse or other devastation but, remarkably, sometimes didn't even break the skin. It was frankly one of the most shocking phenomena of these bombings, the dead sitting upright in café chairs or in burned buses looking perfectly fine but utterly destroyed. There were other casualties as well, the Israeli went on, including an operative in the intelligence apparatus, also expected to live, but they would just leave it at that.

The room went quiet. Someone drank from a water bottle. Aaron stopped looking at the river-crack. His father rearranged his hands, covered the ring. At the other end of the table people were talking. Aaron didn't remember much about his father and Anne's wedding other than the big fight he'd had with his father the night before. He was fourteen then and the idea of his father getting married, of having sex, repulsed him. Because you had to have sex when you went on a honeymoon; his friends said that's what a honeymoon was for. All day, all night. Anne was ten years younger than his father, thirty-two or thirty-three then, and though she wasn't pretty—too skinny, Aaron thought, all elbows and knees—she wasn't ugly. But was she supposed to become his mother or something? What about his real mother? His father had told him he didn't know where she was, but Aaron didn't think that was true. For years he'd heard his father on the phone with relatives saying things like *Visitation rights over my dead body* and figured his mother had tried to get those rights but his father wouldn't let her. He once wanted to ask his father about that but was afraid to get him angry.

One of the Americans was playing with his pen, rolling it between his palms. Aaron looked back at the wall, followed the jagged trail of the crack. If it were truly a river it would be long, like the Nile or the Mississippi, though he'd never seen those rivers. Or many rivers at all. He wished he could see one now, this minute. Put his foot in, or his hand, or maybe his whole self, and be cleansed. Could he be cleansed? It was of course out of the question, the British Israeli was saying, for Aaron or any of his family members to reach out to the relatives of the victims or the other perpetrators, a point that would seem to go without saying but which bore repeating anyway. They presumed Aaron's father understood. He did; Aaron heard him murmur a gravelly consent down the table. It was the first time he'd heard his father speak. He wished he could whisper to him. *Dad. Dad.* He imagined the graying head nodding. *A lion's mane,* someone once wrote of his father's hair, of his generally powerful physique. Aaron had thought it was insulting. *Lionized.* Why talk about his father like an animal, the king of beasts?

Someone lit a match. The sharp smell of smoke. This was particularly so, a new Israeli said, clipped, gruff, probably the smoker, in the case of Barney Reisen, Aaron's co-conspirator who was cooperating with the authorities. Reisen, the Israeli said, was an unstable young man who'd left New York four years before. Mr. Blinder had probably heard about young people like that, disturbed types with glimmers of Jewish sensibility who came to Israel to escape their problems. When in reality they brought their problems with them. Aaron's father offered that, yes, he had heard of that, he was aware of this phenomenon, it was known in Jewish circles in Brooklyn where he was from.

Well, this Barney, the man said, cutting his father off, had spent time on kibbutz and was eventually allowed to enlist in the army in a limited capacity like other foreigners who serve in adjunct units where they're given peripheral tasks. *Lonesome soldiers,* they're called. *Chayal boded.* Military personnel who have no relatives in the country so are assigned a home base on a kibbutz where it's hoped a family will informally adopt them. The system worked with mixed results.

The man took a long pull on the cigarette. Someone shuffled papers. Aaron went back to the crack. A spider appeared halfway down the wall. In Missouri, he thought, if the crack was the mighty Mississippi. At least that's what he remembered from geography. He had not always been a poor student. When did his teachers start to give up on him? They hadn't always thought of him as a waste of time.

Barney Reisen's history was unusually troubling, the throaty Israeli interjected, moving papers around. Aaron couldn't look at the river anymore. He glanced at the small lone window, thought he heard something buzzing outside, a cricket or maybe a rare buzzing bird. Ben-Ami had shown him his army discharge papers. He was proud of them. *With honor,* he told Aaron, who didn't really look at them. Reisen had had some early problems due to suspected homosexual activity, the Israeli said, tapping his pen. Not that such activity was unheard of in the army or on kibbutz, nor, frankly, was it necessarily a problem. But this young man tended to develop obsessive and disturbing attachments to other young men who were—how should he say it?—not mutually interested. In fact, it wasn't clear that all or even most of his relationships took a sexual turn. Which had made things uncomfortable for the communities where Reisen was living. Reisen had been discharged early from the military for this reason and had likewise not succeeded at the kibbutz.

There was reason to believe, the British Israeli added while someone poured water into a glass, that the relationship with Andrew Davidson was along these lines. One-sided. Abnormally dependent. They were divulging this to Mr. Blinder so that he'd appreciate the degree of dysfunction operating here. For while many Americans who came to Israel were upstanding people who made productive lives and contributed to society, others brought with them considerable psychological baggage. More than baggage. Personality disorders of a serious nature. The extremists under investigation, for instance, included a disproportionate number of Americans, who in fact were a very small percentage of the population overall, and this was greatly troubling to the Israelis and—a gesture to the silent buttoned-up officials on the other side of the table—to the American diplomatic community as well. For this reason, they would like to recommend that Mr. Blinder consider the effects of books such as his own on susceptible, impressionable minds. To consider what a steady diet of emotionally inflammatory articles and films and novels portraying the historical enemies of the Jews can do to those looking for a violent cause to which to attach themselves. There was a great deal of research on this topic—they didn't have to explain this to the Americans anymore; they'd had their own brushes with extremism and its disastrous consequences. Teaching history was one thing; generating fearmongering propaganda was another. The Israelis would be the first to say there were genuine and real threats to the security of their country and, by extension, the Jewish people; but visual and reading matter that served mainly to inflame Jewish hatred did not do anyone a service.

One of the Americans cleared his throat, inched up in his chair. He had a crew cut and looked to Aaron like a marine. It was the first time someone from across the table was going to speak. It was for this reason, the marine said in a careful, reedy voice, and in light of the prohibition against discussing the incident, that both governments were requiring that Mr. Blinder refrain from publishing any new work without receiving prior approval from the appropriate officials. This was in order to be on the safe side. The U.S. government's definition of what this incident consisted of was broad. Suffice to say that the subject of Israel would be entirely off-limits, as might anything having to do with the situation of the Jews, historical or current. However, they were sure that Mr. Blinder would eventually find plenty of other things to write about, should he so choose.

The marine sat back. Aaron's father folded his hands more tightly; his knuckles protruded. The typist asked for a moment. Aaron closed his eyes. He was very, very cold. He heard another glass being filled. He was suddenly desperate for a drink. He groped for the bottle in front of him, opened it, tried to sip, and spilled onto his sweatshirt. Would he wear the sweatshirt on the plane home? Would he wear it for the rest of his life? *You also understand, Mr. Blinder, that Aaron will be required to remain in those same black sweatpants and green sweatshirt*

*and black ski cap for the remainder of his days so that he will never forget
what he has done. And everything he touches will die, nothing will flour-
ish. It shall be like the mark of Cain. For the Lord put a mark on Cain
lest anyone who met him should kill him and put him out of his misery.
So shall it be for Aaron, confined to the house of his parents in those same
clothes until the end of his life, and his family shall know the truth about
him but will never free him from its torment. So shall he wander this earth
with the burden of his deeds upon his heart.*

The typist was ready to resume. A chair shifted. Aaron got the
water bottle to his mouth. Where was this young fellow Reisen now,
if he may ask? his father said, his usual booming baritone absent, a
voice Aaron had never heard from him before. Restrained, reserved.
Afraid.

More throat-clearing. Another lit match. Reisen was not doing
well, the British Israeli said. Hysteria. Suicide risk. Heavy medication. Aaron squeezed his eyes tighter. Suddenly he needed to silently
count. *One, two, three, four. See who's knocking at the door. Five six
seven eight. If they knock for you, it'll be too late.* Because, the Americans needed to understand, Andrew Davidson was not only someone
Reisen had developed a romantic attraction to, he was also a close
friend. *Nine ten eleven twelve. Ring the buzzer ring the bell.* Childhood
friend. From when they both lived in Chicago. The families were
close. Kept in touch. Parents devastated. *Seventeen, eighteen, nineteen, twenty, everything broke is fixed by money.* Precarious mental
health. Closely watched. Institutional setting. Best interests, secure
location, the family has been notified.

A pause. The secretary needed another moment, problem with
the machine. Who was this monster? she was probably thinking,
glancing at Aaron. She'd go home to her husband and say over dinner how you would never believe what went on in this world, a perfectly lucky American boy with all the advantages—attentive family,
opportunity for a college education, money to travel, all the luxuries,
no army service looming, no constant war at his doorstep—doing

something horrible, she couldn't say what, ruining his life and the lives of so many others. What was wrong with this world?

A great shuffling. The machine was fixed. Someone announced the time. The flights had been arranged, Aaron and his father would be transported by the two military police to the airport, then escorted by a third, who would wear civilian clothes, onto the plane. He would travel with them to New York and accompany them in the taxi to Brooklyn, whereupon he would take his leave. Anything after that would be handled through the American embassy, whose cooperation they appreciated. They prayed for those whose lives had been destroyed by the events.

Aaron put down his bottle. He wondered if perhaps he could no longer open his eyes, would never have to open his eyes again. He could feel the movement around him, the displacement of air. He didn't think they were shaking hands. Would you shake hands here? The secretary closed up her machine. More chairs scraped the tile. Footsteps by the door.

An eerie quiet. No one had spoken to him. They had roused him hours earlier from the room with the bed and given him a glass of juice and boiled eggs and a roll and butter, then walked him to the room with the bare bulb and left him there. He sat and waited like a prisoner awaiting execution. Half an hour. An hour. Then they brought him here.

Now his father was standing over him, he could tell by the familiar scent, the feeling of the substantial body, a big man, the looming presence that could only be him, for how could you forget the sensation of your own father even with your eyes closed? You would know it the whole of your life.

Aaron's chest pounded. He wished he could be like Ben-Ami, crazy and locked up, put away forever so he'd never have to look at anyone he knew again. Because he didn't think he could bear to see the way they'd see him, how they'd stand slightly apart, and stare: *What is he?*

A tap on the shoulder. He opened his eyes, his head down, saw the black sweatpants, the sandals they'd given him, then his father's shoes, familiar and worn, the soft brown leather kind he would always know, and a fleeting prayer shot through him, a desperate flying prayer that his father might for once look at him kindly, utter some consolation and tell him that it would be all right. That Aaron was still his son, and that despite what he had done, despite everything that was yet to happen, he was still his child. Still, in some small part of himself, deserving of his father's attention and care. His love.

Instead came the only words anyone had spoken to him all day, the voice gravelly and thick. "Get up. Let's go."

The knives. His father wanted only to talk about the knives. The Israelis had shown him Aaron's pack from Ben-Ami's friend's car, had unzipped it, and there, inside, his father said, were the pathetic contents: a toothbrush, toothpaste, a clean shirt, clean socks, clean underpants, his antacid pills, a city map, flashlight batteries, a crumpled letter from a girl, and three pearl-handled antique knives. It had humiliated his father beyond belief. What sort of sick person had his son become? His father had had to stand there, mute and submissive after the awful meeting, first having to beg to get the officials to relent and let him come in the first place, hours of telephoning, calling around the clock, hiring a fleet of lawyers, contacting everyone he knew, anyone with any influence who might have heard of him or his books, after that first chilling call: *Your son is in custody, utmost national security, no further information can be given at this time.* Did Aaron have any idea what that had been like? His father had been in the country for seventy-two hours, had slept for maybe five, had had to plead with the Americans to let him talk to them. Every person his and Anne's family knew had pulled strings until finally the embassy agreed to meet with him. Did Aaron understand? And the tens of thousands of dollars this was costing? What was he talking about—

not tens. Hundreds. Six lawyers were in a Tel Aviv hotel right now working out the documents with the embassy. This was Aaron's life. Did he have any idea?

And then, after the excruciating meeting, while they put Aaron in the car, his father had had to watch the humiliating display of the backpack contents. Had to nod with each raised item: the foolish little pills, the ridiculous underwear and socks and clean shirt, as if Aaron were going on a job interview. And then the knives. These were his son's belongings, they told him. This was his pack found in the car. Had he usually carried knives? they wondered. Not that it mattered after everything else. Still, they were curious. Expensive antiques. Historical artifacts. Were they his? Properly purchased? Did he have documentation, certification? Access to that kind of money? No, he wasn't aware of a history with knives, his father said. Nor of access to such funds. Then they'd best turn them over to the police, the authorities said, in case they'd been reported missing.

Well, his father said to him now, murmuring as they stood facing straight ahead, alone for one brief moment in a cordoned-off area in the airport while the military policeman, six feet away, his gun under his vest, presented their passports, he no longer recognized this son. He no longer knew who this person was. There had been times in his life, his father said, not looking at him, never looking at him, the din of the airport swirling around them like the noise of some festive faraway city, the cavernous call of the loudspeakers in English, French, Arabic, the *whrrrr* of the propellers outside, there were times when he'd told himself that, despite the setbacks—the bad early marriage, Aaron's mother's abandonment, the single parenting, the hours it took away from his writing, the need to crank out the books in order to keep a money flow, books he knew suffered in quality because of it—he had always still believed that having a son, raising that son, was worthwhile, never something to regret. He'd told himself that Aaron, for all Aaron's school difficulties, and for all his own flawed efforts—and oh yes his father knew he was flawed, he was only human, doing the best he could—that Aaron would, despite all that, turn out all right.

But today, his father said, the big policeman walking back, stone-faced, the passports no longer visible but put away somewhere on his unreadable person, this expressionless man in a tweed sport jacket and dark jeans and a giant wristwatch with whom his father had managed to negotiate so that Aaron could sit untethered, without handcuffs, on the plane, Aaron now and forever on every list, their apartment to be watched for God only knew how long, their phones tapped, their travel restricted, his father's writing life over, their personal lives permanently under scrutiny—today, his father said, he was full of regret. Regret that he'd told Anne no children. Regret that his only child had become someone he was ashamed to know. Regret that Aaron had ever been born.

PART 3

37

A cool hand on his wrist, a trace of flowery soap. He heard the miraculous rhythm of his own breath.

The hand went away, a feather of voices beyond the lilac perfume. The *whoosh* of moving bodies. Who was he? Mark Greenglass. He lived in Jerusalem. Chopin Street.

He opened his eyes.

A young woman was folding a blanket at the foot of his bed. She was slender and small, almost a girl. She smoothed it down carefully, adjusting it for evenness, so much on one side, then the other. She paused, surveying her work, tugged gently on a corner.

She turned, saw him seeing her. A hand flew over her mouth.

It had been an explosion. A building right there in Jerusalem seven days before, a place called Olive Branch International. There were burns, damage to a lung, a kidney, a broken leg, some deep wounds. He would need surgery to deal with his teeth. Six shattered or cracked neatly down the middle from the impact of the blast or because he was thrown. Or both.

"From what we see of your dental records, they weren't such great choppers anyway," the doctor said from the little stool. He smiled. His name was Henri Levin and he spoke in perfect English with a French accent. "So now you will get a brand-new set."

Greenglass put a hand to his cheek. A cement-like stiffness, as if his jaws were wired shut.

"So now," the doctor said softly, inching up on the seat, "perhaps you could try to speak a little, yes?" He had watery blue eyes and crinkling around the edges. He probably had a wife, children, maybe one in the army; maybe he'd come there as a teenager in the seventies, or just last year, French Jews nervous, too much violence, too much hatred. And now here he was, heading a trauma unit for the victims of hatred. They treated everyone, Levin had told him. Palestinians, Israelis, African and Filipino guest workers, Jews, Moslems, Christians, Druze. He'd treated arsonists, snipers, Islamic militants brought in in shackles who spat on him and called him filthy Jewish swine before dropping the bravado and letting him stanch the wounds. "Don't worry about sounding funny. It's just the swelling, the missing teeth."

But Greenglass couldn't talk. It wasn't just the stiffness, the tongue that felt like a whale. His emotions were washing over him like a wave. Confusion. Gratitude. Sorrow. He had been to a distant boundary and now he was back, and he was awash in the swell of his feelings. Where had he gone and how had he returned? And why hadn't he slipped away? He had been so close to slipping away.

"I know this is overwhelming," Levin said. "Just try, Moishe." *Moishe.* Like the Yiddish. Like an endearment. The way a parent talked to a beloved child. "Doesn't matter what you say. It can be anything."

Greenglass's eyes filled. He wanted so much to help, wanted to be cooperative, but he couldn't say a word.

"You know what," said the doctor, "first maybe we should make a little blessing. A little thanksgiving." The man was not outwardly religious, he wore no yarmulke, none of the trappings, but he knew. Like Greenglass, he knew: sometimes there were no other words. You just had to reach out into the silent universe and say something because an urgency inside told you to. Not because you were commanded or had been taught, not because it was the custom or the rule or because it had been done for hundreds of years, but because something in you was calling out, and you had to let it, you just had to let it.

Levin took his hand in both his own, then closed his eyes and in perfect Israeli Hebrew said the prayer Greenglass knew was coming. *Gomel.* The one you said after completing a dangerous journey, including the one back to this life from the outer edges of the next.

Blessed are you, Creator of the Infinite, who bestows goodness on us and on all the undeserving, who has bestowed every good thing upon us now.

38

*Y**ona took the noon bus.* The day was hot, the sun merciless. The white van wasn't running, someone in the bakery said. There were no cabs. She asked if anyone was going up the hill, and a heavy-set woman wearing a floral cotton kerchief and carrying a shopping bag of rolls and cakes offered her a ride. Who was she visiting? the woman wanted to know, piloting a cluttered eight-passenger VW van with no muffler up the hill. The smells of apple juice and curdled milk competed with the yeasty scents of fresh bread and lemon cake. The Ben-Tzions on Prophets Street? Of course she knew them. Wonderful people, the wife was an American but spoke like a native. Beautiful children. She herself had eleven, the woman said, waving toward the seats behind them. Everyone squeezes in, she said simply, even with all the junk.

There was no one home. Yona sat on the weedy ground and leaned against the concrete wall, sipping a water bottle. She was strangely calm. What could Dena do to her now? *An unexpected relief,* she'd written to Claudia. *I've let something go.* It was the whip she'd let go. The lash. She'd made a mistake ten years ago, but maybe she'd served her time. The traffic hummed on the main road. She fanned herself with her hand. Twenty minutes later, Dena's Subaru wagon trundled down the street. Yona stood, dusted off her skirt.

"What are you doing here?" Anat said as the children spilled out. The two boys ran to the house. Hila stood by Dena, who was wearing a loose-fitting shift over a long-sleeved white blouse and was bending into the car to unbuckle the baby.

Yona didn't answer. Dena lifted out the sleeping child and handed him to Hila, then turned to walk to the rear door latch, saw Yona standing there.

"Take Daniel inside," Dena said to Hila. "And give the others a drink. I'll be in soon." Anat moved next to her mother, one hand on a hip, and glared at Yona. "You too, Anat. Inside."

"Why? I want to stay here."

"Because I said so. Now go."

Hila extended her free hand to Anat, who ignored it and stomped off. Yona gave Hila a small smile, and the girl nodded, followed her sister.

"I thought you'd left," Dena said. A few spirals of damp hair had escaped her white scarf; Yona thought she saw a strand of gray amid the copper.

"Not yet." On the road below, an ambulance whined. "I need to talk to you."

"So talk."

"You want to stand out here in the sun?"

Dena tipped her head toward the apartment. One of the ties of the scarf rested on her shoulder. White on white. She looked pasty, drawn, the color of the fabric. Perhaps it was a difficult pregnancy. "You want to talk in there with five kids at your feet?"

Yona gestured in the general direction down the hill. "Could we go to the café? The bakery? Get a cold drink?"

Dena seemed to be studying her; her chin jutted out slightly. "I don't have time. I have a lot to do."

Yona glanced around. It was ninety degrees, a broiling sun. How could they stand out there and have this conversation? "What about your car? Can we sit inside it?"

"It'll be an inferno. This isn't America, we don't run the air every second."

Yona kept looking around, trying not to despair. Surely there was something, surely Dena could come up with a place more forgiving than this scorching patch of asphalt. Sweat dripped into the small of her back; her shirt was sticking to her. Finally Dena said, "Sometimes there are a couple of chairs at the end of the street. Unless they've been moved."

They walked down the road. Neither spoke. Piano music drifted out of an open window. Three old plastic patio chairs wobbled on the weeds beneath a stand of young trees. The arm of one had been broken off, leaving a jagged edge. Yona took that one, waited for Dena to sit, then offered her the water bottle. Dena declined.

"I came out here to ask you something," Yona said. They were side by side, facing the hills. They didn't look at each other. "But first, how are you feeling?"

"I'm all right."

"When is the baby due?"

"February."

"Our mother's birthday," Yona said. "February fourteenth."

"I guess. I hadn't remembered."

"Valentine's Day. We used to buy her a big chocolate heart."

Silence. Dena glanced in the direction of her apartment building. A woman on the top floor was hanging wash from an open window, pulling in the laundry lines and sending them out again, clothes dangling. Yona had a thousand questions. How did Dena feel about a sixth child? What was it like to have so much responsibility? Did she

miss having a mother each time she gave birth? Did she ever wonder what might have happened if things had been different between
them? But Dena would answer the way she answered everything.
Of course she would want a sixth child; she'd want eleven, like the
woman in the messy van. Because that's what was necessary: *Be
fruitful and multiply.* One-third of the world's Jews had been murdered by the Nazis; they had to make up for it. Six children weren't
so many. Only in America did people agonize over having a family,
terrified at the thought of caring for another human being. As for
missing their mother or wondering what might have been, what was,
was. You didn't waste precious minutes of your life thinking about
what couldn't be.

The woman with the laundry disappeared inside her apartment.
Dena took a crumpled tissue from a pocket, wiped the sweat above
her lips, put the tissue away.

"I'll be going back to New York soon," Yona said.

Dena put her hands on her belly, watched the hills.

"Though I'm not in any rush," Yona added, and didn't know
why she was talking like this. Dena hadn't asked. But neither had
she cut her off. "I have a job at a gallery but it's not very rewarding.
I think I'm afraid to commit to my own work. I used to draw and
paint. Maybe you remember. I'm thinking of quitting my job, going
to art school. I have the money."

The woman reappeared at the window with a new load of
washing. She pulled in an empty line, began clipping on the limp
garments.

"I've also had a series of affairs with married men over the
years. Which probably sounds appalling to you. I don't expect you
to approve. I'd like to stop doing that when I get home. It was a sort
of self-punishment I administered. Not allowing myself to have a
relationship with a future. Though while I've been here I've come to
appreciate that those men were good to me. They loved me in their
way and treated me well and never deceived me." She paused. "I

don't know why I'm telling you this. Maybe I want you to know who I am."

The clothing jumped on the line each time the woman moved the pulley. The sun bore down; the laundry would dry in fifteen minutes.

"I'm sorry for what I did, Dena. With David. I'm sorry I hurt you. You were so capable and smart and clear about your life, and I envied that. I was confused and childish and jealous." She reached for the water bottle. Her mouth felt like sand. She took a sip, held it out to Dena, who didn't respond. "I'm not excusing my behavior." A pause. "Do you miss our parents?"

Dena kept her eyes on the hills. "I don't think about it."

They sat. Minutes passed. A car came down the road and parked near them on the edge of the asphalt. A man and eight boys piled out—a religious teacher and his young charges, all in white shirts; no one seemed to have worn a seat belt—and headed down a dirt path behind the apartments. Dena looked at her watch. "I need to go, Hila has an appointment. Is this what you came to talk to me about?"

"No." Yona took a breath. She had to do this. "There's an American man in Hadassah Hospital who's gravely injured. Thirty-six years old, originally from New York. He was at the Olive Branch college when it was blown up last week. He was about to start teaching there, had walked over to see where it was. He was a Talmud scholar in Jerusalem."

She stopped. Her chest was hammering and her mouth had dried to salt. But she was afraid to drink, afraid that in the seconds it took to bring the bottle to her mouth Dena would get up and walk away. She persevered. "I believe Naftali Shroeder knew about the plans for Olive Branch and encouraged it. The night the group from Cleveland was at your house I heard him talk about an American kid at Adamah, the son of a well-known writer, who wanted to blow up a school."

She licked her parched lips. Dena wasn't moving. "The authorities are treating the injured man as a suspect, fishing to make a case against him. There are enough coincidences so that they might actually succeed. But you and everyone else here knows he's innocent because you know who did it. Or, rather, you know the person who knows who did it."

Dena took out the tissue, wiped her forehead. She still wouldn't look at Yona. But she wasn't getting up. The teacher and his students disappeared behind one of the buildings.

"I've spoken with one of the investigators," Yona said. "It's probably no surprise to you that the intelligence people are paying attention to you and your husband and men like Naftali Shroeder. It's probably no surprise to anyone out here." She dug in her skirt pocket and pulled out a card. "This is his name. Doron Klein. If you'll speak to him, tell him what you heard Shroeder say that night in your apartment, they'll drop their investigation of the man in the hospital. Klein promises to never divulge the source, won't tell your husband or Shroeder or anyone. There will be no arrests. And if what I heard is true, that only Shroeder had contact with the American boys, your husband will not be viewed as an accomplice. Nor will you."

Yona looked at the card. Her hand was shaking, she could hardly read it. But she had to finish. "If you're willing to come forward, the man in the hospital, assuming he recovers, can eventually go home. But if you're not, he faces the prospect of defending himself against an accusation of committing an act he not only didn't do but was nearly killed by and maybe won't even remember. He could be transferred to a military hospital or a prison, or committed if they think he's mentally impaired. He could lose his freedom for the rest of his life."

Trembling, she handed Dena the card.

Dena didn't look at it. Yona took a sip of water. Minutes passed.

"You realize," Dena said finally, watching the hills, "you're asking me to do a preposterous thing. I wouldn't expect you to understand that my commitment to this movement is total. Just like I can't fathom your lurid serial liaisons with adulterers, you can't fathom my belief in the sanctity of this land and the supreme importance of its redemption."

Dena turned to her, her gaze rock-hard, her eyes icy blue, just as Yona had always remembered them. Blue diamonds. "This is the difference between us, Yona. You live life concerned with your own petty affairs, by which I mean matters other than just sex. You worry about your art and your career and your little love life; you worry about your income and your apartment and maybe even whether you'll ever get married and have a couple kids. Self-actualization. Isn't that the word? The highest level available? Isn't that what you aspire to in America? All over the world. Even here." She gestured with her chin in the direction of the road. "In Tel Aviv and Haifa, all over Israel. It's not just about wanting a big flat and a designer kitchen and trips abroad and the best education for your children, but about human potential. Right?" She waved grandly. "Become yourself. Fulfill yourself. Me. Me. Me."

She turned away, steely-eyed and cold, no trace of the girl Yona once knew. She had always been righteous but she'd also been kind. Why else had she spent all her free time trying to help those failing teenagers in Arad, the struggling old Russians, the dozens of other projects she had been forever starting? But that was gone. All gone.

"That's not what life is for, Yona," Dena said. "It's about being a part of a divine covenant. About God's demands on us. *B'tselem Elokim.* In God's image. We're made in His image to do His work by whatever means necessary, starting right now, by reclaiming this land in His Holy Name."

The words hung there. *In His Holy Name.* Far off, on a distant hilltop, black specks moved. Sheep or goats. Nothing stirred in the hot still air.

"Now, if you think I'm going to turn in Naftali Shroeder," Dena said, and Yona looked at her but Dena kept her eyes fixed on some faraway point, "a man who is nearly a prophet, who saved us time and again from the most vile machinations of our weak-willed and morally bankrupt government, who's done more for the Jewish people than you can ever imagine, then you don't know me very well." She faced Yona, studying her as if she were a stranger. "I don't know why you came here. Today, or two weeks ago. We have nothing to give each other."

"I'm not sure about that," Yona said, and didn't know where the words were coming from. But they were coming. "I refuse to believe you have no compassion for an innocent man. You were the most principled human being I ever knew. I can't believe you'd sacrifice a person's freedom to protect a man who facilitated a murder, maybe two or three murders. Is this what you think God wants? *B'tselem Elokim?* In God's image? What about *tzedek, tzedek, tirdof?* Justice, justice, you shall pursue? Isn't that what our father taught us? Isn't that what we learned all those years?"

Dena turned away, and all Yona had was her profile—the strong jaw, the straight nose, the firm set of mouth. She was like a stone statue. An ancient deity like the life-size Roman figures in all the museums with half arms and broken-off fingers and missing faces, once terrifying and awesome but now relics, only rock.

"You once wanted to save the world, Dena. This is your chance. *He who saves one life.* Well, you know the rest."

Dena stood. Her dress was clinging to her, and Yona saw the small round rise of her belly. A new life entering this comfortless world. "You don't know anything about me," Dena said. "You don't know anything about me at all." Then she handed Yona the card and walked away.

39

The last thing he remembered, Greenglass told the doctor, was riding in the airport van to Ben-Gurion early in the morning of September second to go to the States. He couldn't recall the reason he went.

Levin crossed his long legs. Did he perhaps recognize the name Pinchas Wasserman?

Greenglass didn't think so. Maybe he was once a teacher of his?

How about Seamus Hurley? the doctor tried. He and Greenglass had had an email correspondence, the man had offered him a job at the Olive Branch college.

Greenglass shook his head.

The doctor slowly tapped an index finger against his cheek.

"Is it very bad?" Greenglass asked, and sounded to himself like a stroke victim, his words slurry and thick. It was just the swelling, Levin kept telling him. Nothing permanent. But Greenglass hadn't dared talking to anyone else.

"Your memory? No." Levin uncrossed the leg, swiveled on the stool. "This is how memory is. Fickle. But also protective. Why should you have scenes of the fiery furnace playing in your head? Your mind is trying to shelter you. It's just a little overzealous. Doesn't want you to remember one night, so it plays it safe and curtains off a whole month." A smile. "What can I tell you. It's behaving very loyally to its host. Not a bad thing. Better than the alternative. Constant nightmares."

Greenglass wanted to believe him, but he couldn't help feeling displaced. As if time hadn't quite stood still while he'd been gone,

Rip Van Winkle waking up to discover a hundred years had passed. He wondered for an instant if his parents had died. If maybe everyone in his life had.

"Not to worry, Mark," the doctor said. "Most of the data will come back. Maybe not the explosion, the events of that night, but the rest will eventually return. When it's ready." He should think of it as communications shutdown. A part of the storehouse temporarily inaccessible. The pathways would wake up again one day. Meantime the information was in there, whole, safe, intact.

But how did Levin know about his time in New York? Greenglass murmured. About this Wasserman person. And the extra week he'd stayed on. Had his parents called?

"No," Levin said, tapping the cheek again. "The embassy is having a hard time locating them actually. It seems they're away. Do you know where?" Again Greenglass shook his head. He had no idea. Levin waved a hand. "Doesn't matter, I'm sure they'll reach them. Just as well they didn't come sooner, for their sake. No, it was a friend of yours who told me about your trip. A young woman. She spent the evening with you the day you came back, before you walked to the school."

Spent the evening? She? "A young woman?"

"Your neighbor. Rachel Craft."

Who? Rachel Who? Between September second and now, when entire chunks of his life had become lost to him, a woman had appeared. Or so it seemed. His voice came out muffled, alien. "Don't know anyone, not by that name."

"Well," Levin said. He glanced at the door. "Well." Then he turned back. "Why don't we remedy that? Have you meet her today?" He nodded; he liked the idea. "Might be helpful, maybe jog loose some of that stuck data."

Greenglass raised a hand to his swollen face, murmured something.

"You're worried she won't think you're a catch?" Greenglass felt himself blushing. Still. He had some dignity, didn't he? The doctor moved to the door. "I'll ask the nurse to fix you up. But anyway your friend's been here all week, watching you sleep, half dead, on that bed. You look a hell of a lot better now than you did then."

Her name, like Wasserman's, rang a dim bell, but unlike Wasserman's, which brought up images of a sweaty Talmudist giving out donuts for correct answers, Rachel Craft's reminded him of being sixteen and tongue-tied around the pretty girls at summer camp. But he wanted to know: Who was she? Why had she been in his hospital room all week?

Shula, the maternal-looking nurse in the bubblegum-colored smock, combed his hair, rearranged his pillows, and sat him up with a fresh hospital johnny and a decent pair of hospital-issue glasses. She was everything Felicia was not: ample, noisy, a whirlwind of efficiency who commanded the unit and its mostly male physicians with a potent combination of imperious Prussian despotism and Israeli anarchy. Everyone said it worked great.

"You nervous, Moshe?" Shula said.

He nodded.

"Don't be. She's a very nice girl." She smoothed the blanket, adjusted an IV line. "Every day she comes. From the first night. She's the one who identified you." She moved to the other side of the bed, turned a dial on a machine. "You know why, don't you?"

He shook his head. No. Why?

"Because your ID shows a man with a big beard. Very different. You took it off in America." She checked a monitor. "The police, the hospital, they didn't believe who you are. But she came and found you." She leaned over him, fixed the top of his hospital gown. He caught a whiff of antiseptic soap. She stopped fussing and pointed a long finger at him. "This girl, she likes you. Take my word. Big romances start in hospitals. Very popular." She showed him her wedding band. A rope of thick gold with a Hebrew inscription. "Thirty-two years. Met him right here. I was his nurse. Just like in all the movies." She made a last pass by the bedside table, collected a plastic cup, a paper towel, then swept herself neatly from the room.

"Hello?"

The voice was soft, tentative. She stepped closer. Dark-haired and pretty. She wore jeans and a green top the color of a Granny Smith apple. He had no idea who she was.

"I'm Rachel, Mark. I live downstairs from you."

He nodded. What else, who else, didn't he know? What did it mean to be alive but not be a witness to your own existence?

"It's okay if you don't remember me," she said, taking a seat in the chair Shula had carefully placed by the bed. "We didn't have such a long history anyway." A smile. Warm brown pools for eyes, and a lovely mouth, small precise teeth. "Your doctor thought that was probably a good thing. That way neither of us will be disappointed if you don't remember some detail like my birthday or a great film we saw together. Because we didn't see any films, and I never told you when I was born."

He nodded again. He didn't think he could speak. What if he suddenly started to cry? Levin said it could happen, he shouldn't be alarmed or ashamed. Cardiac surgery patients had it all the time. Sudden inexplicable tears. The heart recalibrating itself after a shock. That's how he liked to think of it.

"So perhaps I should do the talking, yes?"

A nod. Yes.

"Shall I describe our apartment building? Where you live? Chopin Street. Like the composer. I'll tell you about the neighbors, the kid downstairs who was just discharged from the army and blasts Black Sabbath and Metallica to decompress. Or so he says."

Yes.

"And I can tell you what you told me about your trip to New York. The teaching gig there, what you described about your parents. Who, by the way, have been located. Vacationing in the Florida Keys. Bet you didn't remember that." Another beautiful smile. "They're coming to see you. They'll be here in two or three days."

He could feel himself welling up. She was very nice, very kind. And now she was going to see the tears. It was so embarrassing. The heart recalibrating itself right here, right now.

She reached across the little table, handed him a tissue. He dabbed at his eyes. Then he raised his right index finger.

"Yes?"

He held the finger higher.

"First?"

Another nod. He pointed at her.

"Me?" she said.

Yes.

"What about me?"

He put down the tissue, flapped his fingers together. The sign of people conversing.

"Talk? Yes, I said I would talk."

He shook his head, pointed at her again.

"Me? You want me to talk about myself?"

Up went the index finger.

"First? I should talk about myself first?"

Yes. He pointed again and did the thing with his fingers. Her. He wanted to hear about her. Who Rachel Craft was. Where she came from. How they met. And then their evening together. He wanted to hear every detail, the whole story, from the beginning. What they spoke about. Where they went. Whether they ate or drank or walked the streets of their neighborhood. He wanted to know it all, every little piece. He wanted to start weaving the memory.

40

A cool night breeze blew in from the open window above Eyal's bed. Yona lay her head on his chest, took in the musky smell of him. He breathed softly, half asleep, and put his hand over her, slowly stroked her back. She would go home to New York in two days because Claudia was returning and she wasn't ready to stay, not yet, not this soon, but there was email and phone and airplanes, and there were options and choices and now, perhaps, there was also courage.

Plenty of art classes here, you know, he'd told her. *Cheaper rent than Manhattan.*

She knew that. There were also jobs here. And friends. Good friends. Claudia would be thrilled.

She moved her cheek against his silky skin. He was a beautiful person, inside and out. She had come back from Dena's and called him, gone straight over. *I can't tell you where I've been,* she told him. *But I did a good thing. I'm not a bad person after all.*

And because this was true, because she believed it, she let him kiss her and hold her and love her.

And because this was true and she believed it, she let herself love him back.

41

*G*reenglass's parents arrived, escorted by Levin and Shula. Felicia rushed to the bed, took his hand and kissed it. "Oh, thank God," she murmured, then turned to the doctor. Lenny hung back by the doorway. "We are so grateful. Thank you for everything."

The doctor held up a palm. "Please. This is what we do. Your son is going to be okay." Shula brought the second chair up to the bed rail, next to the one in which Rachel usually sat. Rachel had been with him for three days, leaving only at night and now, this morning, so he could be alone with his parents, and already he missed her.

Shula fussed with the chairs. She was being uncharacteristically quiet. His poor parents, she'd told Greenglass that morning while changing the dressings. To come to a hospital six thousand miles away and see your child in such a state: it was heartbreaking. No matter how old your son was, two or thirty-two, a son was still a son, one's child still one's child. All you want is to trade places, take their suffering from them. Shula knew. She had four children herself. "Now Shula and I will go out to the corridor," Levin said, waiting for the nurse. "Call us if you need anything."

They squeaked out on their rubber-sole shoes. Felicia took a seat. Greenglass tried to smile from beneath the gauze; the dental work had begun. Even if he couldn't recall the weeks he'd been with his parents in Manhattan, he would always know them. You could never forget your parents. He was glad to see them.

"You can take a seat here too, Lenny," Felicia said.

Lenny obeyed. He took the other chair.

"You can also say something, Lenny."

Lenny cleared his throat. He suddenly looked to Greenglass tired, aged. The trip had taken the wind out of him.

"Son," Lenny said, and Greenglass thought he was hallucinating. Lenny had never called him *son* in his life. "Son," his father repeated, in what was obviously a prepared speech, "I just want to say that I'm glad you're all right and that if there's anything you need—" He took a handkerchief from his pants pocket and wiped his eyes. Greenglass had never seen his father cry.

Lenny finished with the handkerchief, folded it, placed it back in his pants. "If there's anything, anything at all, you know you can count on me."

Greenglass managed a nod. If he could have raised his arm high enough, he'd have reached over to pat his father.

"And?" Felicia said.

Lenny put a hand up on the rail. It was knobby and punched with liver spots. Seventy years old, his son narrowly escaping death's grasp, and Lenny was confronting his own mortality too. "Also, if there's anything—" A deep breath, he was trying to stay on an even keel. Felicia started to say something but he shot up his other hand. *Let me do it!* "If there's anything I've done to hurt you, I hope you'll forgive me and let us put all that behind us."

It was the hardest thing Lenny had ever done. He looked shaken. *Me too*, Greenglass wanted to say, and would, as soon as he could talk. Lenny retrieved the handkerchief, and Greenglass looked at the flawed, weepy man who was his father. They were the same, two imperfect human beings, trying. *He who seeks love overlooks faults.* Lenny wiped his eyes again. He was terrified. He would need months to recover.

42

Yona's bags were packed. Mark Greenglass had come out of the coma—some memory loss, Doron Klein told her, but nothing catastrophic. She had told Klein everything she knew—again—and still it wasn't good enough. They would run their investigation to its natural end, and all she could hope was that they would eventually conclude that Mark Greenglass, whoever he was, whatever his life had once been, was innocent and that the story was as Rachel Craft recounted it: that he'd walked to the school after their date, a bystander caught in the crossfire.

She made another sweep through the apartment, checking the window locks, the hot water switch, the stove. Her gift for Claudia, the painted goddess, rested on the dining table, colorful ribbons tied around her waist. It hadn't felt right to pack her up and bring her to New York, to the smog and screech of Manhattan and to Yona's fifteen-by-twenty junior one-bedroom among the tainted mementos from Elias and the others, gold and silver necklaces and bracelets that weren't meant to invoke fertility—the opposite; they were rewards for denying it, in all its possibilities—and to the closet full of grim black clothes as if she were some Greek widow. The statue didn't belong there. Maybe Yona didn't either.

She adjusted the tail of ribbons. She hoped Rachel Craft would forgive her. Her deception had produced nothing. And now she could never tell Rachel who she was, never tell her the truth. Klein had warned her: the last thing he needed was for Mark Greenglass's new girlfriend to go to the newspapers and suggest a link to Givat Baruch. All their years of work monitoring such groups would be compromised. There would never be justice. If Yona cared about Greenglass, if she believed in his innocence, and if she cared about the country and the need for the rule of law, she would keep her mouth shut.

A breeze floated in from the open doors of the balcony. She checked her watch. The cab for the airport would come in twenty minutes. She went to the phone, changed her mind. No more good-byes to Eyal. They would just have to see. *Was it so scary to try?* he'd asked her last night. *Wasn't it time for her to take a chance?*

She stepped out onto the balcony and took a deep breath. The city wore the clean sunshine like a coat of fresh paint.

The phone rang.

"Yes?"

The taxi. They were coming early, traffic problems. Could she be downstairs in five minutes?

She moved quickly, closing shutters, locking doors. Down-stairs, the driver loaded her bags. She watched the building disappear behind her as they pulled away. Ten minutes later they were on an unfamiliar side street, cruising for a number.

"Are you picking up someone else?" she said, looking up from her paper itinerary.

No answer. In front of a nondescript building the driver stopped and got out. A small figure emerged from the entry. Yona's heart did its pathetic little knocking.

"Rachel," she breathed as the back door of the taxi opened and Rachel slid inside. Yona glanced at the entry. Doron Klein stood in the shadows. Was she being arrested? She turned back to Rachel. "What, how——?"

Rachel held up a hand. "I persuaded Klein to let me see you. This is what he arranged. He said I have ten minutes, then you leave."

Yona steeled herself. Whatever Rachel had to say—outrage over being deceived, fury for being played the fool—she would hear it.

"They dropped the case."

"They what?"

"Against Mark. They dropped it."

"What happened?"

"I don't know. Klein and another guy came to the hospital and took me aside and said it was over. That someone had come forward with information. And that the people they were investigating were dangerous so everything had to be kept quiet." She took Yona by the shoulders and hugged her. "I don't know who you are or what you did or why, but you saved him." Softly, she wept into Yona's neck, and Yona put her arms around her and stared through her own glassy tears at the ugly building and the still figures in the entry, the musty smell of the cab mixing with the flowery scent of Rachel's shampoo. "You saved his life, Yona. Or whatever your name is. You did it."

No, not me, Yona thought as they hugged in the cramped taxi, the noises of the street swirling around them, her itinerary still clutched in her fist. *No, not me.*

43

Greenglass's parents would be back in the morning. They'd found a furnished flat to rent for a month on Marcus Street not far from his apartment and would stay to help him after he was discharged from the hospital. They were going to the owner's now to sign the papers. Then they would drive to the airport to meet Scott, who was coming in on the evening flight from London.

Felicia was thanking the nurses, the aides. Lenny waited patiently near the door. Greenglass nodded at his father, smiling behind the gauze. *A healing tongue is a tree of life.* Lenny nodded back. Inside Felicia's purse were two letters Greenglass had written that she would take to the post office and mail. The first was to a Pinchas Wasserman, in gratitude. Twice Greenglass had been offered a teaching post at the Olive Branch college, once before the devastation and now, again, for whenever he recovered, after classes got started in a temporary location, thanks both times to the good word of a man he could not recall having ever met. A basket of the season's first fruits, sent by Wasserman's institute, sat on the bedside table next to a box of cookies Felicia had brought from Brooklyn. The second letter was a note and a check addressed to the last remaining synagogue in Far Rockaway, Share'i Chesed, *the Gates of Compassion,* in memory of Regina Berman, may her name be for a blessing and her soul wrapped in the eternal bonds of heaven—for though he didn't know how he knew it, of this he was certain. *Blessed is the Creator of the world, who watches over those who sleep in the dust.*

Lenny signaled Felicia, pointed at his watch. Everyone called goodbye and Felicia blew Greenglass a kiss, then went out the door, Lenny's hand resting lightly on the small of her slender back. It was a great gift his father had given him, and he hoped Lenny would do the same for Scott, and that they, the sons, could give it back. Now he could hear Rachel in the corridor telling them to be careful on the roads, and to call if they needed help with anything. She had told Greenglass that morning that he'd not fled the Olive Branch college the night of the explosion even after he knew it was going to blow. That he'd tried to get into the building in case anyone was trapped inside. That's what the investigators had found.

Pikuach nefesh, the doctor had told her and Lenny and Felicia in a spartan waiting area earlier that morning when the investigators had left. *Saving a soul. The highest value. It's in the Talmud. Avot: Whoever saves one life, it's as if he's saved an entire world.*

Then the doctor put his arms around Greenglass's weepy parents. *Why, you might ask, would anyone try to enter a building he knew was about to explode? The answer: Because how often does a person have an opportunity to save an entire world?*

Greenglass leaned back into the pillows. He didn't think he would have been trying to save a world. But if it was true about what he'd done, he must have had his reasons. There was no sense looking back, either to praise himself or to wonder. You did what you did, and hoped that in the final reckoning it was right.

Rachel was in the doorway talking with Shula. Levin had given the green light to visitors, and Rachel was going out into the hall to greet well-wishers and accept candy and cards and flowers. Greenglass watched her. She had come into his life at the moment he needed her most, and he hoped he would never have to let her go. *Eat your bread in gladness and drink your wine in joy and take happiness with the woman you love all the fleeting days of your life, the days that have been granted you under the sun, for that is the portion given you.* His past was behind him, and whatever he'd lost in it, he was content to leave there, letting it rest in the shadows until the day when the stars were aligned in a certain pattern or the moon was facing Saturn and it came, willy-nilly, dancing back to him.

Until then, together, they would wait.

WHEREVER YOU GO

Joan Leegant

DISCUSSION QUESTIONS

1. Several characters in the book embrace a cause-driven life: Dena Ben-Zion, her husband Aryeh, Naftali Shroeder, Aaron Blinder. What is behind each character's dedication to their cause? What are the rewards of a cause-driven life as presented in the novel? What are the dangers? Conversely, Yona Stern wants to pursue her art and develop more satisfying personal relationships. Is there tension between these differing approaches?

2. The role of religion is explored through numerous story threads. For some people, such as Mark Greenglass, religion can be a life-affirming force; for others, such as Aaron Blinder, religion can justify violence. What do you think explains the different outcomes? Does it depend on the individual? On the type of religious practice or belief? On the community and its leaders?

3. The title *Wherever You Go* comes from the Book of Ruth, and the beginning of the novel features a quote from Ruth. How does this passage relate to the story? What do you think the title means in view of the characters and the events that transpire? Who is pledging loyalty to what, or to whom?

4. Aaron Blinder makes choices in this story that can be understood as immature and reckless at best, and as immoral and criminal at worst. Discuss who and what contributed to his choices. Even if outside factors contributed, is there a point at which an individual bears sole responsibility for his actions?

5. Aaron's father Emanuel Blinder makes his living writing popular but melodramatic novels about the Holocaust. What might the

author be suggesting about the "use" of the Holocaust for literary or artistic purposes? Can remembering the Holocaust through art—film, fiction, theater—spill over into exploitation? Does it depend on the quality of the work? The artist's motives? The commercial value?

6. When the book opens, each of the main characters has a troubled relationship with a close family member: Greenglass and Aaron with their fathers, Yona with her sister. How do those relationships change by the end of the book? What makes for the possibility of forgiveness and reconciliation in a family, according to the story? What makes for a failure to reconcile and the inability to forgive?

7. Art appears frequently in the novel, in Yona's passion for it and at Olive Branch College, which becomes the target of sectarian violence. What might this suggest about the compatibility of art and religion, or art and politics? Pinchas Wasserman wonders aloud whether art can ever be divorced from all that is around it. Do you agree?

8. Mark Greenglass has lost his religious passion before the book opens. What do you think Greenglass's spiritual feelings are by the end? What do you think happened to him during his ordeal that might influence these feelings? What do you think is his relationship with the Divine by the end of the book?

9. Dena makes a decision at the conclusion of the novel that dramatically affects the outcome. Why do you think she made that decision? What does it tell you about her?

10. One of the issues the book explores is the relationship between American Jews and Israel. In addition to the three main American characters, consider the visitors from Cleveland: Ben-Ami, Davidson, and Rachel Craft. How do these (North) Americans view Israel and Israelis? Why are each of them in Israel and what are they looking for? Similarly, how do the Israelis such as Shoeder, Eyal, and Lior view the Americans? How does this portrayal of the Israeli-American encounter differ from what you may have thought previously?

MORE NORTON BOOKS WITH READING GROUP GUIDES AVAILABLE

Diana Abu-Jaber	*Crescent*
	Origin
Diane Ackerman	*The Zookeeper's Wife*
Rabih Alameddine	*I, the Divine*
Rupa Bajwa	*The Sari Shop*
Andrea Barrett	*The Air We Breathe*
	The Voyage of the Narwhal
Peter C. Brown	*The Fugitive Wife*
Lan Samantha Chang	*Hunger*
	Inheritance
Anne Cherian	*A Good Indian Wife*
Marilyn Chin	*Revenge of the Mooncake Vixen*
Leah Hager Cohen	*House Lights*
Michael Cox	*The Glass of Time*
	The Meaning of Night
Jared Diamond	*Guns, Germs, and Steel*
Andre Dubus III	*The Garden of Last Days*
	House of Sand and Fog
John Dufresne	*Louisiana Power & Light*
	Requiem, Mass.
Jennifer Cody Epstein	*The Painter from Shanghai*
Ellen Feldman	*Lucy*
	Scottsboro
Susan Fletcher	*Eve Green*
	Oystercatchers
Paula Fox	*The Widow's Children*
Betty Friedan	*The Feminine Mystique*
Denise Giardina	*Emily's Ghost*
Barbara Goldsmith	*Obsessive Genius*
Stephen Greenblatt	*Will in the World*
Helon Habila	*Waiting for an Angel*
Patricia Highsmith	*Strangers on a Train*
Ann Hood	*The Knitting Circle*
Dara Horn	*All Other Nights*
	The World to Come

*Available only on the Norton Web site: www.wwnorton.com/guides